ONDINE

The Autumn Palace

EBONY McKENNA

EGMONT

We bring stories to life

Ondine: The Autumn Palace first published in Great Britain 2011
by Egmont UK Limited
239 Kensington High Street
London W8 6SA

Text copyright © Ebony McKenna 2011

The moral rights of the author have been asserted

ISBN 978 1 4052 5638 4

1 3 5 7 9 10 8 6 4 2

A CIP catalogue record for this title is available
from the British Library

Typeset by Avon DataSet Ltd, Bidford on Avon, Warwickshire

Printed and bound in Great Britain by the CPI Group

ONDINE

The Autumn Palace

Praise for *Ondine*:

'A wonderfully imaginative debut novel . . . the author's unique blend of the magical and romantic elements of the romantic fairytale gives new life to this long established mode of storytelling.' *Inis*

'. . . on sheer charm alone, *Ondine* is hard to resist. This whimsical romantic fantasy for girls 12-plus simply oozes romantic longing. If you swooned over Edward, you'll likely go gaga for Hamish and Lord Vincent.' *Bookseller + Publisher*

'A debut novel that mixes romance and magic and, for the first time ever, witches turning gorgeous boys into ferrets.' *Bookseller*

'Ebony is an absolute marvel when it comes to humour.' *Bookwitch*

'I can't remember where I first heard about *Ondine*, but I'm certainly very glad that I did.' *Poisoned Rationality*

'I had a hard time putting it down. It was sweet, funny, charming and yet again funny.' *We Adore a Happy Ending*

'I absolutely enjoyed reading *Ondine* . . . Shambles sold the whole story with his wit and charm.' *The Bookette*

'This is a fun, romantic, well written read which would appeal to young girls aged 12+.' *Lovely Treez Reads*

'*Ondine* was an absolute pleasure to read.' *Brizmus Books Blogs*

'Oh man, this book was so absolutely quirkily and wittily fantastic.' Audrey, *Good Reads*

'Don't be a bampot, give this absolutely fantastic book a read, you won't regret it.' Leanne, *Good Reads*

'. . . original and quirky – wonderful use of witty footnotes throughout . . .' *Me and My Big Mouth*

EBONY McKENNA

The decision to leave a career in journalism was a logical choice for Ebony. There wasn't enough time in the day to write the fictional stories she wanted to tell, against the factual that she had to tell. She followed her heart towards writing science fiction, romance and young adult adventures. Ebony now writes full time and lives in Melbourne, Australia, with her husband and young son. She loves trivia nights, train sets and the Eurovision Song Contest. Her first teenage novel was *Ondine*.

www.ebonymckenna.com

Dedicated to my wonderful critique partners, supporters and life-long friends at the Melbourne Romance Writers' Guild for their constant encouragement, brilliant suggestions and unfailing supply of chocolate.

Chapter One

L et's get one thing clear from the outset. Ondine de Groot is not now, nor will she ever be, psychic.

Smart? Yes.

Prone to blurting out the wrong thing at the wrong time? Certainly.

But psychic? Hardly.

However, as she held Hamish's warm hand in hers and walked towards the train station in West Venzelemma, she felt something momentous might happen. Very soon. Possibly in the next few pages.

Hamish was about to take on a job with the Duke of Brugel,[1] who lived two boroughs away in the

---

1 *The Duke of Brugel is the hereditary head of state for the Serene Duchy of Brugel, a former Soviet bloc country in eastern Europe that still hasn't won Eurovision. Venzelemma, where Ondine lives with her family, is Brugel's capital city.*

poshest part of Venzelemma. It would take nine train stops to get there, which meant the next hour could be their last together for a long, long time. In fact, Ondine might not see him again for a whole week! That was far too long to go without seeing the boyfriend she'd only just found.

Giving his hand a squeeze, she steadied her bubbling emotions. In return Hamish gave her his trademark lopsided grin, making her insides go squishy.

'Yer up tae something, lass, I can tell.'

'I was just thinking we might not *have* to say goodbye, once we reach the Duke's place.' Naughty flurries spun in her head as a plan to stay together began to form.

'I thought ye looked crafty.'

Ondine grinned. 'You know how I promised my parents I'd see you to the Duke's, then come home.

Some people might ask, if Brugel was a Soviet state, how did the Duchy survive? Good question. For answers, read The Complete History of Brugel, *by Shaaron Melvedeir — 250 pages of folklore, facts, figures and the occasional photo. Another book,* Everything Shaaron Melvedeir Says is Rubbish, *by Isaak Drixen, 745 pages, is the subject of Brugel's longest-running defamation action.*

And then I also had to promise I wouldn't ask the Duke for a job . . .'

'Och, hen, there's a "but" coming any minute now.'

'But!' And here Ondine beamed with how cleverly she could get around the promises she'd made to her parents without actually breaking them. 'It doesn't mean *you* can't ask the Duke for a job on my behalf.'

'Yer sure yer nae stretching yer arm farther than yer sleeve'll let ye?'

A few cranks and cogs shifted in Ondine's head before she figured out what he was getting at. 'I'm not overreaching. We'll be fine. What could possibly go wrong?'

'I wouldnae want tae get yer parents off-side. When they find out they'll be fair affronted.'

Ondine felt her face crumple. 'You don't want us to be together?'

'Ye cannae look at me like that, it breaks me wee heart. Ye know I love ye more than anything and I'll do what I can for ye, lass.'

The tenseness in her shoulders eased. 'I love you so much. If the Duke says "no", then I'll wear it. But if he says "yes", then we can stay together.'

The cool autumn breeze blew her brown hair over her eyes, spoiling her view. Hamish tucked a stray tendril behind her ear. He gave her such a loving smile she forgot how to breathe.

'Yer sure this is what ye want?' he asked. 'I'll be right busy, what with all the important things the Duke has planned for me. Havtae admit, I'm right jumpy about ma first real gig.'

Ondine could have sworn his chest puffed out with pride. Fair enough, too. The Duke wanted him – for his particular talents – to spy for him.

'I am absolutely sure. Oh, Hamish, we're going to have such an adventure.'

'Aye. I cannae wait.' He grinned at her again and she felt lightheaded with relief.

Fresh emotions bubbled up in her heart. 'Hamish, you are the best thing that's ever happened to me.'

'Aw, hen, yer all that and more tae me.' He gave her a quick kiss. 'But time's wasting, let's nawt keep the Duke waiting.'

Just as they were asking for a couple of City Saver

tickets[2] a familiar voice called out, 'Yoo-hoo'.

Turning around, Ondine saw five suitcases cludder[3] into a neat pile on the ground, as if they'd been levitating not a moment earlier. A lead weight dropped in her stomach at the sight of her Great Aunt Colette Romano standing beside the luggage. How on earth had she packed it, then carried it, then caught up with them so quickly? Oh, that's right, she was a witch.[4]

'What's she doing here?' Ondine said to Hamish behind gritted teeth.

'There you are! Hamish, help me with the luggage,

---

2 *City Savers are very good value, but only for off-peak travel. All visitors to Venzelemma should buy a ten-pack to see the best the city has to offer. The central hospital with its neo-gothic exterior, flying buttresses and vaulted ceilings in the foyer are a must. The hospital is conveniently located within staggering distance of Brugel's largest fish market, so visitors overcome by the stench of rotting seafood can get prompt treatment.*

3 *In Brugel, each dropped object carries a unique verb. For example, dropped cutlery clatters, dropped luggage cludders.*

4 *This was no disparaging comment, merely the truth. Colette Romano was a witch. The fact that she needed less than an hour to be ready for travel – and levitate five packed cases across a street – proved it.*

there's a good boy.' Old Col bustled up to the counter in front of them.

Ondine saw Hamish's brows rise in confusion.

'Col, we are just paying for our tickets,' Hamish said, putting money on the counter. The older woman's hand slammed down hard on his. He winced. Ondine winced in sympathy. For an old bird, she sure packed a wallop.

Old Col grew stern. 'Put your money away, I do not travel second.'[5]

'I'm not asken ye to.'

'Then how am I to be Ondine's chaperone if we are not all in the same carriage?' She made a tisking sound, shook her head and turned her attention to the confused ticket clerk. Then she said in a too-loud voice, 'Three *first* tickets to Bellreeve, thank you.'

Ondine thought, *Chaperone? For a train ride across town?*

Hamish said, 'That is very generous of you, but . . .'

---

5   *Second is the logical yet slightly insulting term used by Bruglers (the residents of Brugel, who speak Brugelish) to describe any thing that is not first. It can mean as much as missing the 100-metre final by a gnat's wing, or losing three sets to love in the first round of the Venzelemma Grand Slam.*

Then Ondine heard the sound of brakes screeching in her head. 'Bellreeve? What are we going all the way out there for? The Duke's right here in Venzelemma.'

'We are going to Bellreeve because that is where the Autumn Palechia is.'[6]

'But –' started Ondine.

'But –' started Hamish.

Old Col breathed in deeply and squared her shoulders. 'Enough!' Just in case they didn't get it, she held her palm up in a stop sign.

Silently, Ondine gave Hamish's hand another squeeze to let him know, *We're in this together, we'll be OK*. Judging by Hamish's pale face, he wasn't so sure. Col had a way of messing up his life. He'd be numpty to think she'd go easy on him now.[7]

---

6 *'Palechia' is Brugelish for 'palace'. It is pronounced 'pe-cha'. Scholars insist the word was originally pronounced 'PAL-e-CHEE-a' as recently as two hundred and fifty years ago. When Wiwyam The Gweat became Duke in 1799, his fondness for removing people's heads from their shoulders made the rest of his advisors wewuctant to cowwect his many speech impediments.*

7 *'Numpty' means 'unwise'. If a witch has previously become very cross with you and turned you into a ferret, you'd be numpty to think you could ever trust her.*

'Come, children.' Old Col had that air of command about her.

Ondine and Hamish could only shrug and follow. All the while Ondine kept wondering about the sudden change of plan. Then Old Col turned and glared at them, which had the effect of chilling the air by five degrees. 'The suitcases aren't going to carry themselves, are they?'

An empty feeling stole over Ondine as Hamish let go of her hand and retrieved Old Col's cases. They looked back-breakingly heavy and there were five of them. Why didn't Old Col levitate them instead?

'Aunt Col, I appreciate your concern for my welfare, but you really don't need to come. I know the way to the Duke's city palace, it's not that far from here,' Ondine said. 'Hamish and I have been there before, you know.'

'You would say that, child.'

Patronising old . . .

It didn't make sense to travel all the way to Bellreeve when the Duke lived so close by. If Ondine were honest with herself, she would also admit that the thought of travelling to the country and being so far away from home made her nervous. Having grown up in the bustling streets of Venzelemma, the city felt familiar. The countryside was another matter entirely. With its dark spooky woods and big noisy animals lumbering about, travelling there felt a bit scary and intimidating.

'Clearly you have not thought beyond your hormonal urges, Ondi. There is a bigger picture here and you are blind to it. You may recall that when the Duke of Brugel graced your parent's hotel several weeks ago,[8] he asked me to work for him, and I accepted.[9] He also invited Hamish into his employ, and Hamish accepted. He has not, however, extended any such invitation to you, and were the two of you to arrive at his city doorstep together, *you*, Ondine, would be returning alone.'

The luggage weighed Hamish dawn. Ondine's

---

8 See Ondine, book 1.

9 *When the Duke met Old Col, he took a shine to her. Naturally, he wanted someone with her witchery skills to be working for him. If not, she might end up working against him, and that was a chance the Duke wasn't willing to take.*

back hurt in sympathy and she grabbed one of the cases to lighten his load. A few paces on, her shoulder felt ready to give out, plus she had a burning strain in her lower back, but she bore it.

Ondine said, 'The Duke will find something for me to do. I'll work for free if I have to.'

'Don't debase yourself like that!' Old Col tisked for good measure. 'Clearly I arrived just in time, before you made a total fool of yourself. If you followed politics at all, you would know the Duke and his family always spend the autumn in Bellreeve. He'll be there soon enough, so we'll be spared the hassle of relocating. If anything, we could scout the area for anything untoward.'

'Oh!' That threw an entirely new light on things.

'When the three of us arrive in Bellreeve tonight, we will have travelled so far and for so long that our gracious host will feel obliged to offer you some kind of employment. No decent person would send a young girl on such a long return journey alone.'

It was almost as if Great Aunt Col was going out of her way to help Ondine. The thought should have been reassuring, but instead it made her uneasy. A few moments ago she and Hamish had been in charge of their destiny. Or as in charge as you can be when you're relying on a duke to give you a job. Now her great aunt had taken over and Ondine didn't like it one bit.

Chapter Two

The train's first-class carriage was at the very end of the platform, directly behind the engine. Negotiating the crowds involved lots of 'Sorrys', 'S'cuse mes' and 'Did you have that bruise alreadys?' as they squeezed their way through. Finally they arrived and Hamish dumped the cases on the ground with a satisfying cludder. Joints clicked and creaked as he stretched his back.

'Oh, look, there's a trolley. Hamish, why didn't you use that?' Old Col put her hand to the side of her mouth and laughed. It was supposed to come out as a giggle, but it sounded more like a cackle.

Although it would be impossible to be inside two people's heads at the same time, Ondine knew she and Hamish shared a thought: *That was deliberate.*

A porter arrived and began loading the cases into the luggage van. It would have been nice if the porter had been somewhere near the ticket counter when they'd first arrived – he could have saved them a lot of backache.

'In you get, children.' Old Col pointed to the carriage door and they climbed aboard.

Inside looked like a plush lounge room. Correction, a *series* of plush lounge rooms, with leather recliner chairs and nifty little tables by the windows. It smelled like money. When Ondine touched the nearest headrest, she felt the soft leather squish beneath her hand.

'It's so lush!' she said. No rubbish on the floor, no graffiti on the walls, no missing light fittings or torn seats. The carpet was so thick she left dents in it as she walked.

'Aye, it's Barry!'[10] Hamish said as he walked behind her.

---

10 *'Barry' means 'very nice', 'great' even. Nice meal, great place, fabulous view, etc. Outside Edinburgh, 'to Barry' means to be sick. It's really important not to confuse the two, otherwise you might end up insulting someone.*

The aroma of walnuts filled the air. Ondine could also smell coffee, honey and a sprinkling of nutmeg. Further up the carriage a passenger sipped a steaming mug of coffee and nibbled a delicate pastry.

They sank into their chairs – no hard bench seats in here – and Hamish smiled at Ondine. Fresh bursts of warmth flurried across her skin.

'Ahh, young love,' Great Aunt Col said, giving them a stern look. 'May I remind you, Ondine, you are only fifteen and not an adult, no matter how much you pretend to be one. Hamish would do well to remember that.'

Defying her great aunt, Ondine planted a kiss on Hamish. Zap! Electricity arced between them as their lips touched.

'Wow!' Ondine shook her head in astonishment.

Hamish pulled away and gave her a wicked grin. He rubbed his old borrowed shoes against the carpet a few times and kissed Ondine again.

Ping!

Static electricity crackled across Ondine's skin and made the fine hairs on her arm stand up. Every little kiss jolted her with bursts of electricity.

'Behave yourselves,' Old Col said, but she didn't sound all that serious.

The electric kisses proved addictive and Ondine rubbed her shoes against the carpet again. She licked her lips and moved in for a kiss.

Pow!

'Ouch!' Hamish said. 'That was really strong!'

'I'm so sorry!' Had she hurt him?

'Och, that's all right. Kiss me better, then.'

She received another delicious electric shock.

'That's enough now, both of you. Remember, you're in public,' Old Col said.

Buildings moved past the window at increasing speed, taking them away from the city at an alarming rate. The summer with Hamish had been truly wonderful, but all too brief. Memories tugged Ondine into backstory, to the time when she and Hamish met. She'd been leaving Psychic Summercamp. He'd been a ferret. A talking ferret who, after an exasperating series of events, finally became a gorgeous lad. Which everybody, especially Ondine, agreed was a rather excellent turn of events.[11]

Ondine was happiest when Hamish was his handsome self instead of his animal incarnation. Over their summer together, the curse had pretty much worked itself out. Hamish could be human as long as he was near Ondine, which suited her just fine. Yet they were about to work for the Duke, and the Duke would probably prefer Hamish to remain a ferret as much as possible.

'This is going tae be so exciting I cannae wait tae make a start,' Hamish said. 'And Col, at first I didnae like yer interfering, but now I can see ye'll help Ondi get a job and then we'll be working together and having adventures, so we will.'

Ondine loved hearing him talk. There was something magical and a little bit naughty in the way he spoke. Just thinking about how they could stay together and work together made her glow. It really felt like everything would turn out wonderfully.

The afternoon tea trolley arrived. Col ordered a pot

---

11 *Usually backstory does not belong at the front of the book. Ondine is aware of this and she has kept her episode of reminiscing brief.*

of Darjeeling for herself and some nibbles for Ondine and Hamish.[12] The waiter made a few deft moves and extracted side tables from within the armrests.

'This is tha good stuff, eh, lass?' Hamish gave Ondine another of his lopsided smiles. The ones that made her go all silly in the head. The next moment he cut a small piece off his marinated artichoke and offered it to her.

There was something so tender and touching about the action, Ondine felt overcome. She accepted the morsel and chewed it as delicately as she could. 'It's heavenly.' She shut her eyes to savour the moment. When she opened them, she found Hamish gazing at her with adoration. They were lost in a bubble of love as she returned the favour, feeding him a tidbit from her plate.

'Easy on tha salad, hen.'

'Oh, sorry, I forgot you're still not used to it.' Ondine picked the leafy greens off her fork and replaced them with chunks of chicken and ham.

---

12 *Darjeeling is expensive fancy-pants tea. It was introduced to Brugel when Marco Polo opened up the spice trade to Asia.*

'It's taking a while tae adjust, like,' he said.

It sure was. As a ferret he ate nothing but protein and fat. Not through choice but necessity, because carbohydrates could put him in a coma. And they didn't like salad. But now he was human, surely he could vary his diet?

As if reading her mind, he added, 'Old habits die hard.'

'They certainly do,' Old Col said, interrupting them. At which point Col tipped the remains of her tea into the saucer and then studied the tea leaves. 'Oh, look, we're going on a journey.'

Ondine rolled her eyes – probably a safer option than going *Pfffft*, because she had another mouthful of scrumptious food. Since when did her great aunt look for signs in a teacup? Col had scorned her old friend Mrs Howser for doing just that at Thomas and Margi's engagement party.

'No, really, look.' Old Col held out the teacup for Ondine to see.

To Ondine's surprise, she saw the clear outline of a locomotive in the wet leaves. 'That's a . . . it really looks like a train. Mercury's wings, I never thought you'd be into reading tea leaves. It's even got a carriage and everything.'

'Really?' Old Col knitted her brows and had another look in the cup. She turned the cup this way and that, then shook her head. 'That's not a carriage, dear, it's a coffin. What a shame, that means somebody's going to die.'

Chapter Three

As much as Ondine didn't want to believe in the power of tea leaves, she couldn't shake the image of that small coffin outlined in Darjeeling in Aunt Col's cup.

On their train chugged, through the valleys of Novorsk Kallun[13] and the dramatic Lake Obski, where sunlight glittered on towers of crystalline rocks.[14] As the sun headed for the hills, they arrived in the northern borough of Bellreeve, where the air smelled like wet leaves. Judging by the puddles on the road, it had been raining. Judging by the dark clouds above, it would rain again soon. There were rows upon rows of

13 *In the process of receiving World Heritage Listing. Knocks Argentina's Ischigualasto for six.*
14 *Not to be confused with Lake Omski just outside Budapest, which has nude sunbathing (in summer only).*

buildings, but none of them over two storeys high. It looked like the kind of place that called itself a city, but was barely more than a town. Aunt Col waved a fan of banknotes at the porters to have their cases brought to the palechia.

Ondine wondered how Col had so much money. First-class travel and flashing the cash to get help had never entered Ondine's mind. Not that her parents were poor, but with three children and a business to run, Ma and Da kept a firm hand on finances. Apparently her great aunt had no such problems. Old Col must have pillows of gold.[15]

'It's not far, we shall walk from here,' Old Col said in her best schoolmarmish tone.

With no bags to carry, Ondine slipped her hand into Hamish's. In return, Hamish gave her a smile that made her knees go squishy. They walked through the

---

15 *An old saying in Brugel, which means you have lots of money. It does not refer to actual pillows of gold, as they are uncomfortable to sleep on. The phrase originates from rich people hiding banknotes and valuables under their mattresses for safekeeping. This behaviour is a result of Brugel's archaic banking system and the protracted recessions of 1972 to March 1987, and September 1987 to early 1996.*

21

quiet streets as shop owners packed up and closed their businesses for the day.

'I cannae wait fer our adventures tae begin,' he said.

Ondine squeezed his hand. Apprehension niggled at her as she silently hoped she could stay with Hamish and not be sent home.

Old Col led them up a tree-lined road that climbed a hill.

'Well, here we are.' Aunt Col stopped at the top, where the landscape opened out before them. Ahead stood the centuries-old gatehouse with its cobblestone path.

Ondine sighed as she took in the velvety green meadows, sprinkled with tiny white flowers. Towering trees dropped their yellow and orange leaves like confetti on the ground. In the middle of the loveliness sat an enormous mansion fit for a ... well, a duke. Three storeys high and forty-five huge windows across, it dominated the estate.[16] It had a soft yellow facade

---

16 *The palechia is one of the grandest estates in eastern Europe and is sometimes called the Versailles of Brugel. A little-known fact: the palechia inspired the redesign of Polesden Lacey in Surrey, England, which is built on a far smaller and, dare we say, more affordable, scale.*

and manicured creepers wound around white columns.

'It's beautiful,' Ondine said with a breathy sigh. On impulse, she leant towards Hamish and rested her head on his shoulder.

'Aw, nawt this, Col, ye goiven!'[17] Hamish said.

'What?' Ondine couldn't believe her ears. How could someone gaze upon such a pretty scene and not feel at peace with the world?

When Col turned back to look at them, her face was all innocence. 'You don't like it?'

Hamish glared at Old Col and said, 'Out of all the places in Brugel, ye had tae bring me here, din't ye?'

With a sinking feeling Ondine looked from Hamish to her great aunt and then back again. 'What is this place?'

'It's the Duke's autumn palace.' Col laughed and winked. The woman was having far too much fun at Hamish and Ondine's expense.

'You've been here before,' Ondine said, 'both of you.'

---

17 *'Goiven' is a word that means nothing, but can stand in the place of a great many swear words.*

Old Col shrugged. 'Why, you're right! We *have* been here, many years ago.' Then she turned and set off towards the gatehouse.

'A great many,' Hamish said, shaking his head. 'Only it wasnae called Bellreeve then. If I'd known, I wouldnae hae come.'[18]

Figuratively, the twig snapped.[19] Ondine rolled her eyes. 'This is where the debutante ball took place, isn't it?'

'Aye. You're a smart lass.' He gave her a smile but it looked tight and strained and his nostrils were flared.

'I didn't realise it was here. I guess I never thought about where it happened,' Ondine said. Taking slower steps to create distance between themselves and Old Col, who walked towards the imposing building,

---

18 *Bellreeve has had several name changes over the generations. At various points it has been known as Trelteman, St Basil and Glückentenk.*
19 *In some countries people might say, 'the penny dropped', which means somebody has finally figured something out. In Brugel, the popular expression is 'the twig snapped', a reference to the sound and effort of someone having to think really hard to arrive at the answer. Next time you ask your parents a really difficult question, like 'Why do I have to go to school?' or 'Where do babies really come from?' listen carefully. Hear that clicking, snapping sound? It's their brains hard at work.*

giggling to herself. Ondine whispered to Hamish, 'Do you think she knew all along?'

'Aye, I do.'

Ondine didn't ask more, because she knew it would upset Hamish very much to speak of those horrible events. She wound her arm around his waist and gave him a hug. He returned it but without the intensity she needed. Despite the picture-postcard scene, her happy mood evaporated. Somewhere in this vast palace was a ballroom, where, decades ago, Great Aunt Col had lost her dental-floss-thin grip on her temper and cast Hamish into ferret form. And in that form he'd stayed for years and years, until he'd met Ondine. The only good to come from his being trapped as a member of the weasel family was that his human physical form had not changed since that day.[20]

They walked to the gatehouse and Ondine let Col do all the talking. The guard looked at the three of them and asked for identification. Oh dear,

---

20 *When Old Col was young, Hamish had embarrassed her terribly in front of high society at a debutante ball, so she had turned him into a ferret. Her spell included the words, 'You can stay like that for all I care,' which explains why she is now old and wrinkly, but Hamish isn't.*

Ondine had none, neither did Hamish.

'They are with me,' Old Col said, 'the Duke is expecting us.'

'Wait one moment,' the guard said, picking up an intercom and pressing a button.

'By the time you do that, we could be inside already. Come children,' Col said, breezing past him.

Eeek, that felt a bit naughty. Hamish took Ondine's hand and they followed Col. Click clack went her feet on the cobble stones, which had fleur-de-lis carved on them.

Wind suddenly howled through the trees. Ondine's dark hair whipped across her face and stung her eyes. A gust pushed her from behind and she lost her footing.

'Steady, lass.' Hamish held her hand as the trees around them twisted and thrashed. His lips kept moving, but the wind stole the rest of his words. Old Col staggered, then turned and pointed.

Ondine looked behind them to see a tornado sucking up everything in its path – buildings, plants and earth. It was heading right for them! The guard fled his post, just before the twister ripped up the gatehouse.

'Run!' Hamish yelled, grabbing her and racing towards the safety of the palace.

The wind clawed at them. Ondine screamed as something exploded beside her and slate tiles flew through the sky. Bang! The twister sucked the doors off the stables and half a dozen terrified horses bolted out.

The next second Col had Ondine by the other hand. The three of them ran towards the palace portico.

Just as someone slammed the enormous doors in their face.

Chapter Four

'Let us in!' Ondine banged her fists on the timber door.

'Stand back,' Old Col commanded. She drew her hands up to the sky and then pushed them towards the door handle. For a heartbeat nothing happened, then the doors burst open to reveal half a dozen terrified staff huddling against the wall.

The wind howled behind them. Ondine turned to see if the twister was following them in. To her enormous relief it changed course at the last second and zig-zagged down the hill towards the lake.

'Phew, that was close.'

The tornado kept vacuuming up everything in its path, becoming a waterspout as it crossed the lake. Then, just as fast as it had sprung up, it lost its power and vanished into the dark clouds. All was still.

'Was that your doing, Col?' Hamish asked, his voice burning with anger.

'Most certainly not. But if you'll pardon the pun, it sure put the wind up me. I've never seen anything like it.'

The nervous staff broke their huddle. One of them stepped forward and held out his hand to Col. 'Pyotr Nillinskovic at your service. I am the seneschal.'[21]

'Colette Romano. Here at the Duke's pleasure.'

Pyotr walked to the door and had a look outside at the damage. 'The school roof's gone and the stables are a mess.' He quickly issued orders to the rest of the staff. 'Find the horses – and find new homes for them, then relocate the school to somewhere with a roof.'

Without missing a beat, or even checking if they had recovered from the shock, Old Col said, 'This is Hamish McPhee, he is also here at the Duke's invitation. And this is Ondine, my grand niece.'

---

21 'Seneschal' is a fancy name for 'housemaster', which is a very important job. The seneschal answers directly to the Duke and therefore wields enormous influence over the rest of the staff. Pick a fight with the seneschal and you'd better start looking for a new job.

The ground slipped a little beneath Ondine's feet. Not literally, for that would be an earth tremor and Brugel is not in a quake zone. The ground slipped figuratively, making her feel a bit wobbly on the inside. She shook Pyotr's hand and with a shaky voice said, 'Pleased to meet you.'

'And I you,' Pyotr said with a welcoming smile that made Ondine start to feel at ease.

Pyotr turned to Hamish and welcomed him calmly with a handshake. Ondine had an inkling she was going to like this man as the colour returned to his lined face. He had the most obvious comb-over she'd ever seen. The wide parting began just above his ear and stretched his slick brown hair right over to the other ear. She had to give herself a mental kick to stop staring at it.

'How old are you, Ondine?' Pyotr asked.

'Fifteen, sir.'

'I see. Then you can work in the afternoons, and attend the palechia school in the mornings. Once we find a new home for the school, of course. Please come with me.'

She couldn't believe how quickly Pyotr had recovered his composure.

The moment Pyotr turned away, Hamish squeezed Ondine's hand. Not to demonstrate his love – it was all about keeping a straight face while they gazed at that astonishing head of hair. Or not-hair. As much as she loved looking at Hamish, it took all her effort not to look at him right now, because if she did, she'd collapse in a fit of giggles.

Their feet clacking on the mosaic-tiled floor, the three of them followed Pyotr inside. Delicious aromas of roasting meat and vegetables wafted through the air. They must be somewhere near the kitchens.

'Do you have any work experience?' Pyotr asked Ondine.

'My parents run a pub and I help out a fair bit,' she said.

'You know your way around a kitchen, then?'

'Of course.'

Hamish squeezed her hand again. She kept her giggles in check as she answered more of Pyotr's questions while politely looking him in the eye and trying very hard not to look at his hair. Odd that the seneschal wasn't asking Old Col or Hamish any questions. Then another twig snapped – Hamish and Col already had jobs. She, however, was at a loose end and the kind man was trying to find her something to do.

'If the three of you would come this way, I'll take you to your lodgings. Then I shall inform the Duke of your attendance.'

'He's here already?' Ondine asked.

'Yes. A last-minute change of plans,' Pyotr said.

Aunt Col's brows shot up in surprise. 'A good thing we came directly, then, otherwise we would have been cooling our heels in Venzelemma.'

Ondine couldn't help thinking her great aunt knew a lot more than she was letting on. Pyotr's acceptance of them was so fuss-free that Ondine began to wonder if something was afoot. Ondine might lack a lot of what might be called 'life experience', but she trusted her instincts, and those instincts were telling her to be very careful. Which meant no gasping at the priceless paintings, no ooh-ing and ah-ing at the intricate decorations and the luxurious furniture as they walked past open sitting rooms. She kept her eyes firmly fixed on the middle of Pyotr's back – not looking down in case he turned around and thought she was acting sullen. She dared not look up because of that tantalising bad hair.

'This will be your room, Ondine,' Pyotr said, as they stopped outside door 404.

It was smaller than her bedroom at home. There were two narrow, single beds, one made up with a well-loved teddy bear sitting on the pillow and a crocheted blanket on the top. The other bed – which would be Ondine's – had plain white sheets and a beige quilt. Each bed had a matching white side table and a small white chest of drawers at the foot of the bed. The window looked out to a narrow, cobbled courtyard where washing flicked and flapped on the clothes lines.

Drab-tastic!

Pyotr continued, 'Your bags are yet to arrive. We'll walk to the laundry, where I'll introduce you to Miss Matice. She is the Master of Domestic Services, which is one of the most important jobs we have here.'

Nice that he tried to talk up the job description, but Ondine wasn't fooled. As they walked away from the kitchens and headed towards the laundry, those lovely cooking aromas faded away, replaced by strong smells of bleach, floral detergent and something that might almost pass for green apples.

'I'm very happy to do laundry,' Ondine said, because she didn't want to seem ungrateful. OK, laundry was a drudge, but Pyotr could have given her plenty of worse things to do, like scrub floors or toilets. 'But, if you don't mind me asking, how come you wanted to know about my kitchen experience?'

'Because, if you've worked in a kitchen, you'll know all about wine and food stains, and how to get them out.' Pyotr gave her a big grin.

Old Col snickered into her hand.

Hamish looked despondent and slightly worried. 'You'll be OK.' He leant forward and gave her a kiss on the cheek, which had the temporary effect of making her forget all about her imminent menial work. The drudgeny would be worth it if she and Hamish could be together.

'Young love. Bless,' an unfamiliar voice said.

Ondine felt heat rising in her face as she turned.

Pyotr introduced her. 'Miss Matice, this is Ondine, she will be starting here today. Would you be so kind as to take her under your wing?'

Miss Matice's hair was pulled into a tight blonde ponytail that made her head look alarmingly thin, like the rest of her reed-thin body, which almost seemed to disappear when she turned sideways.

'Delighted,' Miss Matice said, extending her bony hand to Ondine. 'Please, call me Draguta, we friends now, yes?'

'Y-yes.' With a mental hiccup, Ondine shook hands and tried to keep a straight face. Honestly, what kind of parents burdened their kid with such a horrible name? An uncharitable thought arrived – maybe she'd been a really ugly baby.

'Bye, then,' Hamish said, giving Ondine a lopsided smile.

She wanted to throw her arms around him and kiss him silly, but that would not go down so well with her new employer. And she really needed to make a good impression so they would see how useful she was and allow her to stay.

With a small wave, she bid him farewell and made ready to face up to her new job.[22] Pyotr, Old Col and Hamish turned and walked away.

'Start with baskets. Is about to rain, get washing off line,' Draguta said in her strangely clipped style of talking. Ondine wondered if perhaps Brugelish was her second language.

Through the open doorway, Ondine looked out at the courtyard and saw a small team of workers removing washing from the line. She walked out and reached up to the first peg.

Something wet and smelly slapped her hand.

Urgh! It was a fish! A woman next to Ondine

---

22 *Which was remarkably similar to her old job. You may have noticed it was a Sunday afternoon and there were people working. Just like hotels, weekends are the busiest times at the palechia, so laundry staff take their weekends on Tuesdays and Wednesdays.*

Ondine's timetable looked like this:

Monday	Tuesday	Wednesday	Thursday	Friday	Saturday	Sunday
School	School	School	School	School		
Laundry			Laundry	Laundry	Laundry	Laundry

screamed and came running inside, dropping her basket of laundry in the process. 'It's raining fish!'

Plop! Flop! Splat!

Like some bizarre dream, fish fell all around her, landing with wet spluds on her head and shoulders and the ground. Some of them kept wriggling and flipping. And oh, the putrid smell!

Argh! Horrified, yet compelled to stay on task, Ondine grabbed the washing from the line and threw it into the basket. Wet projectiles kept hammering her. *Ooof*, her head. *Ouch*, her shoulder. *Biff*, her face.

All around people were screaming and crying and huddling under the eaves to get away from the hideous rain.

Ondine picked up her laundry basket and charged inside.

'Where is laundry?' Draguta demanded.

Looking down, Ondine gasped. Her basket was full of fish. 'It must be underneath!'

'Is crazy! Crazy!' Draguta threw her hands up in the air in frustration. 'Will have to wash all over again!'

'Or, looking on the bright side, I've caught us dinner,' Ondine said.

'Ha! I like you!' Draguta slapped her on the back. 'Now, get rid of fish and get washing. Here, take basket and sort for colours.' In the next breath, Draguta caught the attention of another laundry worker and told her to take all the fish to the kitchens.

Feeling bewildered by the strange turn of events, Ondine could only shrug and get to work, sorting clothes. Draguta tended to an industrial-sized machine that had just finished spinning. Not for the first time, Ondine wondered whether she would ever get used to calling Draguta by that harsh name. Strong veins popped out on Draguta's sinewy arms as she pulled wet bath sheets and towelling robes from the machine. At the same time, another laundress moved towards a small door set into the wall. Dirty clothes spilled on to the floor.

'A laundry chute! That's cool,' Ondine said.

'Not nearly,' Draguta said. 'They be lords and ladies, but live like slobs. They put down chutes in one day what regular people use in week. Get used to it.'

'Draguta, do you have a middle name?' Ondine asked as she separated the dirty clothes into their respective piles.

The laundry master's face turned to a scowl. 'Elena. Named after grandmother, may she rot in hell!' Draguta turned to her right and spat on the floor.

A slither of fear slid up Ondine's spine and she mentally ruled out ever mentioning the name Elena again.

Should she try another tack? Why not. 'Do you have a nickname?'

'No.'

Ondine gulped. 'Well . . . most people call me Ondi for short, so feel free to call me that, I don't mind.'

'My name is Draguta. Is strong name.' Draguta hefted a basket of wet washing on to where her hips would be if she had a gram of fat on her. A strong name for a strong woman.

It took two workers to heft each of the remaining baskets of washing out to the courtyard, where the rain had stopped just as fast as it began. Draguta managed a whole basket on her own. Ondine stayed inside, sorting the remaining dirty clothes.

'You need to go through pockets,' Draguta instructed, as she came back into the laundry. 'They filthy, leave tissues behind. Lost count of times to rewash dark trousers because of shredded tissue. Don't be shy, shove hand in there. Ferret around.'

Ferret?

Panic surged through Ondine. 'Jupiter's moons! *Ferret!*'

Chapter Five

How far had Hamish gone? What if he transformed into a ferret in front of the seneschal?

'I have to go!' Ondine shot up, knocking over a pile of silk blouses. Charging down the hallway, she yelled out, 'Hamish, wait!'

On she ran, hoping she wasn't too late. All that time on the train and they hadn't spent one moment discussing how they were going to manage Hamish's ... *issue*. They had been together so much during summer, she'd become used to him being human whenever she was around. What if he'd lost the ability to control his transformations? A familiar groan of pain and a filthy Celtic curse carried up the hall. Ondine's vision blurred as tears threatened to leak out. Skittering around the corner, she saw Shambles the ferret lying on the floor. Clothes everywhere. Old Col cast Ondine a dark look, as if this were all her fault. Pyotr merely cocked one eyebrow and swallowed, waiting for an explanation. Ondine herself struggled to find a reason.

For a moment she opened and shut her mouth, but nothing came out. Pyotr had just witnessed a terrifying weather event and now a man turning into a ferret. She wondered if she should tell him about the fish rain? It would be a lot to take in. Dread crawled through her body. She didn't have to be psychic to know they were in serious trouble if she didn't think of something quickly.

The something she thought of was: 'You've never seen a man turn into a ferret before?'

'Can't say that I have.' Pyotr scratched his temple.

'You have now,' Ondine ploughed on. 'You can see what a great asset he'll be to the Duke. After all, Shambles is the one who foiled the assassination attempt against him. The Duke wouldn't even be here if not for him. That's why he offered him a job, because he saved his life. And if Duke Pavla goes under, Lord Vincent would take control, and who wants that?'

'Thank you, yes.' Pyotr nodded slowly, closing his eyes as he did so, indicating he'd heard – and possibly seen – quite enough.

'If ye could all turn around for a wee bit, I need tae straighten meself out,' Shambles said, wincing as he budged and fudged his way into a sitting position to become humanly Hamish again. Ondine felt a fresh pang of longing for him. He looked like he was in so much pain.

They turned their backs to give him privacy.

'I have seen many things in my years . . .' Pyotr started.

Ondine waited for him to finish his sentence, but after a few breathy pauses with nothing between them, she realised he wouldn't.

'Great Aunt Col did it to him, in the ballroom here at the palechia. Years ago when she made her debut.' Ondine turned to see how the seneschal was taking it. A flicker on Pyotr's face, a raised eyebrow, then his features were back in place, as if they were discussing nothing more than the weather.

With a small cough Old Col said, 'You are the epitome of discretion, sir, and we are in your debt.'

Once he had his trousers on the right way, Hamish stood up. He sat down again straight away and looked a bit woozy.

Ondine knelt beside him and put her hand on his shoulder, 'You're hurting.'

'Naw lass, I'll be fine.'

She didn't buy it, and gave him a tender kiss on the forehead to salve the pain.

Pyotr spoke up. 'I think it would be best if he returned to his animal form.'

'But –' Ondine started.

Pyotr said, 'As much as it appears to pain him, I believe the Duke would prefer him to remain a ferret.'

'Dinnae fuss, it will just be for a wee while,' Hamish said.

Ondine began to fret. They were at the Duke's palechia because they wanted to be together. But the Duke only wanted the ferrety Shambles side of

Hamish. It hurt to know the only way they could be together was to be apart.

Ondine flung her arms around Hamish's neck and hugged him, hard. 'We'll work something out,' she said, and kissed him again.

Pain lanced Ondine as she watched him revert to his animal form, but it was nothing compared to the physical pain he must be feeling.

Pyotr said, 'By the way, what is that smell?'

'It's trout,' Ondine said. 'Lots of them fell from the sky as we took in the laundry.'

Pyotr stopped and stared at Ondine. 'Do you mean to say it has just rained fish?'

'Yes, sir. But we've cleaned most of it up.'

'Just a moment,' he said as two men walked down the hall towards them. Pyotr asked them to remove any stray fish from the lawns, trees and rooftops. 'And see that you clean out any debris that may have fallen through the school roof.' They looked startled.

'I meant what I said,' Pyotr added, dismissing the workmen. He returned his gaze to Col, Shambles and Ondine, his face showing no sign that he'd asked the workers to perform anything out of the ordinary. 'Come this way. The Duke does not like to be kept waiting.'

Chapter Six

'Delighted to see you!' Duke Pavla said as he took Old Col's hand in his. They were standing in his gleaming study. The leather chairs looked so shiny Ondine thought she'd slide right off them. Not that she had permission to sit down yet. The Duke – and the Duchess Kerala was here too – hadn't invited them to do so.

The Duke looked the same as he always did – dressed in an expensive, dark suit, his hair swept back from his widow's peak. His high-maintenance split moustache looked so neat it might have been stencilled on. 'Dare I say you have arrived just in time. Somebody tried to poison me with seafood,' he said.

'My Lord Duke, you have no cause for alarm.

Falling fish are a natural phenomenon, caused by the twister turning into a waterspout over the lake,' Old Col said. Then she added, 'Although it was a startling event.'

For a palpable few seconds Duke Pavla stared at her as if she had said something really strange. Well, she had.

'Falling fish?'

'As a result of the twister, Your Grace.'

It took him a few moments to compose himself. 'I was referring to earlier events at the fish markets,' he said.

Now Ondine was really confused.

With a wave of his hand the Duke invited them to sit. He also dismissed Pyotr, so it was just the five of them in the room. Ondine did her best not to fidget. To her dismay, Shambles climbed on to Col's shoulder, not hers.

The Duke sat behind his desk. The Duchess remained standing behind him. She looked im-maculate, as only the seriously rich can. Perfectly applied make-up, shiny mahogany hair, a tailored suit that complimented her hourglass frame and soft dainty hands. She wore an imperious look on her face, a mixture of revulsion and concern. Obviously not a small-animal lover. It was hard to explain why, but Ondine had the feeling the Duchess was one of those people who preferred her animals without a pulse.

'This is too much of a coincidence. You've heard about what happened at the fish markets yesterday?'

Old Col coughed softly. 'No, Your Grace.'

The Duke looked bewildered. Ondine felt incredibly uncomfortable. Surely at some point things would start making sense. Wouldn't they?

The Duchess placed a comforting hand on Pavla's shoulder.

'I was due to open the new sushi bar,' Pavla said. 'They would have made me eat the stuff, too. A good thing I changed my schedule. I sent my dear wife to the markets in my place. They had a listeria outbreak but thank the stars she was unharmed. If anything had happened to you, my love . . .' his voice trailed off as their eyes locked.

A pang gripped Ondine. They looked so very

much in love. Would she and Hamish ever have that? Impossible if he remained a Shambles-ferret.

'I'm fine. I have an iron constitution,' the Duchess said.

'I can't help thinking someone has cursed me. Yesterday bad food. Today a twister, now you're saying there was fish rain? If this is the result of dark magic, I'm glad to have you as an ally, Miss Romano,' the Duke said. He turned to Shambles, who was still on Old Col's shoulder. 'And you, Shambles, I can see you will be a valuable asset.'

'Aye. Ready, willing and able. Where would ye like me tae start?' Shambles said.

'I think you should begin with the most obvious. The kitchens,' the Duke said. 'Watch them closely for the next week and report anything unusual directly back to me.'

'Or me. If the Duke is unavailable,' Kerala added.

'Yes, good idea, my love.'

The Duke still hadn't addressed Ondine, which made her feel insignificant. Then again, maybe if he ignored her, she could slip under the radar? If he didn't directly send her home, did it mean she could stay?[23]

Unexpectedly, the Duke winked at Shambles, which was not endearing. If anything, Ondine felt even more unsettled.

The Duke moved towards a pile of letters, picked up a gold paper knife and began slicing the envelopes open. He talked the whole time, reading one thing while discussing another. Meanwhile, the Duchess walked over to a side table and poured herself a glass of wine.

The Duke opened the next envelope. Brown powder fell from the papers it contained.

Poison?

'Get back!' Shambles yelled. 'Dinnae breathe it in!'

The Duke coughed and reeled away in shock. Instinctively Ondine grabbed a rose bowl off the side table, tipped the flowers on to the floor, then slapped the upturned bowl over the envelope and powder.

The Duchess's mouth fell open as she stood in mute

23 *This kind of thinking began after the Soviet days, during the time of new freedoms and transparency, when 'everything not expressly forbidden is permitted'. A marked change from the gruelling days of 'anything not expressly permitted is forbidden'.*

shock. Her eyebrows shot up and stayed there.

Inside the bowl water dripped on to the powder, turning it into a dark brown liquid that oozed across the desk.

'What is it?' the Duke said.

Confusion made Ondine feel dizzy. 'Looks like coffee,' she suggested.

'We don't know that for sure,' Col said.

'I feel so terribly foolish,' the Duke said, wiping his brow.

Perhaps they'd all overreacted. What a mess Ondine had made of the Duke's study.

The brown liquid stopped oozing and started sinking into the table, eating right through the veneer.

'Not so foolish after all,' Col said. 'It's some kind of acid.'

'Who sent it?' Shambles asked.

'There is no return address on the envelope,' Col said, picking it up. 'Your Grace, call the police, this needs to be tested.'

'Wait,' the Duchess said, stepping closer to the table. 'Let me see it.'

Great Aunt Col handed the envelope to the Duchess, who held it up to the light as if she might make out something the others had missed. 'The stamp has not been franked, so we do not know from which sorting office it came. Maybe if I try this . . .' She took out a pack of matches from her handbag and lit one, holding it beneath the envelope. 'Saw it in a movie once, there was a secret message written in – ouch!' The envelope caught fire and she dropped it hastily.

'Are you all right, my love?' Pavla rushed to his wife's side and checked her hand. 'You'll need a cold compress.'

As the burning envelope fluttered to the ground, Shambles raced down Col's shoulder and stomped his paws on the glowing paper. 'Weil, there goes that,' he said.

'I was trying to help,' Kerala said.

The Duke's skin turned grey. He took a small breath, then adjusted his tie. 'Colette, you and Shambles – and Ondine, it seems – have arrived just in time. I want you to be my eyes and ears here in the palechia. From now on you will open all my correspondence. If there is no return address, incinerate it immediately.'

Uneasiness morphed into dismay in Ondine. When she'd set out with Hamish, she'd had visions of being with him and having a great time. Not for a moment did she think they'd have to work that hard. Not harder than she already did at her parents' pub in Venzelemma. Now she felt as if they were responsible for the Duke's very survival. And she didn't have a clue how they would do that.

'You wouldn't credit it, but I used to think I was paranoid,' Pavla said. 'However, I have come to accept that somebody really is out to get me. As much as Vincent knows he will one day succeed me, he is far from ready. As they say, "Fate chooses our relatives, we choose our friends".[24]

The mention of Vincent's name sent fresh ripples of worry through Ondine. Lord Vincent was the Duke's teenage son and heir, but he was also a total prat and had tried to bring on his father's heart

_____

24 *Jacques Delille, 1738–1813. He had loads of friends in high places, but his own father refused to acknowledge him.*

problems so he could inherit the title ahead of time. At least he was now in a military academy fifty kilometres away and couldn't do anything directly. But what if he had spies in the palace?

'Your safety and continuing good health are my paramount concern,' Old Col said to the Duke.

'Ondine.' Duke Pavla turned his full attention to her. Worry filled her stomach with concrete. 'I appreciate your swift action, but you are so young. You should be with your parents.'

'I –' Ondine made a start, but she couldn't finish.

'She has the gift of sight, Your Grace,' Col said. 'She will prove very useful.'

'Really, now?' Pavla's eyes widened.

Not really, she wanted to say, but Col had dropped her in it and the Duke was interested. If the Duke wanted to believe in it, then why not? What some people called psychic powers, others called 'cold reading' or 'being really observant'.[25] If he thought she could be useful, she'd get to stay.

---

25 *Or watching every episode of 'Lie to Me' and applying it to your real life.*

'Aw, yeas, she's brilliant at it,' Shambles added, climbing back on to Col's shoulder.

The Duchess moved to stand beside her husband, placing her hand on his arm. Her knuckles turned pinky white as she squeezed him that little bit too much. Ondine thought Kerala wanted to say something, but she kept silent.

'How very useful,' Pavla said. In the next breath he summoned Pyotr back into his study to show him the mess. Pyotr nodded and ushered them into the anteroom while he cleaned it up.

The Duchess murmured in Pavla's ear. Despite her low voice, Ondine heard everything she said: 'Are you sure about this? They turn up in a storm, then it rains fish and now you have a toxic letter. It's too much of a coincidence.'

Old Col coughed into her closed hand. 'Please forgive my rudeness, Your Grace, but I am inclined to agree with the Duchess. This really should be a matter –'

'For the police? Of course it is. I will put Brugel's finest on the case. They are continuing the investigation of the attempt on my life at the railway station. But from all accounts the scallions under arrest are taking the blame upon themselves and refusing to implicate anyone further. They will, in time. Given the right motivation, everybody talks.'

A disconcerting look crossed his face. He dropped his voice low. 'Here, among family, friends and staff, I need something . . . less overt. Men and women in uniform won't loosen tongues. If anything, it would make the schemers behave impeccably and everyone else miserable. I need whoever is out to get me to feel as if the authorities' attentions are otherwise . . . *diverted*. Are we on the same page? Good. The three of you will gather information on everyone at the palechia and report back anything you see, hear or suspect.'

'We'll get started right away, so we will,' Shambles said.

With a pang of longing, Ondine looked at Shambles. As a ferret, he could slip into rooms and listen to conversations without anyone noticing. He'd be the perfect spy.

'Do you have a list of suspects?' Old Col asked.

'Hand over the phone book,' Shambles said.

Ondine clamped down a grin. This was not the time for jokes.

To their credit, the Duke and Duchess ignored the quip. Pavla said, 'A couple come to mind. Lord Vincent is all too eager to assume the reins of power. Or should that be reigns?'

Crickets chirped in Ondine's head, because the Duke's pun only worked in print form.

Pyotr walked past them with a trolley full of boxes and lumpy plastic bags. Evidence, Ondine guessed, as Pyotr nodded to them that his work was done.

'No matter,' the Duke said as he ushered them back into his study. 'My son and heir has learnt his lesson. His supporters, on the other hand, could well be plotting my downfall. Another I suspect is my eldest sister, Anathea.'

'The Infanta?' Old Col asked.

The Duchess coughed as she sipped her wine.

Looking about the study, Ondine could see no trace of their recent drama. Only a notebook lay on the table to conceal the burn in the wood.

She gave a mental shudder.

Duke Pavla continued: 'All this would have been hers, you see. But fate intervened and I was born. She begrudges me the right that is mine by birth. Words are her poison of choice. Makes mischief. Most right-thinking people take anything she says with a slice of lemon.'[26]

The Duchess made a moue with her mouth and wrinkled her nose at the mention of her sister-in-law.

'Miss Romano, you and Shambles shall attend dinner tonight, ostensibly as my guest, but privately I want you to be on the alert for signs of discontent. Ondine, you will be needed in the laundry.'

Oh, thanks, I get sent to work and Col gets a free meal, Ondine thought.

'Yes, Your Grace,' Col said.

'The entire family is in residence. It should provide ample opportunity to observe the various personalities at play.'

After they were ushered out, Ondine checked

26 *With a slice of lemon is how Bruglers traditionally take their tea. In some cultures the expression is 'with a pinch of salt'. This makes no sense at all because tea with salt tastes awful!*

to make sure nobody could overhear them before she spoke. 'I can't believe he's making the three of us responsible for his safety! He should bring in the experts.'

'Thank you for your vote of confidence,' Old Col said.

'I didn't mean it like that.'

'Of course not. What you really mean is you're only fifteen and you have the burden of a nation on your shoulders.'

An invisible weight descended on Ondine as she let the truth of Col's statement settle. 'How much does he really expect us to do? We're not trained detectives.' *What we are is a scared girl, a ferret and an old witch*, she thought.

'Ah, my dear, that is why we shall be so effective. I am the batty old lady with a pet on her shoulder, and you are an innocent girl. Nobody will suspect a thing.'

'Right.' Ondine mulled it over. 'You're being quiet, Shambles.'

'Aye, I was thinking about Pyotr. Nothing seems to faze him.'

'Hmmmm,' Ondine said.

Col gave a most disarming smile. 'You're thinking like detectives already. Nobody should be above suspicion.'

'In that case, Vincent is still at the top of my list,' Ondine said. 'Mercury's wings, I've just realised something. Pavla said Vincent had learnt his lesson, past tense. Does that mean he's not at the academy any more?'

'Oh dear,' Hamish said.

'Oh double dear,' Col said. 'He won't be happy that we're here either. We'll have to try our best not to antagonise him. Right, Ondine, you should get back to the laundry. Shambles, we need to dress for dinner.'

Shambles leant over and gave Ondine a whiskery wet smudge on the cheek, but it didn't comfort her at all. If anything, it made her wonder when she'd next see him as proper Hamish again.

Chapter Seven

amish wanted to be human all the time, but he knew the only way to make progress in their hunt for suspects was to remain a ferret and allow people to call him Shambles. He'd much rather be with Ondine in the laundry, but that wasn't an option. He'd also love to be able to talk more, but he exercised extreme control and stayed mute as Pyotr announced Old Col's arrival at dinner.

'Your Grace, honoured guests, ladies and gentlemen, I present Miss Colette Romano.'

Perched on Col's shoulder and blinking away tears from her strong perfume, Shambles was able to check out the room from human eye-level. Over to one side he noticed two small boys. They were well dressed for their age, wearing cut-down suits like mini-gentlemen.

The boys exchanged sly looks and Shambles instinctively knew they were up to no good.

A waitress offered drinks to some adults near them. One of the boys stuck out his foot and tripped her up. She yelped in surprise, her face filled with horror. Then the most bizarre thing happened. Pyotr, who was standing close by, turned around at exactly the right moment, put his hands out and caught the falling tray. Some of the drink sloshed out, but the glasses didn't fall.

Everyone around them looked momentarily stunned. Pyotr kept his composure and handed the tray back to the grateful waitress. She then carried on serving guests as if nothing had happened, but Shambles could tell by her rapid breaths that she hadn't fully recovered.

No sign of the Duke, which was odd – he'd invited them, so surely he'd be here by now? The Duchess, holding a glass of red wine, approached Col. Suddenly the world dropped from beneath Shambles, and he hung on for dear life.

What the?

Old Col was curtseying! After her graceful bob, things righted themselves and he was back to eye-level again.

'My Lady Duchess, it is an honour,' Col said.

The Duchess enunciated her words far too carefully as she said, 'You. Are. Too. Kind.'

Duchess Kerala wore her dark hair in a neat helmet shape. Light bounced off her hair, it was that shiny. The hand holding the glass of wine looked soft and fleshy, as if she'd never performed a manual task in her life.

The waitress appeared and asked the Duchess, 'Your Grace, may I offer your guest an aperitif?'[27]

'Thank you, but soda water is fine,' Old Col said.

Surprise jolted Shambles. He felt sure Col would help herself to the best of whatever was on offer. The twig snapped – Col wanted to keep a clear head.

The two young boys who had tripped up the waitress were now eyeing Shambles with undisguised glee. Thank goodness he was out of their reach. Oh

---

27 *Invented by those gourmets the French. An 'aperitif' is a pre-dinner alcoholic drink, designed to get the appetite going.*

great! Old Col decided to walk towards them. In the time it took the thought *I'm still safe up here* to travel from one side of his ferret-sized brain to the other, Col had bent down to the boys' level.

'Hello, there,' Col said, 'this is my pet ferret, Shambles. He's very friendly. Would you like to pat him?'

Wrong on so many counts, but if he uttered a word to them it would blow his cover. He turned his head towards Col's ear and murmured, 'If they pull my tail, I'm out of here.'

'He's funny looking,' one of the boys said.

One of the little snipes pulled his tail, while the other clonked him on the head with a forceful pat. The impact was so great his teeth crashed together.

From across the room, Duchess Kerala said, 'Boysh, be gentle.' She didn't take a step closer to intervene; instead another woman stepped in and calmly directed the boys away. Shambles rummaged around in his brain: had the Duchess slurred her words? When she spoke again, he was sure of it.

'Thank you, nanny. The boysh can have their

dinnersh now,' the Duchess said.

Looking at the boys, Shambles could see them growing into little Lord Vincents, attitude and all. He made a mental note to keep clear of every one of the Duke's offspring, even if he was supposed to be a docile 'pet'. He scanned the room, but saw no sign of Vincent. He didn't know if that was a good thing or not. If he were here, he could keep an eye on him, but Vincent knew he was a ferret who could turn into a man, and might blow his cover.

At the other end of the room, the double doors opened. A woman wearing a starched white apron over black trousers and a black shirt nodded to the Duchess. The Duchess handed her empty wine glass to the nearest member of staff and announced to the room, 'Dinner is sherved.'

Shambles licked his chops. Wonderful aromas of caramelised onions, roast meat and crispy potatoes wafted in.

The dining room looked decidedly blue. Blue walls, and in the middle of the room, a long table with a blue-and-white tablecloth. A swift team of waiters, all dressed in black with starched white aprons, placed several bowls of salad at intervals along the table. The bowls were filled only with green leaves, thin slices of spring onion, shavings of Parmesan cheese and white beans.

Shambles saw the table was set for eighteen. A quick headcount told him there were a couple of spare seats. Hope sprang as he wondered if he might get fed. He'd be extra nice to Col. She'd give him some food. He might even charm some of the guests into feeding him as well. With so many people, and such large silver domes over all the plates, surely there would be plenty of leftovers?

Duke Pavla entered from another set of doors. Everyone bowed their heads as he walked in. He stepped towards Kerala and kissed her tenderly on the cheek. A lump formed in Shambles's throat. They made such a lovely couple. He hoped he and Ondine would still be as affectionate when they were that old.

They stood waiting for the Duke to be seated. To Shambles's surprise, the Duke did not sit at the head of the table. Instead, he chose the centre of one of the long sides, opposite the Duchess. The seat beside the Duchess was empty, and Shambles wondered who would sit there, if not the Duke?

'Good evening. As of now, fish will no longer be on the menu. Be seated.'

As soon as the Duke sat down, everyone else followed. The waiters lifted the domes off the plates to reveal the banquet beneath.

Shambles's stomach did a double take. *What tiny amounts of food!*

Even for a man the size of a ferret it was a measly serving. Half a boiled egg, sliced. Two slivers of roast chicken, so thin you could see through them. A tiny clump of fried onions. Sautéed courgettes and more of those white beans. Oh yes, and three thin scallops of potato. All arranged in the middle of a large white plate with a thick band of blue around the edge.

'This better be the entrée,' he murmured to Col as his stomach grumbled.

Old Col coughed, then lifted him off her shoulder and placed him on her lap. It got him out of sight, so he could slip under the table, unnoticed, and report back on anything he overheard.

Despite the small portions, Old Col came through for him and let a chunk of egg fall from her fork. With a leap he met the food mid-flight and swallowed it before he landed.

Somewhat recharged, he set to work, ears on alert. Avoiding people's feet became his main priority. Above the table, the dinner guests looked composed and serene, but underneath there was a fair amount of fidgeting and fenudging[28] going on.

Heading for the end of the table, Shambles saw a pair of legs crossing nervously back and forth at the ankles. He strained his ears to snapping point.

'Murmur, murmur, food, murmur, right, murmur, murmur, tennis.'

Not much help there, so Shambles decided to walk behind the twitching feet and sit directly under the speaker's chair.

'Murmur, murmur, rule out murmur the food,' one male voice said. 'Murmur, never enough of it.'

---

28 At the risk of turning this into a manual on Brugel's unusual grammar, 'fenudging' is a common adverb describing the flickety fidgety movements of people who otherwise ought to be sitting still.

A person sitting beside him gave a low chuckle. 'Murmur, murmur, Infanta.'

It sounded promising. Shambles listened some more and heard someone whisper, 'running out of time' and 'need to move soon' but nothing that made a cohesive whole. A staccato march announced the return of the waiters, who removed the empty plates. He strained to hear more conversation but the sound of feet drowned it out.

Moving about under the table, he searched and listened for more interesting conversations. Someone arrived late and took the remaining empty seat. He recognised the smarmy voice say, 'Good evening, Mother,' and heard him kiss her on the cheek.

Vincent! Shambles scurried back over the parquet to get away from Vincent's heavy boots. The last thing he needed was to get too close. All the same his ears stayed on high alert as he heard the Duchess mutter to her son, 'One day, all this will be yours.'

Really now? That was interesting!

Without warning, pain seared Shambles's insides. Panic shot through him. He silently cried out for

Ondine to take away his agony. In his mind, he fixed an image of her sweet face to help him focus. How had this come on so quickly? His black furry arms buckled and bleached and turned into skin. His legs grew and grew. Just in time he pulled himself away from someone's twitching foot. Any moment now, Vincent might drop a fork or a napkin, reach down to get it and see him lying on the floor, bare as the day he was born.

He kept thinking of Ondine. When he angled his head so he could see through the forest of legs, he thought he'd died and gone to heaven. There she was, standing by the door with a tray of steaming hot hand towels. Her proximity must be why he'd changed. Slapping his forehead, he felt like a silly wee daftie! He could be a ferret any time he liked, but when she came near him, he turned human. Or, if he were already human, and she walked off, he reverted to ferret. If he didn't start controlling it soon, he'd be in serious trouble! He also knew if he wanted to do his job properly without detection, he'd have to keep away from her.

Ondine caught a glimpse of him and momentary shock played over her lovely features. Just as quickly, she reset her face, as if she hadn't seen anything at all.

Hamish felt a fresh surge of pride at how well she handled herself, considering the crazy circumstances.

'Your Grace,' Ondine said, walking towards the Duke.

Galloping agony pummelled Hamish from the inside, but now his biggest worry was fear of discovery. He had to change back or he'd be exposed. All the time he said not a peep, made not a single groan or even a loud panting noise.[29] Watching her feet move around the table and stop at each person was another form of torture. But the motivation to remain undetected overrode all else. Revisiting the pain, he willed his body back to ferret form.

Through blurry vision, he saw Ondine's feet approaching the Duchess and Vincent and nearly miss a step. Oh no, this was hardly the quiet sneaky start he'd hoped they could all make. Vincent now knew

---

29 *Quite frankly he deserved a medal. Next time you do something mild like stub your toe or get a paper cut, see if you can remain completely silent.*

Ondine was here, so they'd have to be extra careful.

Staggering on to his four paws, Shambles wobbled and hobbled back to the safety of Old Col. Lovely meaty aromas assailed his senses. When he looked up, he found a tiny lamb cutlet dangling from her fingers.

'Aye, yer a good woman.' He kept his voice quiet, so that only Col could hear.

He buried his face in the meat, biting off chunks and swallowing them without chewing. He heard rather than saw Ondine leave via the servant's door. A pang gripped his heart at her departure, but he knew that she'd want to get as far away from Vincent as possible.

A furious barking sound came from the guests' entrance. Two of the waiters opened the double doors. In stepped the Infanta Anathea holding a white ball of fluff under her arm. It barked and yapped like a lunatic. (The dog, not the Infanta.) With the frozen expression of a woman caught in a wind tunnel, the ash-blonde Infanta looked around at everyone seated at the table. For a while Shambles tried to work out what was wrong with her face. Everybody knew the

Infanta was at least a decade older than the Duke, but her eyebrows were up near her hairline and her forehead looked ironing-board flat.

Keeping that imperious look on her face, perhaps because she was incapable of any other expression, Infanta Anathea turned to the Duke and snarled, 'You started dinner without me?'

Everyone stopped talking. The room reverberated with clunks and clangs as they put their cutlery down. A flash of silver caught Shambles's eye – he turned to see someone dropping a small fish knife into a clutch bag and clicking the top closed. Shambles snuck over to the patent-leather bag. It was so shiny he could see his furry reflection in it.

The Duke rose from his chair. 'Dear sister. Dinner is at seven sharp. Just as it always is. Your seat is waiting.'

'You're so rude,' the Infanta said.

Shambles used the distraction to his advantage, the Infanta's voice drowning out the quiet 'snick' as he opened the clutch bag. He grabbed the stolen knife with his teeth and brought it to an empty spot under the table, well clear of anyone's feet.

At that moment the Infanta's little dog spotted Shambles under the table. The dog wriggled and spasmed like he'd been struck with an electric prod.

'No, Biscuit,'[30] the Infanta said, attempting to calm her pet.

Biscuit paid the Infanta no mind. With a blood-curdling 'ru-ru-ru-ru' the white hairy thing launched itself into the air. He landed on the ground and charged for Shambles.

'Biscuit! Heel!' the Infanta commanded, but Biscuit had another master – blood lust!

For a terrifying quarter of a second Shambles considered transforming into a human to gain an advantage over the dog. Panic surged through his furry body as he looked up to see Old Col's worried face. With a lunge he shot up the leg of the chair, but his claws tangled on the hem of Col's skirt.

'Ru-ru-ru-ru,' Biscuit barked.[31]

Quick as a flash, Old Col's hands grabbed

---

30 *Biscuit's real title is Cardrona King Ivanovich, five times Best Breed, twice Best in Show, Venzelemma Ducal Dog Show.*

31 *He snarled too, but the Brugelish spelling of dog snarls is too complicated to print here.*

Shambles around the middle to pull him to safety. Biscuit hurled himself into the air, his mouth open, white teeth and red gums bared.

The pretty white dog sank his fangs into Shambles's ferrety neck and chomped down hard.

Chapter Eight

Being neither a witch nor a woman possessed of supernatural powers to see into rooms without being in them at the time, Ondine remained oblivious to Shambles's current plight. To her credit, she had realised her presence in the Duke's dining room during the evening meal had been a huge mistake. She knew Hamish and Old Col would be at the dinner, but she couldn't refuse Draguta's request to take the towels in. Guilt spread through her at the huge amounts of pain it must have caused Hamish for her to appear like that and make him transform. It didn't help that Vincent had been there too. Thankfully he only gave her a greasy look and had kept his mouth shut. The moment she'd done her job, Ondine had nodded to the Duke and Duchess and quickly scarpered out of there. Her assumption being that Hamish would revert to ferret form and remain safe and undetected, if a little green around the gills.

Not knowing Hamish was bleeding from the neck after Biscuit's attack, Ondine followed Draguta to the staff lounge and ate a bowl of vegetable soup and a multi-grain dinner roll. Unaware that the Infanta was screaming profusely at Old Col about the chance 'that revolting *thing*' had given her champion rabies,[32] Ondine accepted a second bowl of soup.

She was also completely insensible to the next development, where Old Col made an incantation to the powers of the earth, stars and moon, at which

---

32 *Rabies is a particularly nasty virus transmitted via bites from infected animals. The virus attacks the victim's central nervous system and sends them completely mad. In later stages of infection, the victim foams at the mouth as their body produces copious amounts of saliva. If not treated quickly, it is almost always fatal.*

In an attempt to placate nervous tourists, Brugel declared itself rabies free in 2005. However, neighbouring countries Slaegal and Craviç make no such claims. As everyone knows, wild dogs and bats (which are the main carriers) cannot read, and frequently walk or fly straight past the signposts advising them to keep out.

point Biscuit's teeth fell out.[33]

The Infanta's high-pitched screams that could open a can? Ondine heard them loud and clear. Just about everyone in the palechia heard them. They ripped through the halls and the thin plaster walls like daggers of foul temper. The piercing noise reached the staff lounge, where Ondine's second bread roll beckoned, but ultimately lay untouched.

In a heartbeat Ondine took flight and ran towards the horrible sounds of chaos and terror.

Only to find herself face to face with her worst nightmare. OK, her second worst nightmare. Her first worst nightmare was being separated from Hamish. But her second worst nightmare was Lord Vincent.

He was standing right in front of her. His eyes glinted with anger as he scraped his blond hair back from his forehead. A gleam of satisfaction stole through her as she saw remnants of a blue stain on his hand, left over from the night they'd caught him robbing the family hotel. Did he not wash, or was it

33 The little doggy's teeth did make a noise as they hit the floor, but as this sound has never happened in the recorded history of Brugel, there is no word for it.

sheer guilt keeping the stain there? Not for the first time, Ondine wondered what she'd ever seen in him. He might have been handsome if he weren't so ugly on the inside.

'What are *you* doing here?' she asked.

'What are you doing *here*?' he asked straight back. 'And don't stand there like an idiot. Bow to your betters.'

Just because you've got a title it doesn't mean you're better than me, Ondine thought. The memory of the night he slapped her hard on the face came flooding back.[34] In defiance, she kept her back ramrod straight. 'Aren't you supposed to be in Fort Kluff?'

'It didn't take.' He examined a fingernail and said, 'Why are you here?'

'I'm working.'

Vincent mimicked, '*I'm working.*' He made no sideways movement to let her pass.

Frustration surged through Ondine. 'May I pass?'

Silently he stepped to the side and made room. Ondine took a step but something smacked her hard in the shins. A lurching, falling sensation lasted all of

---

34 *Bet you wish you'd read the first book now, eh?*

half a second before she hit the floor with a thud. She looked up and saw a smirk on his face.

'Not quite a bow, but it will do.'

Picking herself up, Ondine brushed away the hurt in her palms. 'You're a –'

'Tut tut! When I'm Duke, you'll show me more respect.'

'When you're Duke I'll emigrate to Slaegal!'[35] Ondine stomped off as best she could, head high, limping slightly, but all the same savouring the victory of getting the last word in.

Just as she turned the corner Vincent yelled out, 'Witch!'

His tone carried such a sting, it was the first time Ondine heard someone use that word in a derogatory sense. Indignation on behalf of her great aunt surged through her. A retort sprang to her lips just as Old Col arrived, carrying a prone Shambles in her arms. Around his neck she'd wrapped a white linen napkin.

---

35 *The capital of Slaegal is called Norange. It's the only known word that rhymes with orange. Some people dispute this and say 'strange' is close enough, and, indeed, it is a strange place.*

Correction, some of it was white but mostly it was covered in deep burgundy stains.

'Shambles!' Ondine cried.

Lurch. Ondine's stomach did that horrible sinking-with-fear thing as she looked at him. Then *lurch* again as another nagging, awful, this-is-not-right feeling took hold. She was standing right next to him, close enough for her to touch his head and say, 'Oh, you poor darling.'

So why hadn't he changed back into a man now that they were close again? Did he not want to? *Gasp.* Was he too injured?

'Quick, let's get to my room,' Old Col said. They ran up the stairs and rushed down the hall, and shut the door behind them for privacy.

Ondine grabbed a couple of towels and placed them on the bed, so they could lie Shambles down without staining the duvet.

With a waver in her voice, Ondine asked, 'How did it happen?' All the while she gently stroked Shambles's soft ferrety head and even kissed him twice. Did his eyelids flutter open? Did he mutter even one saucy comment about kisses? No.

Which made Ondine worry even more.

'Jupiter's moons, he's dying.'

'He's not dying,' Old Col said, unwrapping the cloth to reveal Shambles's matted wet neck.

His furry body gently rose and fell with his breathing.

'But there's so much blood,' Ondine said.

'That there is. Fortunately, most of it belonged to Biscuit. That's the Infanta's crazy dog, by the way. Thank goodness the dog bite missed anything vital, otherwise Shambles would have bled to death.'

Fresh pain seared Ondine and her tummy curdled like lemon juice in milk. She felt like she might stop breathing. Her strapping, handsome lad was simply lying there in his fragile ferrety state and there was nothing she could do about it.

Old Col related the entire sorry tale to Ondine. About how the champion show dog had gone the full-beserker on Shambles and how she had used ancient magic and ripped the little mutt's teeth out. Every last one of them.

Old Col looked ashamed. 'In the panic of the

moment, I wanted Biscuit's teeth out of Shambles. I must have said the spell not quite right. Maybe I had a senior moment?'

Hope surged in Ondine. If that nasty dog had no teeth left, Shambles would be safe from future attacks. 'Will he make a full recovery?'

'Undoubtedly. He's sleeping it off. When the dog attacked, Shambles was about to let fly with enough profanities to strip the wallpaper. There wasn't time to think. I cast a spell to make him appear dead, so that I could get him out of the dining room.'

Relief washed over Ondine like a tidal wave. But there was one more unknown factor in the sorry adventure, not counting all the unknown unknowns.[36]

'Aunt Col, why is he still a ferret?'

---

36 *From former US Secretary of Defense, Donald Rumsfeld:*

   'There are known knowns. These are things we know that we know.

   There are known unknowns. That is to say, there are things that we know we don't know.

   But there are also unknown unknowns. There are things we don't know we don't know.'

   Feb. 12, 2002, Department of Defense news briefing.

   Mr Rumsfeld forgot to add that there are 'unknown knowns'. These are things that you did know, but have forgotten.

Col shook her head, pursed her lips as if in deep thought and said, 'We'll have to wait and see.'

Waiting is awful. There's the waiting for a meal to arrive when you can smell it cooking, and your stomach is saying 'hurry up'. There's the butterflies-in-the-tummy waiting for a gymnastics score from the fussy judges who are not sure if they should deduct half a point or a whole point for stepping outside the white lines. Then there's the hopeless I-feel-completely-sick kind of waiting, as a young girl looks upon the hopeless shape of an injured ferret waiting to see if he'll ever become handsomely human again.

An hour dragged by. When Ondine looked at Old Col's watch, it lied and said only eight minutes had passed. Fifteen more of Ondine's hours passed over the next two real hours. There was no change from Shambles at all, just the rise and fall of his furry little tummy as he breathed in and out. Every now and then his paws twitched. At one point, his eyelids flickered and seemed ready to spring open, but it was just his eyes quivering. Dreaming.

'You need sleep yourself, you've got school in the morning,' Old Col said.

'But it's got no roof.'

'Pyotr told me they'll make do with one of the barns.'

'Do I have to go?'

'Of course you do. If you don't, the Duke will send you home. By the way, your parents are furious with me for letting you stay and work here.'

Gulp. Shambles had taken up so much of her head space she hadn't given a thought to her parents. 'It didn't go down well?'

'You should have heard your mother scream when I phoned her and told her where we were. They wanted you to go home immediately. I told them you'd get a better education here. So you'd better prove me right or we're all in strife. And another thing, make sure you call them every now and then, just so they know you're safe and well.'[37]

---

[37] *In Brugel, it is mandatory for all children to attend school until the age of sixteen. You can stay on longer, of course, and many people do. It's common to find senior-school students in their twenties. The rise in mature students became so alarming in the 1990s the education*

Rubbing her eyes and finding gritty things in the corners, Ondine agreed to return to her room. Some people have worried so much about another's fate they have lain awake all night with the stress of it. Ondine was not such a person. Yes, she fully planned to worry all night about Shambles and whether he would ever be Hamish again. The new bed felt strange and cold; a recipe for further fretting. Her body, however, had other ideas and she fell asleep two pico-seconds after pulling the covers up.

Tasting a mouthful of dust, Ondine half-woke and prised her eyes open. It was dark – hardly surprising as it must have been the middle of the night. The true surprise was trying to swallow. Her tongue felt dry enough to leave splinters in her cheeks.

I must have fallen asleep with my mouth open, she thought. Quickly followed by another important thought: *I need a drink*.

Eyes adjusting to the low light, Ondine saw

department had to allocate designated campuses for twenty-somethings. It also created the uniquely puzzling situation of some students being older than their teachers.

no refreshing glass of water on her side table. She attempted to swallow again and felt the ash-dry results. Wincing at the night chill, Ondine pulled her top blanket over her shoulders and did her best to be as quiet as possible so she didn't wake Draguta the laundry boss, who was asleep in the bed beside hers. She closed the door with a soft click and made her way to the kitchen.

At this time of night, she expected to be alone. No such luck. There in the kitchen, standing at the central galley bench, was a woman dressed in a shimmery satiny nightgown, with a whimpering fluffy white dog. A white dog with soft red gums, full of gouges where his teeth used to be.

The Infanta! Ondine tried to work out the correct form of address to use. Your Grace? My Lady? Her father would have known, but he wasn't here to help.

'Your Highness.' Ondine quickly dropped into a curtsey. In any case, she couldn't say much more because her mouth was as dry as week-old bread. The woman smiled and Ondine felt a surge of relief at getting it right.[38]

At first Ondine thought she'd surprised the woman, judging by the Infanta's shocked expression, but after a while it became obvious the woman's eyebrows sat up like that permanently.

'Were you sent to the kitchens at this late hour, child?'

Croak, rasp. 'No one sent me. I need a drink of water, Your Highness.'

The Infanta nodded her head towards the taps and put a spoon in the dog's mouth. For the smallest moment Ondine felt sorry for Biscuit. Straight after that she thought the dog deserved everything he got for attacking her beloved Shambles.

Glass of water safely in hand, Ondine decided to

---

38 *In some European countries, it is correct to address an infanta as 'Your Highness', but only if she is the daughter of the ruling king or queen. As Brugel is ruled by Duke Pavla, and the Infanta is Duke Pavla's older sister, this is not the case. Brugel tradition requires her to be addressed as 'My Lordship', even though she is a woman. Thereafter she is referred to as 'Ma'am'.*

By calling her 'Your Highness', Ondine promoted the Infanta to a station above the Duke, and the Infanta had no intention of correcting her.

get out of there before she said anything stupid. When she turned around, she saw the Infanta make a quick movement away from the large stockpot bubbling over a low flame.

'What?' The Infanta's gaze bored into her.

Ondine was hardly going to say she thought the Infanta had put something in the soup. A queef of disgust[39] spread through her at the thought that the Infanta was feeding the dog with the soup spoon. Or was the soup just for the dog? In which case it would be all right, if a little unconventional. However, if it was the communal soup, she should probably warn everyone it had Biscuit slobber in it.

Hot on the heels of that internal soliloquy, Ondine had another thought that pushed disgust aside and let fear in. Maybe the Infanta didn't put the spoon back in the soup. Maybe she put something else in the soup?

'Sorry, I just . . . my eyes are still half shut. Please excuse me, Your Highness, I must get back to bed.'

Those imperious raised eyebrows made Ondine

39 *'To queef' is to mentally have a little puke, without producing anything. You might also press your lips tightly together and blow your cheeks out like a bubble-headed goldfish.*

uneasy. Somehow, Ondine felt sure the Infanta had put *something* in the soup and she had to tell Old Col the moment she got the chance.

'What are you named, child?'

'Ondine, Your Highness.'

'And what did you see, Ondine, hmm?'

'I . . .' She took a gulp of water and thought desperately for something convincing to say.

The dog provided inspiration as it licked the offered spoon. 'I'm so sorry to stare, but I saw that your puppy has no teeth. I really wasn't expecting that.'

No change at all in the Infanta's expression. It was hard to know if this was deliberate. 'No. Earlier this evening I wasn't expecting my dog to be mauled either,' she said. 'It was my baby brother's new friend who did it. This had better be set to rights or there'll be trouble.'

Something else Ondine wasn't expecting – the Infanta paid no attention to her audience and put that licked doggy spoon back in the soup, confirming her earlier guess at the slurry of dog bacteria swilling in the pot.

Ondine's face must have betrayed her disgust, because the Infanta said, 'He has a better pedigree than anyone else under this roof.'

Yes, but his mouth is still teeming with germs, Ondine thought. How unfair that the Duke had set the health inspector on her parents' hotel, when all along he should have been paying closer attention to his own kitchen![40]

Again and again, the Infanta spooned soup from the pot to the dog. The dog stood on the galley bench, licking away. A few drops of soup landed on the bench, right where the kitchen staff would be preparing food in the morning. The dog licked that up as well.

The Infanta stopped spooning and looked at Ondine. 'You are new here, aren't you?'

'Yes.'

'Far too many people are being hired of late. I don't approve, but the Duke won't listen to me. Work hard and keep out of trouble. Plenty of people think

---

[40] *This happened in Ondine's previous adventure, and, luckily for her family, Hamish gave everyone ample warning that the health inspector was on her way.*

they know what is going on but they don't. You think you might know something, so you go and tell the Duke. Save yourself the bother. He isn't interested. If you see anything or hear something strange and you want to know what it means, you come to me instead, you hear?'

Ondine gulped and gave a meek, 'Yes.'

Chapter Nine

Morning? Isn't that when it's light? No such luck. Ondine woke to find Draguta giving her a gentle nudge on the shoulder and saying, 'Time for get up.'

Darkness filled their room.[41] In the distance Ondine could hear people stirring and getting ready for the new day. There were noises of feet scuffing down the hall, the hiss of showers and the scrape of cutlery on crockery in the staff lounge as people had breakfast.

---

41 *Brugel had not yet turned the clocks back and was still in Summer Time. In spring, Bruglers turn their clocks forward two hours on the first Sunday in April, then have the Monday and Tuesday as public holidays, to help them get over the shock. In the autumn, they wind the clocks back one hour on the first Sunday of October, and another hour on the first Sunday of November, so they get two sleep-ins.*

Hamish! Ondine's mind sprang into action. Some teenage slugabeds cannot get themselves right in the head or body before midday. Ondine surprised herself and her generation by getting dressed, cleaning her teeth and brushing her hair into a tight ponytail in record time. All the while she fretted. What if he had woken in the night and she wasn't there? Would he think she'd abandoned him?

When Ondine arrived in Col's room, she found her great aunt looking fresh and lively, ready for a new day. Unfortunately, when she clapped eyes on Hamish, he was still a Shambles-ferret.

'Shambles, you're awake. Are you OK?'

'All the better fer seeing yer beautiful face,' Shambles said as he climbed up on Col's shoulder so he could be eye-to-eye with a blushing Ondine.

'You two, you're incorrigible,' Col said.

'Then stop *incorriging* us,' he said.

Ondine giggled. Even though she was looking at a ferret, in her mind she could see Hamish's devilish grin and imagined his sparkling green eyes full of fun.

Old Col made a scoffing noise, then said, 'I'm glad

you're here. We need to confab.'[42]

'You've found out who's trying to kill the Duke?'

'I'm good, dear, but not quite that good. However, Shambles has discovered that people are helping themselves to silverware and probably anything that can fit in your hand. So please take care when you're doing the laundry to go through people's pockets and remove anything valuable.'

'Of course I will,' Ondine said, gazing longingly at the ferret-that-should-be-her-sweetheart and wishing he'd become human again.

'And you're sure you're feeling OK?' Ondine asked.

'Aw yeas, all ticketeyboo. Best sleep in ages.'

He certainly sounded confident, Ondine thought. 'But, you're still a ferret, even though I'm right here.'

'Aye, yer a smart lass. Isnae she a smart one, Col?'

Aunt Col rolled her eyes. 'Quite.'

Shambles gave the widest grin in a ferret's arsenal and winked at Ondine, 'Sheer willpower. I've goat it in spades. Worked it out while I was under the table

---

42 *Quickly discuss things, so that everyone knows what everyone else is up to. But not talk for so long that people get bored and fidgety.*

and ye walked in at dinner. Had tae think on me feet. And it feels bettah staying like this instead of changing back and forth all the time. Sure and the Duke needs me tae be like this on account of being able tae do me job, lass.'

Niggling worries started niggling and worrying Ondine. 'But . . . you like being human, don't you?'

'Aw, I *loave* being human.' He winked again. 'But ye know I have so many responsibilities now, and I cannae very well sneak aboot if everyone can see me. Now, as much as I love tae see yer smiling face, it's past seven, lassie. Classes start at quarter past. Ye'd best make yer feet yer friends.'

Giddy hope and confusion churned in Ondine's heart, which wasn't difficult considering the stress of the previous day, the earliness of the current hour and her bizarre conversation with the Infanta during the night. Which reminded her.

'Don't drink the soup.' Keeping things short and simple, she explained her encounter with the Infanta, the spoon, the dog and the soup pot.

With a shudder, Old Col said, 'I will inform the

Duke. Now, best you get to school. I will be taking a stroll near the arch of crepe myrtle trees on the western lawn around three this afternoon. Meet me there.'

'OK. I'll see you then.' Ondine gave her great aunt a kiss on the cheek and gave Shambles a peck on the top of his head. They walked off in different directions – Old Col and Shambles towards the conservatory for breakfast, Ondine to her new classes. More nagging worries followed Ondine all the way to the school barn. Worries that went along the lines of, *I know Shambles needs to be a ferret most of the time, but when nobody else is around, he really ought to be my Hamish.*

The barn looked like it had been converted in a hurry. It had a portrait of the Duke on the wall, dusty windows, creaky floorboards and tables and chairs. Enough for a teacher and a dozen students aged between eleven and fifteen. One large, portable white board stood at the head of the room.

A woman who looked about the same age as Ondine's eldest sister Marguerite came up to her. 'Good morning, you must be Ondine. The seneschal has told me all about you. I'm Ms Kyryl. You can take a seat next to Hetty if you like. Let's begin.'

Ms Kyryl had dark hair pinned tightly at the back of her head. She wore conservative pleated blue trousers, flat black shoes and a buttoned-up white shirt under a v-neck jersey, which matched her trousers. On her hips she wore an intricately braided leather belt, with tassels at the ends and tiny brass bells that tinkled musically as she walked.

Ondine sat down next to the smiling Hetty. Hetty had ramrod-straight black hair, tied in pigtails either side of her head, which made her look about ten, although she was clearly Ondine's age. Hetty had the tiniest little button nose. When she smiled, her cheeks turned into round cushions and her scimitar[43] eyes almost closed.

'I shouldn't be glad about the storm, but I am,' Hetty said. 'The thing is, I've always wanted a pony and now I've got one. Just looking after it, of course, until they rebuild the stables. But I've finally got a pony!'

'A horse is a lot of extra work,' Ondine said. 'Where do you keep it?'

---

43 *A nifty and terribly dangerous curved sword from the mystical east.*

'In our lounge. We've moved all our furniture out and laid down straw and it's so wonderful.'

Ondine's jaw nearly hit the table.

'Ha ha, got you! We're keeping it in our barn for the meantime. Sorry to tease you! I'm so glad to finally have a friend my age.' Hetty then fired off a series of questions: 'Have you moved here with your parents? What jobs do they have? Are you staying permanently or is it a seasonal contract?'

'I'm here with my great aunt . . .' Ondine started. She nearly added that she'd also come with Hamish, but she wasn't sure what to call him. She thought 'my boyfriend who turns into a ferret at the most inconvenient times' was a bit of a mouthful. And hard to explain. She didn't know how to answer the rest of the questions because she didn't want to reveal Old Col's job description, nor how long they would be staying. Hopefully not for ages because she wanted to go home with Hamish and resume her normal life. Hetty looked so pleading, Ondine didn't want to dash her hopes by saying they wouldn't be here for long.

'Good morning, class,' Ms Kyryl said.

'Good morning, teacher,' the students said as one.

'I was born here and the whole time there have only been two other children who were my age.' Hetty rolled her eyes as she added, 'And they were both boys, who came and went.'

'I've always gone to school here. Well, not here in the barn, back in the proper school house. My parents run the chicken farms. They supply the palechia and most of Bellreeve with poultry. My brothers and sisters were all born here too. I have two older brothers and one older sister. My sister does the accounts for a toy factory in Norange and my brothers are at Venzelemma University.'

Ms Kyryl interrupted them. 'Hetty, I know you're excited, but it's class time now. Everyone, please stand for the national anthem.'

Scraping chair noises echoed around the room as they all stood, hands on heart as the teacher pressed a button on the portable CD player. The opening strains of *Oh Brugel, My Heart* rang out.[44]

44 *Over the centuries Brugel has had several national anthems. During Soviet occupation they sang (through gritted teeth)* Sing to the Motherland, Home of the Free. *These days people sing* Oh, Brugel, My

Everyone sang, even Ms Kyryl (who sounded off-key). Despite the stirring words and rampant patriotism of a people whose spirit yearns to be free, whenever Ondine sang the words 'my heart', she thought of Hamish rather than her country. When she sang about the 'young and the strong' she also thought of Hamish. When she sang about 'hallowed fields' and 'wealth for toil' she had no idea what they meant, so she thought about Hamish for good measure.[45]

Once the anthem finished, they recited the *Pledge of Brugel*. Ondine ran the words together in a light drone: 'I love God and Brugel. I honour the flag. I serve the Duke. I cheerfully obey my parents, teachers and the law.'

Ms Kyryl said, 'Thank you, children. Once they fix the roof we'll move back to our old rooms, but this will

Heart *with gusto and pride. Except at the Olympics, because they have yet to win a gold medal in any event. They do have a chance if lift jumping ever becomes a recognised sport. Lift jumping involves cramming people into a lift. Everyone jumps just as the lift moves up or down. Last person standing wins.*

45 *A great many national anthems contain confusingly 'poetic' phrases that make little sense to the modern citizen. As Brugel is almost land-locked, it has been spared the ridiculous lyric 'girt by sea'.*

do for now. This is always a lovely time of year, because we have the Harvest Festival to look forward to. Once again the Duke has asked us to stage a pageant in the ballroom, to entertain the visiting dignitaries. The great and the good of Brugel will all be there, so I know you will do your very best on the night.'

Ms Kyryl handed out sheets of paper with a list of characters, including Farmer One, Farmer Two, Cabbage, Turnip, Apple, setting Sun and Harvest Moon.

Ms Kyryl continued, 'It's traditional for the festival to follow the full moon, which this year will begin on Thursday the twenty-ninth of October. The Harvest Ball and pageant will be on the Saturday. Now, children, who would like to play the role of Harvest Moon?'

Ondine worked out the dates. The Saturday would fall on October the thirty-first, Halloween.[46]

---

46 *The way Brugel celebrates Halloween is different to the rest of the world. There is no 'trick or treat, give me lollies' palaver, and there are no pumpkins – because Brugel's Halloween pre-dates the arrival of pumpkins from the Americas by several hundred years. Bruglers hang wreaths of wheat in their windows and place apples on the sills for good luck. They eat copious amounts of turnips and cabbage, (fried, in scoups, roasted, etc.) then venture outside in the full moon and gather around the*

Several hands shot up in the air. Ms Kyryl's eyes alighted on Hetty and she gave her the role. Hetty looked delighted and beamed with pride. Ondine felt a bit silly that she hadn't raised her hand fast enough.

Ms Kyryl cast more speaking roles. Each time, Ondine shot her hand up, only to miss out. Until it came to Cabbage. Nobody wanted to be Cabbage.[47] Ondine sighed, raised her hand and felt the sting of defeat. 'I'll be Cabbage if you like,' she said.

The boys giggled.

'Hush, class. Thank you, Ondine, you are very gracious.'

They read through the play. Each time Ondine came to do her lines the boys sitting on the other side of the classroom made squelching noises with

---

village square for Bonfire Night. Bruglers write down their bad habits or regrets on notes, and cast them into the fire, as a way of saying goodbye to the past and cleansing their futures.

It's considered tremendous bad luck to remain inside on Bonfire Night. Because of the mountain of turnip and cabbage consumed, and the lower-body explosions that ensue, staying outside is not just tradition, it's vital for good health.

47 *The word 'cabbage' is Brugelish slang for 'fart'.*

their hands in their armpits.

Hetty murmured, 'Don't let them get to you. They are just snotty boys.'

'Thanks.' Ondine hadn't known Hetty for long, but already she began to feel she had an ally in this strange palace.

Miss Kyryl said, 'Very good everyone. OK, put your scripts away and we'll have a history lesson.'

Ondine and Hetty took out their notebooks.

Ms Kyryl smiled to the class. 'Now, children, who can tell me when Brugel was founded?'

Everyone's hands went up. Not to be overlooked, Ondine shot hers in the air too because she knew the answer.

The teacher's eyes alighted on Ondine and she answered with satisfaction, 'Brugel was declared an independent state in twelve sixty-four.'[48]

Giggles rippled through the classroom.

What? How could the answer be wrong?

---

48 *Ondine is not wrong per se, but the general area Brugel occupies on the map of Europe has been around in some form for centuries. The specific date to which Ondine refers is the signing of the Treaty of Venzelemma, the site of Brugel's capital city.*

'Not to worry,' Ms Kyryl said. 'Who can tell us the real answer?'

Looking bright and perky, Hetty responded with, 'Brugel was the first land found after the flood.'

'Correct.'

WHAT! Ondine felt her eyebrows nearly shoot off her forehead. Keeping her voice low, she murmured to Hetty, 'There was a flood? When?'[49]

'Who founded Brugel?' Ms Kyryl asked.

Ordinarily Ondine knew the answer, but she kept her hand down this time.

Another student said, 'The four mountain tribes joined together to defeat the barbarians.'

Ms Kyryl said, 'That's right. And the leader of the tribes?'

Another child this time: 'Became the first Grand Duke.'

'Very good. And how many Grand Dukes and

---

49 *Just about every culture has a backstory involving a flood. Floods are handy devices. You can pretty much make up any story of life 'before the flood' because there's very little evidence around to prove you wrong. Geologists, palaeontologists and archaeologists would disagree, but that's their job.*

Dukes have we had?'

'Two hundred and seven,' another child said.

'And have we ever had a Duchess lead Brugel?'

This time the students kept their hands down, but after a bit of thought, Hetty raised her hand and answered, 'Elmaree the First became Grand Duchess in seventeen forty.'

'Very good,' Ms Kyryl said. 'And during her reign the Russian empire annexed the Grand Duchy of Brugel. After Elmaree, what happened? Anyone?'

No hands went up, so the teacher supplied the information: 'Her son Leopold led a rebellion to secure autonomy for Brugel. After that, Brugel lost its status and became a Duchy instead of a Grand Duchy, but it regained its independence. Have we had any more Duchesses?'

Some of the children shook their heads, not entirely sure.

The teacher supplied the answer. 'In nineteen eighteen we had Duchess Yalene. During her reign, can anyone tell me what happened?'

Ondine's hand rose in the air, because she had

a fair idea of the answer. Not from the name of the ruler, but from the date. It was ingrained in Brugelish DNA.

'Yes, Ondine?'

'Brugel became part of the Soviet Union.'

'Very good!'

Relief crashed through Ondine at finally getting something right.

'We nearly had another Duchess more recently, can anyone tell me?'

All hands shot in the air.

'The Infanta Anathea,' Hetty said.

'Correct. She was heir presumptive and would have been Duchess . . . until what happened? Can anyone tell me?'

Just about every child recited, 'Lord Pavla was born and Brugel rejoiced.'

'That's right. Lord Pavla the Fourth is Duke of Brugel.'

'And we've got our independence,' a boy across the room said. 'And that is why Brugel is always better off with a Duke.'

Ondine blurted, 'That's hardly fair.'

Ms Kyryl's eyebrows shot up in surprise. 'That's quite a statement, Andreas. Care to elaborate?'

Andreas looked smug and arrogant. He had to be at least two years younger than Ondine, but that precocious look on his pale, lean face told the world he knew everything. 'The facts speak for themselves. The times Brugel had a Duchess, we lost our autonomy.'

'But . . .' Heat roared through Ondine. 'They just happened to be Duchesses during really difficult times.'

Andreas gave her a look of utter superiority and scratched the side of his nose. Ondine could have sworn he sneaked the edge of his thumb inside and had a pick as well. 'We have had Grand Dukes and Dukes during very difficult times as well, but they didn't lose their country.'[50]

His smugness reminded Ondine so much of Lord Vincent that she couldn't help wondering if they

_____

50 *You could argue that a sample size of two women versus two hundred men is hardly a comparison at all, and leaves a very wide margin for error. The current Duke of Brugel would argue that this interpretation of history is completely sound, and that having a Duchess at the helm is proven bad luck for Brugel.*

might be related. No sooner had the thought crossed her mind than she pushed it aside. She would not let Vincent unsettle her, she'd put all that behind her.

'An interesting debate,' Ms Kyryl said, 'but there were also times when Duchesses, although not ruling in their own right, acted as regents to their sons who became Grand Dukes. Brugel did not lose its autonomy then.'

'Doesn't change the facts,' Andreas said with the self-satisfaction of someone who was too young to know anything but already knew everything.

Ondine thought about her encounter with the Infanta the previous night. Maybe some people thought Brugel was better off with the Duke at the helm, but she knew Anathea didn't see it that way.

Chapter Ten

That afternoon Ondine's ears rang with censure as she put another coin in the payphone to keep the call going.

'You will come back on the first train, young lady.' Her mother's voice ripped into her.

The coin-warning light on the old phone flickered again. It wanted more money or it would cut out. How unfair that she had to pay to listen to Ma scream at her.

'Everything is fine, really. And I have an important job to do, and Col is taking very good care of us.'

'I don't care. You get back here this instant!'

'I'm sorry, but I can't.' Who would want to go home with such a screaming reception waiting for her? Besides, she needed to be with Hamish. 'Sorry, Ma, the light's flashing again and I've run out of money. Can you send me some?'

'I'm not going to fund your escapades!'

'Well, then, I'll have to keep working so I can save up enough to get the train ticket back. Sorry, Ma, but the phone –'

The line went dead. Light-headed with relief, Ondine replaced the receiver and headed to the laundry. She worked hard with Draguta, washing and hanging clothes and sheets on the lines. The fishy smell had almost gone from the courtyard, which was a definite plus. The sun gave some warmth but the wind had a cool bite to it. When it was time for her tea break at three o'clock, she dashed off towards the crepe myrtle trees, her skirts whipping at her legs. The papery flowers were in their last flush of bloom. Their pink, white and red petals looked so beautiful against the green leaves and marble grey of the trunks. Dried petals sprinkled the ground like confetti. The trees were so old and well looked after, they formed a flowery tunnel to walk under. More importantly, they offered a secluded place to meet.

As she walked under the trees, Ondine's heart caught in her throat. Standing there like a groom at the altar was Hamish.

Not the ferret, but proper Hamish, wearing freshly pressed black trousers and a white shirt. Sunlight filled her as she raced to him and threw her arms around his neck. 'I'm so glad to see you,' she whispered into his ear.

'And it's always so lovely tae see ye, lass,' he said as she pulled away to get a good look at his gorgeous face. He stroked her cheek with the pad of his thumb. 'Although I see yer face every time I close me eyes.'

Ondine felt herself beaming all over at the compliment. For a moment she didn't know what to say. All she wanted to do was gaze adoringly into his sparkling green eyes for a while. So she did. Then she touched the delicate skin on his neck where last night she'd seen only matted fur and dried blood. To her surprise, his skin looked unharmed. 'It doesn't have a scratch!'

'Aye.'

'Did it heal when you changed?'

'It must hae.' Hamish gave a shrug. 'There's got tae be an upside tae all of this.'

Ondine kissed the spot anyway. 'Now you're all better.'

She felt his muscles tighten under her lips and he gave a soft groan. 'Don't be so sure. If ye do that again, I'll fall apart at the seams.'

She giggled and kissed him again in the same spot.

'All right, you two, that's enough.' Aunt Col suddenly made her presence known, her words mentally dousing Ondine with cold water. In the cool autumn air, Aunt Col looked pale, her hair a little more salt than pepper, and was that a wattle forming at her neck? A pang of sadness gripped Ondine. Every time her great aunt looked at Hamish he probably reminded her of her lost youth. Would the same happen to Ondine? Would Hamish stay young as she grew old?

Col cleared her throat. 'We need to compare notes about last night. Vincent is not happy we're here, so let's do our best not to antagonise him.'

Ondine rubbed her shin at the memory.

Hamish's hand slipped into hers behind her back. The contact made it hard for her to think straight.

'So, let's report,' Aunt Col said.

'Um.' Ondine had a think. 'Apart from the soup incident with the Infanta, nothing else so far. Everyone here seems to have a lot of work to do. I think they're too busy to plot the Duke's downfall.'

'Yes.' Col chewed at her bottom lip and her forehead seemed to develop more wrinkles. 'All the same, disgruntled staff can bear a grudge.' Col yawned. 'Oh, bless me. I need more coffee. Now, what was I saying?'

Behind Ondine's back, Hamish entwined his fingers in hers and she felt her brain go fuzzy.

'It's early days yet, but keep your eyes and ears open,' Col said. 'I'd hazard a guess there's no love lost between Duchess Kerala and Anathea. You were under the table at the time, Hamish, but I saw them look daggers at each other at dinner.'

'Aye, I was busy liberating silverware from someone's handbag. Who was sitting down towards the kitchen door by the way?'

'That would be one of Anathea's daughters.' Old Col rubbed her temple in frustration. 'Which is another black mark for the Infanta.'

'I will be extra vigilant in the laundry and keep a lookout for stolen things too,' Ondine said. Meanwhile Hamish kept playing with her hand and she came over all silly.

Old Col huffed in frustration. 'Stop it, you two. We're not getting very far just yet, but I think it's important to compare notes as often as we can. Ondine, you should get back to work before you are missed. Hamish, we need to check the Duke's mail.'

'Yes, Col.' Ondine made to move away, but Hamish gently tugged her hand and brought her back to him. Despite her great aunt watching. Ondine kissed Hamish firmly on the lips. The contact sent jolts of electricity through her.

'Love ye. See ye soon, lass.' Hamish winked at her.

Ondine's tummy turned to jelly and she giggled. Then reality crashed through. 'Wait. You're opening his mail?'

'Yes, and the afternoon post has just arrived,' a commanding voice said.

The three of them looked up to see Duke Pavla himself approaching, arm in arm with Duchess Kerala. They were taking an afternoon stroll in the gardens together. As they stopped, Kerala tilted her head to rest it on Pavla's shoulder.

Just in time Ondine remembered to make a quick curtsey.

'My Lord Duke, Lady Duchess,' Col said.

Remembering she wasn't supposed to speak unless spoken to, Ondine kept quiet and let Old Col do the talking. All the same fear poured down her spine. She hadn't had a chance to think about this the day before, but surely professionals in a secure facility should screen the mail, not her great aunt and the man she adored. But she also knew the Duke wanted everything to appear completely normal so that whoever was out to get him would not realise anyone was on to him. Or her.

It was completely bonkers.

The Duke looked at the three of them and

said, 'What news, Miss Romano?'

'We are continuing with investigations, Your Grace,' Col said.

The Duchess asked, 'Have you found anything?'

'Not yet,' Col said.

'Shambles, you look well enough,' Pavla said.

Ondine wished the Duke would call him Hamish when he was in proper Hamish form. It seemed demeaning.

'Aw yeas, much better thanks, Yer Graces.'

'Good. I was worried for a moment there. You're not . . . stuck as a human, are you?'

'Aw naw, I can change back whenever I need tae.'

'Then please do so. I do not want people to see you like this. The fewer people know about your presence, the better. When you're finished with surveillance in the kitchens, I want you to focus on the gardeners and farmers. Make sure the produce is safe. If there is something untoward happening in the food chain, I need to know.'

'Right, Yer Grace.'

'Good day.'

The Duke took his Duchess for the rest of their walk.

Col exhaled with relief the moment they left. 'Holiday's over, we have serious work to do.'

'Aye,' Hamish said.

Fear constricted Ondine's chest. Her breaths came in staggered jumps. 'Please, be careful.'

Hamish tucked a stray lock of hair behind Ondine's ear and gave her the softest kiss on the tip of her nose. 'I wasnae going tae, but now ye've said it, I'll take extra care.'

'You're making fun of me.'

He kissed her again, this time on the lips and her heart staggered behind her ribs. 'Dinnae fuss yerself, although it warms me wee heart tae know yer thinking of me.'

As he let go of her hand, Ondine shivered. Hamish could be seriously hurt. If anything happened to him, she'd never forgive herself.

Chapter Eleven

As the days went by things settled into something of a pattern for Ondine. Lessons in the morning, half an hour for lunch, then laundry in the afternoon with Draguta. A good amount of Ondine's work consisted of going through every pocket for snot rags, snuff boxes and stolen silverware, before putting the clothes in the cavernous washing machines.

I wonder what Hamish is up to, Ondine thought as she pulled out a small key from a jacket's inside pocket one afternoon. No sooner had this thought formed in her head than the man himself appeared. Except her heart sank, because he was only the ferret of the man.

'Come here, little fella, the laundry's no place for you.' What she really wanted to say was, 'Oh,

Shambles, I'm so glad to see you. Every time I see the post van arrive I can't stop the panic rising in me.'

In a blur of dark fur, Shambles raced up Ondine's side and stood on her shoulder. He gave her a whiskery wet kiss on the cheek. 'Aye, lass, I missed ye and I wanted to see how ye were gettin' on,' he said in a low voice. 'The Duke's goat me checking up on laundry now.'

Draguta dropped her bundle and stared at them.

Gulp, gulped Ondine. Had the laundress heard him?

Shambles shifted his weight from left to right. A difficult thing to do considering he had two of each foot, and Ondine's shoulders were hardly large.[51]

Draguta found her voice: 'No dirty animals here! Out! Now!'

Relief engulfed Ondine – Draguta had said 'animals' not 'talking animals'. She hadn't heard him

---

51 *Swimming is not a major sport in Brugel, so most women maintain the narrow shoulders they were born with. In 'big swimming' countries like Australia you can spot the serious swimmers, they're the ones who have to turn sideways to fit through doorways. Olympic champion Libby Trickett's shoulders were so wide she became stuck inside a marquee tent on her wedding day.*

speak. Their secret was safe. 'He's my aunt's pet. He's perfectly harmless. And clean.'

'No break rules. Duchess strict on that. You get me in trouble when bring animals in here.' Draguta shook her head and picked up the most enormous load of wet washing. The bottom of the basket bowed under the weight, but Draguta didn't even grunt. Instead, she looked at Shambles with a steady eye and kept her voice stern. 'Don't shed fur on the clean linen.'

'She's good value, that one,' Shambles murmured as Ondine got back to work.

More workers brought clean washing in from the line and then set to the industrial machines, ironing the creases out.

'Ondine, take to Duchess's suite,' Draguta said.

Ondine gathered the neat stacks of freshly laundered sheets and towels. They were so heavy she had to use both hands. There was no room for Shambles, so he had to run along beside her.

With a grunt of frustration Ondine said, 'If you were Hamish again, you could help carry some of this.'

'Good idea, lass. Let's go past Col's room and I'll get some clothes.'

Thank goodness, she'd see her lovely Hamish again. And her arms wouldn't feel like they were about to drop off.

When he emerged from Col's room as his handsome self, her heart flipped over. He took half the load but the linen formed a big white barrier preventing them from sharing a proper kiss. Instead he leant over and kissed her cheek. It would do. For now.

They walked towards the palechia's south wing.

'I've been so busy, lass,' Hamish said with a grin on his face. 'I found out the farmers hae cheated on cleaning the vegetables. All sorts of manure and muck on them by the time they reach the kitchens. The Duke was right pleased with me help.'

'Nice one,' she said. At least cleaning vegetables was hardly a dangerous pursuit.

'Aye, and I checked tae make sure the only fertiliser they were using was the stuff from a cow's belly.'

'Fertiliser? How can that be dangerous?'

'Aw, lass, yer so innocent.' He gave her a smile and a wink.[52]

Boggled for a moment, Ondine felt he was patronising her. She felt sure he didn't mean to. 'What about the mail?'

'Aw yeas, that's settled right down, but still very important.'

The pride on his face told Ondine how much he loved his job. Which was good, but it also niggled at her in ways she didn't want to examine too closely.

'And now you're spying on the laundry?' Did it mean she'd get to see more of him? Perhaps yes. But perhaps it meant she'd only see him as a ferret.

'Goat it in one,' Hamish said.

When they arrived at the Duchess's chambers, the opulence took Ondine's breath away.

Incredible, magnificent, ornate, overblown and fabulously expensive were the first thoughts that came to mind.

Breakable was the next.

---

52 *Don't even think of googling this or there'll be a SWAT team at your door faster than you can say, 'I need a lawyer.'*

They took extra care negotiating the sitting room – specifically the narrow path between all the polished tables and desks with their curvy legs. Not being an expert on timber, Ondine didn't know they were made from Brugeloak,[53] but her nose tingled at the overpowering scent of furniture polish. The furniture itself wasn't the problem, just everything on it. Every display table and bureau had tall vases filled with fresh flowers, while the desks were overflowing with photo frames and antique inkpots and silver boxes of all shapes and sizes. There were so many *things* Ondine didn't even know what to call them. All she could do was hold on to her tower of linen and make sure she didn't knock anything over.

---

53 A Brugeloak tree is quite remarkable. It matures in six years, producing large edible white berries that taste like a cross between apples and peaches. The large seeds inside taste like hazelnuts and can be ground to make paste. However, close to ninety per cent of people develop an allergic reaction to the paste and therefore sales of Brugeloak butter are low.

For more information about Brugel's unique flora, grab a copy of the bestselling What Caused This Rash? by noted botanist Kerk von Dennegelden.

A series of gilded photographs of Kerala and Pavla on their wedding day adorned the wall. The Duchess had the same dark, shiny helmet of hair she wore now, and a serene, confident expression on her face. The Duke's hair was darker and his face younger and more hopeful. In most of the photographs, their posture looked regal and stiff, but in one the photographer had captured them in an unguarded moment. Their bodies were angled together and they gazed adoringly at each other.

'It's well posh, eh, lass?' Hamish said.

'Mercury's wings, I've never seen anything like it.' Every wall had niches for yet more antiques. Along the length of one wall were more books than a person could read in a lifetime. Along another wall stood wine racks filled with more bottles than a person could drink in a lifetime. Scattered around the room were a dozen fancy chairs that looked far too old and expensive to ever sit on.[54]

Every window overlooking the south lawn had the

---

54 *This is very true. Just as every generation gets taller, every generation gets heavier. Take out a mortgage, then sit in a chair from Brugel's renaissance and see how easily it breaks under your weight.*

thickest curtains, held back with rich twists of gold-coloured cord.

'But no tassels?' Hamish winked at Ondine. 'I do love tassels, they really complete the look and add that wee touch of grandeur.'

'What?' Ondine stared at Hamish for three pico-seconds before he cracked up and she started laughing too. It was so nice simply to be with him, she almost didn't mind the drudgery of work.

'Come awn. Let's stop gawking and get the beds made.'

The bedroom raised the opulence bar another notch. Of course the Duchess would sleep in a four-poster bed with heavy curtains. Of course she would have more tables stacked with framed photographs and antiques and more of those elegant vases that would break the moment you touched them. Fresh flowers stood tall in each vase, filling the air with a heady aroma that reminded Ondine of cloves and apples.

Arms aching from carrying the stack of sheets, Ondine dumped them on a footstool and rolled her shoulders. 'Right, which one of these enormous wardrobes is a linen press?'

A door Ondine opened revealed fabulous clothes hanging on padded wooden hangers. All were the same colour.

'She must like wearing yellow,' Hamish said, scratching his head.

Ondine opened the next door. 'Or blue. Saturn's rings, look at this.' Each door she opened revealed a new colour. Taking a closer look, she saw each hanger had a tag with a date and event written on it. One had several dates on it, all but the last crossed out.

'Jupiter's moons, she keeps track of when she last wore something and what she wore it to. That's very organised.'

'Organised or anally retentive?' Hamish said.

Ondine opened the door of the next wardrobe, still hoping to find where to put all the clean linen. This door revealed shelves and a pull-out desk, complete with an old-style ledger. Did she dare look at it?

Of course she dared. They were here to spy, weren't they? With shaking fingers she opened the ledger. Each page contained lines and lines of information about staff. The day they started and how much they earned each month.

'Saturn's rings, look how little I earn.' At least she wouldn't be lying to her parents about not being able to afford a train ticket home. Amazed, she sat down on the floor to continue reading the ledger.

A strained squeak escaped her mouth.

'What, no planets this time?' Hamish knelt beside her.

'She's got everyone here. The chefs take home a pittance but look how much Ms Kyryl earns. That's a lot for a teacher.' Ondine scratched her head. 'Great Pluto's ghost, here's a column dated a few months ago that shows how much everyone weighs.'

'Why would she do this?'

'She likes tae keep track of everything?'

She flicked through the pages and found some recent diary entries.

Ondine de Groot. Arrived with Colette Romano
and a ferret.

Ondine's jaw fell open. 'That's it?'

'Ye havenae been here long,' Hamish reminded her.

They both read the lines about Colette Romano. Her arrival date, her job description as 'advisor' and her staggeringly huge wage. Beside those notes, the Duchess had written, *Overpaid and overfed.*

Ondine laughed, then stopped to listen for footsteps. No, just her imagination and racing heartbeat making her feel guilty. 'We really shouldn't be reading this.'

'Yes, we should. The Duke wants us tae get information, this is information.'

'But surely he knows what's in here? I mean, she's his wife, she's probably written all this down for his benefit?'

'Mebbe she's keeping secrets from him.' Hamish flicked a few pages back and found an entry for Draguta Matice. Because she'd worked at the palechia for so many years, there were several notes. One of them said:

Approaching second long-service leave. If we don't get rid of her soon she'll cost us a fortune.

'Oh, Hamish, how could she say that? It's so unfair. You can't just sack someone because they've got holidays coming up.'

Hamish turned on the sarcasm. 'But the Duchess is *always* right, Ondi.'

'I have to warn Draguta.' Ondine stood up to leave. In the process, she tipped over the ledger and a piece of paper fell out from the back of it. The handwriting was so small Ondine had to squint. It had columns of dates and details of cash deposited, adding up to a steadily growing balance.

'Ye've hit the jackpot, lass, the Duchess has a secret bank account!'

'But . . .' It didn't make any sense. 'If this is a bank account, why is it all hand-written?'

Hamish scratched his forehead. 'Mebbe it's not a real bank? Mebbe she's stashing it under the mattress for a rainy day?'

'We have to tell the Duke,' Ondine said.

'But we'll havetae be careful how we do it. Ye've seen how loved up they are. It would break his heart tae find out she's keeping secrets from him.'

Something went a bit woozy in Ondine's head. The bank balance was enough to buy half the country. How nice of Hamish to start rubbing her back. She felt instantly soothed as he gently massaged her shoulders.

They heard footsteps in the hall. 'We'd better pack this up before someone walks in,' she said.

In a blur of papers, Ondine tucked the piece of paper into the ledger and shoved it back in its rightful home. Then Hamish resumed rubbing her shoulders.

'Left a bit, lower . . . oh, nice! But Hamish, how do we know if we've put it all back the right way?'

'Eh . . . too easy. We'll put a half glass of wine in there with it.'

'What's that going to achieve?'

Hamish's eyes narrowed with a glint of mischief. 'When she next looks at it, she'll think she put it away in a hurry. She won't remember because the wine glass will remind her she was drinking at the time.'

'Or she'll know someone else has been here, going through her things.'

'Time will tell.'

While Ondine chewed her bottom lip in apprehension, Hamish left the bedroom, then came straight back with a clean glass and a bottle of sauvignon blanc. He unscrewed the cap. They only needed a little wine for the bottom of the glass. Hamish replaced the cap and put the bottle beside the ledger as well.

'Would she do that?'

'Mebbe. Mebbe not. Mebbe she'll open the cupboard door and be so distracted by the bottle she won't care.'

'There were far too many "maybes" in that.'

They closed the wardrobe and Ondine made for the door. She didn't want to spend another minute up here.

'Aren't ye forgetting something? We have tae change the sheets.'

Ondine slapped her forehead. Not changing the sheets was a sure-fire way to make the Duchess angry. Plus, she'd probably blame Draguta for the mistake and sack her.

Working together, they stripped the old sheets,

making sure not to knock the antiques over in their haste, then grabbed new sheets and remade the bed, taking extra care to straighten out creases. Hamish lifted up the top mattress and shook his head. 'No money under here. Just thought I'd check.'

In the bathroom – more marble everywhere and gold taps, for goodness' sake – Ondine bundled up the used linen and shoved it down the laundry chute, then did the same with the old towels. In a few minutes, there were clean towels hanging over the rails where they should be.

'Here it is,' Hamish said from the bedroom.

Ondine stuck her head out of the bathroom door and saw Hamish standing next to a bureau. Marble-topped, of course. He'd found the linen press.

'Good one.' She grinned. He'd already stacked the rest of the clean linen in there.

'I think our work here is done,' Hamish said, giving Ondine a smile that made her feel a bit wonderful all over. 'Now, hen, whatever we saw in that book has tae stay between us. I mean, we'll tell Col and she'll be fair astounded, but nobody else.'

'But I have to warn Draguta, she needs to know Kerala has it in for her.'

'But if we tell her, she might change her behaviour and then the Duchess will think she knows more than she does. She might even think it was Draguta looking at the secret bank account.'

'Which will give her a reason to sack her.'

'Exactly.'

'Even though Draguta would be completely innocent,' Ondine exclaimed.

'Aye.'

'But if we don't warn her, the Duchess will sack her anyway. And she doesn't deserve that.' This whole spying caper gave Ondine a headache. On top of that, keeping secrets from people she regarded as friends had set up a nasty ache in her heart.

Chapter Twelve

Another day. Another pile of laundry. Hamish was off somewhere else, spying on staff. Ondine's job stayed the same. Going through people's clothes for lost objects felt wrong, but the Duke wanted her to work in here and report anything suspicious. Surely it was an invasion of privacy? On the other hand, it had to be done. Ondine pressed her fingers into a pocket and felt something small and chunky. Urgh! In her hand lay a crusted tissue that had something wrapped inside it. A voice in her head said, *Look away, look away!* but she couldn't.

Teeth. Several of them. All small, off-white and triangular. The exact sort of teeth Biscuit the dog no longer had in his mouth.

'I'm going to be sick!' Ondine said, dropping the

dirty parcel on the floor with a soft *fwob*.[55]

Draguta came back at that point. 'You have Infanta's basket. She is worst. Never know what you pull out of pockets. Last week, I found dirty spoon and sticky lid from medicine bottle.'

Ondine nearly placed her hand over her mouth to stop herself queefing. In the nick of time, she remembered her hand had touched the gritty tissue. The laundry trough, soap and hot water beckoned.

'She's really winning me over, that Infanta,' Ondine said to Draguta. 'I met her one night, in the kitchen. She was spoon-feeding her dog soup, and I swear to Pluto and back she kept putting the dog spoon in the pot.'

'Excuse, please.' Draguta pushed Ondine out of the way and promptly vomited in the trough. 'You should told me before ate soup. So much leftovers. I have double helpings.'

Mentally, Ondine filled in Draguta's speech with

---

55 *In most cases dirty objects are placed in baskets or rubbish bins. On the odd occasion you throw them towards the bin and they miss their target, they make this noise on landing.*

all the definite and indefinite articles the laundress had left out.

'I'm so sorry, I didn't think.' Guilt ebbed through Ondine as she took in Draguta's pale grey face. 'You must be on a hair trigger. I only just said it and you puked, yet you've been eating the soup every day.'

'Urgh.' Draguta wiped her face with a cold wet towel, then draped the cloth over the back of her neck for good measure. 'Feeling rancid last couple days. Thought coming down with something. Now I know. Dogs have more bacteria in mouths what are people in Brugel.[56] I surprised more are not sick.'

Draguta's words proved truly prophetic. For the next few hours, a great many people in the palechia were sick, most of them staff, who regularly ate soup because there wasn't much variety on offer. Of those who were sick, most were caught completely by

---

56 *Brugel is often used as a unit of measurement amongst the eastern states of Europe. For example, 'Every day, an area of rainforest the size of Brugel is bulldozed in the Amazon.' It is true that a dog's mouth is a total bac-fest, but the exact number of bacteria is anyone's guess. If the dog's had a good clean-up at the vet, the numbers will be lower. If the dog has snaffled week-old road-kill, it's time to get out the hazmat suits.*

surprise and nowhere near a laundry trough or basin at the required moment. This in turn translated into an increased number of dirty towels, sheets, pillow cases, blankets and rugs arriving in the laundry. Another problem with so many people being sick? Fewer able-bodied staff to do the cleaning up.

Old Col appeared at the doorway, her face drawn and pale. 'Ondine, I need clean towels and bedsheets.'

'What's wrong?'

'Nothing,' Col said, noticing all eyes in the laundry were on her.

'Are you sick?' Ondine asked.

'Of course not. Whatever gave you that idea?' Col said as beads of sweat appeared on her top lip.

Panic sliced through Ondine and she ushered her great aunt out of the laundry and into the hall so they could grab a word in private. 'You look terrible.'

'I'm only pretending it's for me. I was trying to tell you that, using ESP, but you're mentally deaf.'

Smackdown! 'Gee, thanks.' Ondine rolled her eyes. 'So why do you need linen? Is Hamish sick?'

'Ixnay on the icksay, it's the ukeday.'

139

Confusion creased Ondine's face. 'What on earth are you talking about?'

Old Col kept her voice to a low murmur: 'We're pretending the Duke has only lost his voice so that nobody panics. He's here, confined to bed. Tell nobody.'

Oh dear! Oh dear, oh dear, oh double dear! Checking the hall to make sure nobody was within earshot, Ondine asked, 'Is the Duchess here too?'

'No. She left for the city yesterday evening, and will be back tomorrow. She took Vincent with her, he's going to stand in for the Duke at the Opera.'[57]

'But that's terrible!'

'He's lucky. It's one of the shorter productions, only three hours.'

'Not that! I mean Vincent's acting as if he's the Duke already!'

'Keep your voice down. I'm sure this is one of those

---

57 Attending the opera should be a beautiful night out. In Brugel, however, their opera is monumentally bad. Noted Slaegalese critic Zarah Bragiç likened it to wailing cats. In a cement mixer. Which is why it was far too dangerous to allow Duke Pavla to attend – the shock to his system might kill him. There is a silver lining: where Bruglers fail in the singing department, they more than make up for it in earplug manufacture.

twenty-four-hour things and Pavla will be all right again. Now get me the clean linen.'

Ondine did Col's bidding, then quickly told her what they'd seen in the Duchess's ledger. As she got back to the laundry she couldn't help wondering if they'd completely failed in their mission already. Vincent wanted to take over; standing in for his ill father was the first step.

Back at work in the laundry, Draguta scolded her. 'If told more people about dog soup, we not have such mess.'

Ondine felt chastened, even though it wasn't exactly her fault. 'But it was the first night I was here. And people are suddenly sick now? It doesn't make sense.'

'Infanta making dog soup each night I bet.'

That could be it. One night of bad food might not make too many people sick, but night after night, week after week? Then again, Hamish had said the farmers hadn't been cleaning the vegetables properly, so perhaps that was part of it? When she swallowed, she felt something niggling in her throat, like the start of a cold. Definitely the time of year for it at any rate.[58]

Draguta hauled wet washing into a basket. 'No chatty-chat with me, not in mood.'

As Ondine hosed the sick off yet another rug, she hoped the mess and illness would all be over soon. Lost in thought, she very nearly hosed the blur of fur as it ran towards her. 'Shambles, what are you doing here?' she cried.

Draguta stared daggers at Ondine. 'I said no pets!'

Gulp. Ondine grabbed Shambles and took him outside, so they could chat in private.

'Is it the Duke? Is he all right?'

'Aw, lass, ye've never seen so much sick. Col's doing her very best tae get him through it.'

'And Kerala's not here while everyone else is throwing their guts up.'

A thoughtful look crossed the little ferret's face. 'Now that ye mention it . . .'

---

58 A traditional Brugel cold remedy involves equal measures of fresh milk, plütz, tomato juice and gunpowder. Mix and drink immediately. After that, a sniffly cold is the last of your problems. It's also expensive, as fresh milk can sometimes be hard to obtain.

'Do you think – but no. It can't be her. Do you think? I mean, why would she harm him? She loves him. And if anything happened to him, it would all go to Vincent anyway. She's not in line. Maybe . . .' Ondine kept thinking out loud. 'Maybe it's Vincent making the Duke sick?'

Just thinking about Vincent turned Ondine's stomach. She had once fallen for his charm. What if Vincent was working his charm on someone here at the palechia? Someone young and naive like Ondine had been.

'Aye, Vincent's a dirty wee bast –'

'H'hem!' Ondine cleared her throat as she saw laundry workers approaching with clean washing.

Shambles kept his voice low. 'And another thing, the teacher is giving ye a test first thing tomorrow. Overheard her the day before yesterday at afternoon tea with the Duchess.'

'You're taking afternoon tea with the Duchess? Half your luck.' Ondine looked at the laundry flapping in the breeze and wondered what had happened to her plans for a grand adventure with Hamish.

'Dinnae be angry with me, lass. I would have told ye earlier only I've been busy with all me responsibilities.'

Ondine couldn't help thinking Hamish loved having such an interesting job, with all those responsibilities.

Shambles gave Ondine a scratchy kiss on the cheek. 'I know ye'll give it yer all. It's maths and yer a big win at that.'

If only it were proper Hamish, not ferret Shambles, kissing me, Ondine thought with a sigh. 'Thank goodness it's not a history test. I'd suck at that.'

'I thought ye liked history?'

'Not any more.' Ondine felt guilty taking a break while everyone else was working so hard. 'Sorry, Shambles, I need to get back to work.'

Shambles gave her another whiskery kiss.

'Thanks for the warning, I'll swot up tonight,' she said.

'Yer welcome. Oh, and I nearly forgot another thing. So much going on, so little time. Tomorrow, yer invited tae afternoon tea.'

'Really?' Ondine said, feeling a rush of excitement. Finally, something more interesting than laundry!

'Wow, that is such an honour to get an invite. Oh dear! I've nothing to wear.'

'Col has something for ye. It will look well on ye, too.'

Chapter Thirteen

The next morning, Ondine arrived a few minutes early at the school barn door. Hetty was already there, smiling as Ondine approached.

'It's so nice to have another girl my age at school. I'm so glad to have a best friend again. Someone to share my secrets. You'll share all yours too, won't you?' she said, smiling, her cheeks plump and round.

Something caught in Ondine's brain. Sharing secrets reminded her of lazy summer afternoons with Melody, pretending to read their futures in a pack of cards as they divulged all sorts of family stories. Now with Hetty, the rules were different, but she had to pretend everything was normal. Putting on her best secret-sharing grin, she said, 'Sure.'

'I probably sounded a bit desperate just then.

Sorry about that. It's so weird, this place.' Hetty gave a hesitant smile. 'There are so many people, but it's so lonely at times.'

Ondine found herself nodding, but she started to wonder if maybe Hetty had some kind of agenda. Immediately she slapped that thought away. Since coming here she'd been off-kilter. Hetty was just being friendly, in an anxious kind of way.

Ms Kyryl arrived and opened the barn door for the students. Hetty talked all the way to their desk. She seemed so desperate for friendship. A bit too naive. What if Vincent had convinced Hetty to do his bidding? Ondine mentally shook the thought away. Hetty might be immature, but she wasn't silly. Or at least, not as silly as Ondine had once been. *Then again, she lives on a farm*, Ondine thought. Chickens were a fine source of salmonella if they weren't handled with the utmost care. Perhaps the illness ripping through the palechia originated with the chickens?

Ms Kyryl said good morning and announced the maths test. The class groaned. Ondine groaned, too, because she had to pretend she was just as surprised as everyone else. In fact it was a convincing groan, because she'd studied into the night and still felt half-asleep.

The test itself hurt her brain, but she felt pretty confident she'd done a good job. There were a few questions where she didn't have a clue. The ones involving parabolas. They always turned her brain to concrete.[59]

It was over soon enough and they took out their textbooks to work though the next chapter of maths problems while Ms Kyryl marked the papers.

'I love maths,' Hetty said to Ondine. 'When my sister was at home, she used to help me with my homework and I really got the hang of it. I'll definitely be doing things with maths when I'm older. How about you?'

When Ondine thought about her future, she suddenly realised she hadn't given it much consideration. 'I'm not sure what I want to do. I guess I . . .'

---

59 *Another problem with parabolas is pronunciation. Is it PA-ra-BOWL-a or pa-RA-bo-LA? You can waste a good five minutes in class arguing that one.*

'Don't leave me hanging. What is it? You can tell me. I'll keep your secrets.'

There was that word again, secrets. Secrets Ondine couldn't share, no matter how relieved she'd feel if she could unburden herself. Ondine couldn't deny the bond developing between them. Hetty was the only other girl her age in the whole palechia. They had to be friends, otherwise she'd have nobody. And perhaps if they became really good friends, Ondine could find out if Hetty was working for Vincent.

'OK. The thing is, I'm not really sure what I want to do. Probably work in my family's hotel and then maybe later I'll branch out. I guess as long as I'm with Hamish I know I'll be happy.'

Hetty's eyes grew round in surprise and she made a little squeak. Just as suddenly, her voice dropped lower. 'You've got a boyfriend already? Oh, my gosh. You city girls grow up fast!'

An opportunity revealed itself. 'What about you? Any handsome boy caught your eye?'

Hetty blushed furiously and lowered her head

in embarrassment. 'I don't know the first thing about boys.'

'But there must be one you like?'

She shook her head.

At that moment, Ms Kyryl handed back the test results. There in the top right corner of Ondine's paper was 'D+' in green pen, followed by the number fifty-eight.

That sinking feeling of failure pulled her down into her seat.

'D+? But I –' Just in time, Ondine reeled in the words that threatened to fly out. She couldn't admit she'd studied. But to get less than sixty per cent? What a burn. All that studying for nothing.

'But you what?' Ms Kyryl asked.

'But . . . I thought I got most of them right,' she said. Oh, how embarrassing, her voice sounded so whiny.

'You did very well considering your lack of formal education. Your great aunt tells me you attended a psychic camp during your summer holidays, which I understand was not a great success.'

Giggles rippled through the classroom. Embarrassment raced up Ondine's neck and face. Even her ears burned.

'It was Ma's idea,' Ondine started. Sure, she'd thought it a great waste of time, too, but now the class was laughing at her, she felt strangely protective of her family's choice. After all, regular school terms are mandatory, but surely what you do in your holidays is free choice? Otherwise why call them holidays?

Ms Kyryl asked the students to open their textbooks to a set page and they embarked on a new set of quadratic equations.[60]

Hetty leant over and whispered, 'Don't feel bad. We went to maths camp over the summer.'

'Oh.' That would explain why they were all so good at it.

'But I bet you had more fun,' Hetty said.

After school Ondine dashed to Old Col's room in the hope of seeing Hamish. To her continuing disappointment, she found him in Shambles form, sitting atop a small table crammed with platters of

---

60 *Another term for parabolas.*

food. Old Col sat beside him, making notes.

'Smells great, I'm starving.' Ondine reached for a slice of cheese.

'Not so fast.' Old Col's hand slapped her on the wrist. 'We haven't approved it yet.'

Shambles piped up, 'Hullo, lass. Pavla's goat us taste testing. Best job in the world. That lamb's tae die for.'

'You're tasting his food? But what if someone really is out to get him and they put something in it!' Fear twisted her tummy.

'That is the whole point, dear child,' Old Col said. 'Considering how sick the Duke is, we should have done this earlier. He's turned the corner now, thanks for asking. Although he's a long way from being at his best.'

'I meant to but ... I'm glad he's feeling better. That's such a relief.'

Col said, 'He's banned all seafood since it rained fish and he's banned coffee. He very nearly banned soup as well, but then they'd have nothing to feed the staff.'

'There's sandwiches,' Ondine said, wishing she had something solid to eat. Then the reality of the situation hit home. 'But what if you get really sick?'

'Aye, goat it worked out too,' Shambles said with his ferrety mouth full. 'Ye noticed how me neck injuries all healed when I changed. If there's anything wrong with the food, I'll change intae meself and I'll be all better.'

'Does this mean you don't have time to open his mail anymore?'

'Not in the slightest,' Col said, then laughed. 'We're very busy, keeping the Duke hidden in his sickbed, opening mail and eating all day.' Taking up a knife and fork, she cut a morsel from the edge of the hard cheese and gave it to Shambles. The two of them chomped away happily.

Squelch. A cramp of hunger twisted Ondine's tummy. The need for food overrode her fear of what might be in it. She snatched a hunk of cheese and wolfed it down.

'There you are! Where have my teeth gone?' a voice demanded from the doorway.

The three of them turned to see Infanta Anathea

standing there with that ironing-board-smooth face of hers, holding no-teeth-Biscuit under one arm.

Thank goodness Hamish was presently in his Shambles form, otherwise they'd have a lot of explaining to do. Unless the Infanta had been there for a while and eavesdropped on their conversation?

'That spell must be reversed,' Anathea said. She had a look on her face that was hard to read. 'And that *thing* on the table needs to be put down.'

Calm as you like, Col said, 'Do you have the teeth?'

Guilt made Ondine gulp. She'd had the teeth. But she'd thrown them away.

The Infanta said, 'Do I look like the kind of person who has a set of dog teeth in her bag?'

Ondine thought she looked like the kind of person who carried around all sorts of crazy things in her bag. Probably a fair bit of emotional baggage in her head as well.

'I can't do much without the teeth,' Col said.

Was she baiting the Infanta? Surely her great aunt would not be so rude.

'Fix it, now, or so help me something will be done!'

'Yes, yes.' Col held her hands out. 'Give me the dog.'

'Ru-ru-ru-ru,' Biscuit wailed.

Shambles tensed.

Anathea held on to him tightly. 'No, he will not be abused again.'

With a resigned voice, Col said, 'I'm not going to abuse him. I'm going to help him. I'm sure he has more teeth in his gums that can come through soon –'

'He's a champion breed, not a shark!' Anathea protested, handing the dog over.

'Ondine, will you get my travelling bag, it has some nifty potions in there.'

Doing her great aunt's bidding, Ondine fetched the carpet bag. The medicine bottles clinked and rattled as she picked it up. She handed the bag to Col, who passed her Biscuit. Ondine really didn't want to hold the dog who'd nearly killed her dearest love, so she gave him back to Anathea.

'Ru-ru-ru-ru.'

In a flash of fur, Shambles dashed off the table, raced over to the bed and climbed to the top of the bedhead. Then he leapt even higher and balanced on the lampshade. Ondine didn't blame him wanting to be out of reach when Biscuit got his teeth back.

'It's all right Shambles, his bark's worse than his bite,' Ondine said.

'How dare you!' Anathea said.

'Ooops, sorry.' Ondine found something interesting on the floor to look at.

'Let's have a look,' Col said, taking Biscuit back into her arms and not caring that he snarled and wriggled. 'There, there. *Kleine denta wachsen, kleine denta wachsen.*'[61]

'What is being said?' Anathea demanded.

'I'm encouraging his little teeth to grow. Now, Ondine, my hands are full. Grab me the tin marked "salamander".'

Rifling through the bag Ondine found bottles and boxes and an assortment of strange things. 'Found it.'

Tucking the dog under one arm, Col flicked open the tin and shook a little powder into Ondine's palm. She dabbed the tip of her finger in the powder and

---

61 *This is Old Brugelish, which has origins in German and Latin. The language is so frustrating and illogical that studying Old Brugelish is the leading cause of nervous breakdowns in modern scholars.*

proceeded to rub it on the dog's gums.

A wince of disgust creased Ondine's face. 'It's not real salamander, is it?'

'It's their dried eggs. Right, that should do it.'

'The teeth are fixed now?' Anathea said as she took her dog back.

'I'm a witch, not a dentist. You'll have to wait and see.'

Anathea held Biscuit close to her chest. 'I will not be made fun of! You mark my words, make an enemy of me and you will never know a moment's peace!'

With that, she stormed out.

Shambles leapt off the lamp and landed on the bed. 'She's going tae the top of me list of suspects.'

'Agreed,' Col said. 'I've been looking at the line of succession. Vincent is too young to succeed but if anything happened to the Duke, Anathea could make a play for power.'

'Is that such a bad thing?' Ondine said. 'Surely anyone's better than Vincent?'

'No argument here,' Shambles said, climbing back

on to the table, where he helped himself to a bite of roast lamb. He swallowed it in one gulp. 'Mmmpfh, aw, very good, yeas.'

'What about the salad?' Ondine asked. 'Aren't you going to try that?'

'Aw no, lass. Ye know us ferrets cannae stand it,' he said.

'Then perhaps you should be Hamish again, and then you could eat a bit of everything and –'

Old Col chimed in. 'I know what you're getting at, child. You'd like to see more of Hamish, because you can't think beyond your own needs. But we've got it worked out. He eats fat and protein, I eat the fruit and veg, and together we have all the bases covered.' Col picked up a leaf from the salad then took some red powder from a small metal box and sprinkled it over the food.

'Is that a magic antidote?' Ondine asked.

'Paprika. I love it. Mmm, interesting . . . I thought that was spinach but it must be something else. In any case, it's fine, if a little bitter.'

'Can you please take this more seriously!' Ondine

wanted to stamp her feet. They were eating potentially poisonous food. When they weren't eating they were opening potentially explosive mail. They didn't seem the slightest bit worried.

'Oh dear.' Shambles ducked away from the table and scurried into the bathroom. In a few moments he returned as Hamish, dressed in a shirt and dark trousers. 'Bad news. I think the lamb is off.'

Fear turned Ondine's tummy to lead at the thought that her darling Hamish could be sick. But it was so good to see Hamish as his human self again. 'Are you feeling OK?'

Beads of sweat broke out on his brow but he smiled anyway. 'All the better fer seeing ye.'

'I worry about you.' She reached forward and gave him a hug.

'Oh dear, that's turned,' Col said behind them as she sniffed the leftover lamb. 'Hamish, I'm surprised you couldn't smell it.'

'Aye, weil, I could, only it smelled good because I was hungry.'

'Hamish, you must be more careful,' Ondine said.

Col pushed the offending pieces onto a side plate. 'Not even the Infanta deserves that. Looks like lamb's off the menu now as well.'

Ondine hugged Hamish more tightly. 'I can't believe it, someone really is trying to poison the Duke.'

'Perhaps,' Col said.

Ondine turned to her. 'You've got a bit of . . .' She touched her tooth.

'Thank you.' Col removed the stray greenery from between her teeth. 'But I hope it's not as sinister as that. Maybe some well-meaning idiot in the kitchen has served up something they should have thrown out a few days ago.'

Despite Hamish's arms holding her close, a cold shudder rippled through Ondine. 'This place is giving me the creeps.'

Col folded her napkin and got up from the table. 'No time for that, child. We must all ready ourselves for afternoon tea with the Duchess. Hamish, you know what to do.'

It broke Ondine's heart to watch him change into a

ferret again. Maybe when afternoon tea was over, they might find some time to be themselves again?

There I go again, wanting the impossible, she thought.

Chapter Thirteen-A[62]

Ondine felt like she had to pass another test as she and Hetty took their seats at one of the small tables in the conservatory that afternoon. She felt like a princess wearing the dress Old Col had picked out for her. It was made from floaty peach-coloured layers, which twirled and swished with each step. Her great aunt had even bought her the sweetest pair of low-heeled slippers, all sparkly and lovely. They were strapless shoes, so walking in them took a bit of getting used to, because she kept thinking they were about to fly off her feet each time she took a step. Sunlight streaked through the conservatory windows.[63]

---

62 *This book has two chapter thirteens because there is so much bad news.*

63 *Compared to Ondine's schooling and laundry work, Old Col and Hamish have scored the much better deal so far. Sampling food,*

Outside, the autumn wind flickered through the row of liquid amber trees, making their orange and yellow leaves twist and spin into the air as they fell from their boughs.

There were about twenty small tables here, all made from lace-iron.[64] Ondine recognised the tablecloths from her time in the laundry. It didn't take a psychic to know most of them would be covered in wine and tea stains by the end of the day and she'd have to wash them again. Old Col and Shambles sat at a different table, closer to the Duchess. The Duchess, her glossy mahogany hair perfectly coiffed, sat at the head of a longer table in the centre of the room.

Nobody made any introductions to Ondine or

opening mail, eavesdropping, partaking in a little gossip. All far too easy. However, they do have the burden of the Duke's welfare on their shoulders, and they need to find out who is plotting his downfall. And they might want to hurry up with that, because things are about to get a lot worse.

64 Brugel is famous for its lace-iron work. Lace-iron is a process of super-heating iron until it bends, giving it a stretch so it becomes thin, but not so thin that it breaks, and lacing it together to create a decorative flat surface. Many unwary customers are fooled into buying shoddy knock-offs made from a flat circle of iron with a lace pattern stamped into it.

Hetty, but Ondine didn't mind. It was enough to be all dressed up, sitting in such lovely surroundings, eating delicate sandwiches and crisp, sweet biscuits, washed down with tea.

'We're seat filling,' Hetty said in a soft voice. 'It happens from time to time. The Duchess can't stand to have an empty table, so she lets us come as long as we behave ourselves.'

'Why not move the empty tables and seats out?'

'Because they are screwed to the floor.'

Ondine placed her hand on the edge of the table and tried to move it. Not even a slight budge. She tried the same with her chair, with the same result. 'Who screws furniture to the floor?'

Hetty leant closer and kept her voice low. 'A few years ago, some tables and chairs went missing. My parents helped search the farmhouses and barns to try and find them. They never showed up. The Duchess ordered the rest of the furniture to be bolted down. It's been that way ever since.'

'Lucky us, then,' Ondine said as she helped herself to a cheese finger sandwich from the neat little display tower in the middle of her table. Glancing across the room, Ondine saw Hamish-as-Shambles appearing to sleep on Col's lap. His ears strained back and forth like a radar dish, listening for morsels of information.

'We don't get the fancy sandwiches either,' Hetty said, 'just cheese or jam for us, but it's nice all the same to be here. It's a bit like playing dressing-up, don't you think?'

Ondine smiled. 'Quite!' She took another cheese sandwich and pretended it was chicken and avocado. A tuft of white fluffy mould clung to the side of the cheese. Back at her family's pub, she'd eaten mouldy cheeses all the time – but they were proper mouldy, with a mottled blue coating. This was hard yellow cheese and all kinds of wrong.

Out of the corner of her eye, she saw a guest at another table slip a dessert fork into her handbag. Stealing cutlery? Ondine picked up one of the spoons at her place setting and turned it over. The maker's stamp indicated sterling silver. The good stuff.

As politely as she could, Ondine tried to get her great aunt's attention. She coughed a little into her closed hand. That did nothing. So she made a 'psst' sound, which also achieved nothing. Finally she threw caution to the wind and said, 'Aunt Col, may I give your pet ferret some cheese?'

That got her attention. And Shambles's. Ondine quickly excused herself from Hetty, and took the slice of the expired cheese to Shambles. When she reached them, she murmured to him, 'Show the mouldy bit to Col. Meanwhile, there's a nicked fork in the blue bag.'[65]

Ondine quickly made her way back to Hetty, whose eyes were as round as the saucers beneath their teacups. 'The Duchess doesn't normally allow pets in here. Your great aunt must be very special.'

'You have no idea,' Ondine said and added a giggle.

Across the room, Shambles disappeared under the tables. A few moments later, he appeared at Ondine's feet with a silver fork in his mouth. Ondine leant down and held out her hand as he deposited the cutlery in her palm. He disappeared again and a few

---

65 *If you need to keep your voice low while getting a message to someone, murmuring is far more effective than whispering. Whispering involves far too many 'esses' and people will overhear you and want to know what you're talking about.*

moments later reappeared with a teaspoon. Ondine cast a glance around the room, pretending to admire all the finery. What she really did was check nobody was looking her way, then she snuck the extra items beside her cake plate.

The side doors opened to announce a new arrival. Hetty gave a high-pitched shriek as Lord Vincent walked in.

Ondine hissed, 'Calm down.'

Such was her excitement, Hetty sat there and silently vibrated in her chair. Try as she might, Ondine couldn't stop her eyes rolling towards the ceiling.

Looking relaxed and charming, Vincent made the rounds of the room, shaking hands with guests and making small talk. Between Hetty's gasps, Ondine made out a few words. Something along the lines of Vincent standing in for his father, who was unavailable.

More squeaking from Hetty. 'He's coming over here,' and, 'OhmygoshI'mgoingtodie.'

'Good afternoon, ladies,' he said, his face showing no sign of upset at the fact that Ondine had scored a seat in here. If anything, he seemed almost . . .

pleasant. It had to be an act, especially considering the way he'd treated her last time.

Hetty giggled.

Knowing all eyes were on them, Ondine played along. 'Good afternoon, My Lord.'

'I have a pony!' Hetty gushed.

Ondine slapped her palm to her forehead.

Vincent turned the charm on full blast. 'Really now? Are you kindly taking care of one of my father's horses?'

'Eeeee –' Hetty said, furiously nodding her head.

'Then I thank you for your troubles. I hope we can have the stables repaired soon.'

Please pull yourself together, Ondine silently begged. It reminded her of how she'd lost her head over Vincent way back when, but surely she hadn't acted quite as silly as Hetty.

Hetty grinned and made a weird sound in the back of her throat.

Vincent smiled again and said, 'It was a pleasure meeting you,' then he moved on.

It was impossible to get anything coherent out of

Hetty while Vincent was in the room. After what felt like half an hour, but was probably only a few minutes, he finished his circuit of the room, spoke a few words to his mother and left.

'Ahhhhh,' Hetty said with a too-loud sigh. 'Isn't he amazing?'

Ondine coughed water into her nose and grabbed her napkin. By the time she finished, Hetty still wore a double-glazed expression.

'Come on, snap out of it,' Ondine said.

As if her words had done the trick, Hetty suddenly remembered where she was and her hand came up to her mouth. 'I have no idea what I just said then. Tell me I didn't say anything stupid.'

'He seemed impressed you had a pony.'

Hetty buried her face in her hands. 'I want to die.'

At that moment, the Infanta walked in with Biscuit tucked under her arm. Try as she might, Ondine couldn't see if the dog's teeth were growing back yet.

The Infanta wore a sky-blue tailored suit, several years out of date, and eye shadow to match. On her face she wore an imperious, you-started-without-me look.

The Duchess put down her glass of wine. 'Anathea, you're not in the diary. To what do we owe thish unecshpected shurprise?'[66]

It was only mid-afternoon, but Ondine heard the slur in Duchess Kerala's words and wondered how much she'd had to drink.

The Infanta kissed the top of one of the female guests' heads and said, 'Hello, dear.'

It must be one of her daughters, Ondine thought. It also happened to be one of the women stealing cutlery. Then the Infanta looked at the Duchess. 'Since when do I need an appointment to see my sister-in-law?'

Ondine had been thinking the same thing. Afternoon tea was a regular event, and they seemed to have spare tables – or at least enough spare seats to invite school children. So why was there no spare seat for Anathea?

Unless her distaste for Anathea ran so deep Kerala went to extraordinary lengths to make sure there were no spare seats?

---

66 *If it was expected, it wouldn't be a surprise. The Infanta's arrival at meal times was one of those 'known unknowns'. You know she'll turn up at some point, you just don't know when.*

An uncomfortable silence cloaked the room. Nobody wanted to say anything, probably because nobody knew what to say. The Duchess drained her wine glass and touched a hand to her hair, as if to set it in place. A stalling tactic – there was no way her dark lacquered hair had come the slightest bit loose. She turned to her social secretary, who handed over a leather-bound diary. The Duchess flicked a few pages forwards and backwards, pursed her lips and frowned.

'I have shpace at three tomorrow afternoon. Can it wait until then?'

'After midday? What's the point?' the Infanta said.[67]

The cold look between the Duchess and the Infanta dropped the temperature in the room by ten degrees. Biscuit wriggled in the Infanta's arms and made a 'ru-ru-ru-ru' bezerker bark, trying to get at Shambles.

Ondine feared for her beloved.

Shambles stood up on Old Col's lap and made his

---

67 *In other words, the Infanta thinks the Duchess is a drunken lush. If you want to talk about anything sensible with her, you'd best do so early in the day before she's had too much to drink.*

own, 'ru-ru-ru-ru' sound back at the dog.

Biscuit yelped and tried to burrow into the Infanta. Everyone, including Ondine and Hetty, laughed. The distraction helped break the icy tension in the room. The Duchess accepted another glass of wine from the waiter.

Old Col spoke up, 'Did I mention, Your Grace, that I can read tea leaves? I'm very good.'

The Duchess smiled and appreciated the diversion for what it was. The Infanta still didn't have a seat and nobody offered her one. While the waiters brought out pots of freshly brewed tea, Anathea and her crazy dog took their leave.

Old Col poured tea and the conservatory regained the atmosphere of a garden party.

'My niece is proficient at reading palms,' Old Col said. 'Ondine, would you be so kind as to share your gift?'

'Really?' Hetty said. 'Wow, you should have told me! I'll get you to read mine later.'

'I'm not that good,' Ondine said.

'You're too modest,' Old Col said.

With a flagging heart, Ondine approached the Duchess.

'I will need both hands, Your Grace,' Ondine said. Inside, she trembled, but she did her best to control it.

The Duchess put down her glass of wine and gave her palms to Ondine. The nail on her left pinkie finger was so long it had started to curl inwards. It mildly grossed Ondine out to see the yellow stains underneath it. This close, she could see Duchess Kerala's blue eyes, but they didn't shine. If anything, they looked cold and calculating.

'Thank you. You're right-handed.' Ondine had seen the Duchess make a note in her diary with her right hand, so it wasn't guess work. 'That means your left is the life you were given, and the right is the one you've made for yourself.'

Then Ondine made the mistake of looking at those soft, pampered palms. Instantly she regretted it, because she didn't like what she saw. Clean, simple lines on the left hand, but a right hand filled with complicated scribbles, slashes and crossings out. As if her present life was trying to scratch out the past. The words 'secret', 'deceit', and 'danger' immediately came to mind.

Looking up, Ondine saw Old Col give her a satisfied nod.

Ondine summoned every ounce of diplomacy she possessed and began the reading. 'You are so generous, Your Grace, and so concerned for the welfare of others it almost reduces you to tears.'

The Duchess smiled and said, 'Go on.'

Complete mince, as Shambles might say, but it seemed Ondine's kind words met with approval. She really wanted to say, 'I think you're as cunning as a sewer rat,' but that would do her no good at all. Meanwhile, others at the table drank their tea, swilled their cups and turned them upside down on their saucers. Old Col looked for omens in the mush.

Out of the corner of her eye, Ondine saw one of the guests offering Shambles the last piece of mortadella[68] from her plate.

Ondine felt even more uncomfortable as she

---

68 *A type of inexpensive processed 'meat' with huge portions of fat. Each slice is so full of fatty chunks it resembles crazy paving.*

continued with the reading. 'I see your marriage continuing happily, for a great many years into the future.'

The Duchess gave Ondine an unreadable look, as if she'd told her something she hadn't wanted to hear. Her tone stayed deadpan. 'A charming divershion, I'm shure.'

Ondine's stomach dropped to the floor. Old Col must have read the distress in her face because she made a timely interruption: 'Some tea, Your Grace?'

Thank you, Aunt Col, Ondine silently said. She looked about the room and saw Hetty serving tea to several women seated nearby. It seemed everyone here wanted to know their futures. From under the table, Shambles liberated a cake fork from another handbag. It was going to be a long afternoon.

The early evening chill teased Ondine's skin as she dashed towards the crepe myrtles. Her feet came loose in the pretty sandals, so she kicked them off on the grass and ran in bare feet, her skirts swishing and swooshing around her knees. The swirling wind blew leaves and petals off the branches, making her feel like she was inside a snow-globe.

Joy burst through the gloom the moment she saw Hamish standing there. 'Oh, sweetheart!' she cried and wrapped her arms around her beloved.

He felt stilted as he returned the hug. Worry wormed through her. This was not the warm welcome she'd expected.

'It's g-good to s-see you.'

She was wearing a gorgeous dress, but Hamish's smart clothes felt damp and stuck to his skin. The twig snapped. 'You're freezing!'

'I'm a wee bit wet, lass.'

'Oh, my stars, what happened?'

'I left me clothes behind the trees fer next time, but they goat smothered in dew.'

'Oh, you poor darling. I should have brought you a coat or something. Or a mug of soup.'

'Not the d-dog soup, I hope,' Hamish said.

When Ondine kissed him, his lips felt so cold it shocked her. She trailed kisses over his cold cheeks, doing her level best to warm him up.

Old Col interrupted. 'We'd best keep this brief, the Duke will be wanting information soon. Ondine, what news do you have?'

'I've been thinking about how sick everyone was after eating the soup. It couldn't all be dog germs. If the Infanta is in the kitchens at night, maybe she's putting something else in the food, not just the dog spoon.'

'Aye.' Hamish held Ondine close to him, as if she were a hot-water bottle. 'The Infanta is bonkers.'

Old Col nodded. 'The Duke is right to think she is up to something. But we have no proof yet. Afternoon tea today provided more information. The tea leaves were very good. The Infanta's eldest daughter has not lodged her income tax for the past seven years. One of the Duchess's friends and the Infanta's other daughter are stealing silverware and selling it on Bee-Bay.[69] The visiting ladies from the hospital charity lie about their age, but that's a small thing. They're also terrible gossips and tell all their friends at the bowls

69 *Brugel's answer to e-Bay, where the auctions work in reverse. The seller nominates a high beginning price, then reduces it by increments. The first bidder to put their (electronic) hand up 'wins' the bid. Many Brugel estate agents try the same technique, with mixed results.*

club about who has come in for what type of surgery and how often.'

Surprise jolted through Ondine. 'You got all that from tea leaves?'

'No. But I have excellent hearing. Eavesdropping is one of my hobbies,' Old Col said. 'Now, Ondine, what did you really see in the Duchess's palms?'

Ondine gulped. 'I didn't like it one bit. I mean, I was just telling her what she wanted to hear, but at the same time, I felt she was hiding something. This horrible feeling came over me and I felt a bit sick.'

'That could be the alcoholic fumes from her breath,' Hamish said.

Ondine laughed. Hamish was still cuddling her and it felt wonderful.

'The Duchess certainly likes the sauce,' Old Col said. 'But I'm fairly sure the Duke is aware of that. We should keep an eye on her, but my gut feeling is to hold off saying anything about her to the Duke at this point. If we sully the reputation of the woman he loves, without real proof, we'll be out of here faster than you can sneeze.'

'But surely the ledger I told you about, surely that's proof she's up to no good,' Ondine said.

'Aye, lass, but mebbe he doesn't want us to know she's goat a savings account. I think he wants us snooping intae other people's affairs, nawt his.'

The cool wind blew around Ondine and the warmth from Hamish evaporated. She turned to find him transformed into Shambles, standing on top of a pile of crumpled clothes.

'But I was enjoying that,' Ondine said.

'Me, too, lass, but Col's right. We need more proof, and I'm going tae get it.'

Did he need to get it right now? She'd been so happy to see him as himself again.

Col smiled with approval. 'Excellent idea, Shambles. Follow the Infanta and see what she's up to in the kitchens.'

'Be careful,' Ondine added, 'Biscuit's teeth may grow back any moment.'

'Aye, lass. I shall blend intae the shadows.' He gave her a ferrety wink and dashed off.

'Don't be sad, dear,' Col said as Ondine headed

back across the lawn to pick up her shoes. 'He's doing his job.'

'Yes, but does he have to enjoy it quite so much?'

Chapter Fourteen

At this point in time, the chances of the words 'model student' and 'Ondine de Groot' being used in the same sentence were slim. However, when it came to laundry work, she excelled. Growing up in her family's hotel had given her all the training she needed for long working hours and little free time.

'Thank you, Ondine, you doing great job,' Draguta said as they folded the clean clothes into neat bundles.

Ondine grinned. 'You're welcome.'

'Here. Take sheets and towels to Infanta and make up room.'

Ondine accepted the bundle of linen and headed up the stairs to the Infanta's wing.

'You took long enough,' the Infanta said as Ondine arrived.

'My apologies, My Lordship,' Ondine said, using the correct form of address this time. She looked around the Infanta's rooms for an empty surface so she could put down her linen, but there were none. It looked like burglars had ransacked the place, but surely if they had, the Infanta would have been screaming the house down and calling for the police? Then Ondine realised the Infanta had opened the door herself.

'Ma'am, where is the butler?'

'She quit. Rude girl.'[70]

'I see,' Ondine said, looking around. In his basket, Biscuit lay on his back, paws akimbo, snoring contentedly. A pang of jealousy shot through Ondine at how much she'd love to trade places with the dog. She spotted a small patch of clear space on the floor and put her linen down. Then she headed for the bed and began stripping it.

'You needn't take that "high and mighty" attitude with me, girl,' the Infanta said. 'I know what you're thinking.'

---

70 *Female butlers are common in Brugel and also in neighbouring Slaegal, but Craviç is having none of it.*

'Ma'am, I'm thinking I have a lot of work to do today.'

'Don't answer back.'

Great Pluto's ghost, no wonder the last butler quit!

Without prompting, the Infanta said, 'You don't know what it's like to have your life ripped away from you. To have your hopes and dreams dashed.'

Ondine kept busy changing the bedsheets. Last time she was stuck listening to the Infanta, in the kitchen, she had had nowhere to avert her eyes.

'I was going to be married to a prince, you know. Not one of those Slaegal princes, they're a schlip[71] a dozen. Over there, you lift up a rock and you find a prince. My prince was a real one, from the house of Hollenstotder-Betansk. The arrangement was already made. The date set for the week after my sixteenth birthday.'

The Infanta gave a noisy sigh. 'Am I going to have to pour the tea myself?'

Far from finished with her present task, Ondine stopped making the bed and walked to the table.

---

71 *Brugel coinage.*

She lifted the lid and found the teapot empty. Great, she'd have to start from scratch. On the dresser she found the kettle, also empty, so she walked to the Infanta's kitchenette and filled it. When it boiled, she tipped some of the water into the pot, swirled it round to warm the porcelain, then poured the water out.

With a note of surprise in her voice, the Infanta said, 'You know what you're doing.'

'Thank you, ma'am.' Ondine put two teaspoons of leaves in the warm pot. The moment the kettle boiled again, she poured the scalding water over the leaves and the water turned a satisfying dark brown.

'How do you like it, ma'am, weak or strong?'

'Strong and stewed.'

Ondine nodded and checked the milk jug. The leftover milk in the bottom had formed a thick band of dried scab around the inside wall. Ick! Back to the kitchenette then. Scrub, scrub, nearly done. Just for a cup of tea!

'At this time of day, I take it with lemon. I only like milk first thing in the morning.'

Ondine thought, *You could have told me that before I wasted my time scrubbing the jug!*

In the fruit bowl she found three lemons. She chose one, washed the skin and cut it into thin slices. Then she put a slice in the teacup, grabbed the strainer and poured the Infanta her cup of tea.

'May I return to making your bed, ma'am?'

'Of course. You know, if things had been different, I would have been in the south wing, instead of up here on the draughty north face.'

Ondine got straight back to work and finished with the bed, then carried all the dirty linen to the laundry chute in the bathroom. The fabric made soft *dadud* noises as it fell against the chute's angled walls.

'When they thought I'd be the ruling Duchess, I used to have my linen changed every day. Now I'm lucky if it's changed once a week,' the Infanta said.

My heart bleeds, Ondine thought as she scooped the Infanta's used towels off the floor and dropped them down the chute. All she had to do next was put the clean towels on the rails and get out of there. Being around Anathea made her twitchy and nervous. If she stayed too long, the Infanta would make her clean the bathroom. As far as Ondine was concerned, her job was done.

'And another thing. This is a fine cup of tea, Ondine. Thank you.'

'You're welcome, ma'am.' The batty old cow had said something nice! Ondine decided to return the favour as she made her way to the door. 'I hope you have a lovely day.'

'Come back here, I haven't finished with you. Here, let me pour you some tea.'

To Ondine's surprise, the Infanta poured her a cup. 'Do you take sugar?'

'Yes, two please.' Why didn't she just excuse herself and walk out? Her job here was done. Draguta needed her back in the laundry.

'Do you know what it's like to have to bow, scrape and curtsey to someone you despise, Ondine?'

Lord Vincent appeared in her mind. 'Yes, ma'am.'

'I believe you do.' The Infanta looked at her for a while, then a slow, knowing smile spread over her face. 'You've met Vincent, haven't you?'

'Wow, you're good.'

'He's a piece of work, let me tell you. Far too eager to take over. Thinks he's got it all worked out. With Vincent, the fire's burning but the cow's still in the field.'[72]

A giggle escaped Ondine's lips. She couldn't think of anything sensible or non-committal to say, so she drank her tea.

'I was thirteen years old when it was all taken away,' the Infanta said. 'Thirteen! Old enough to understand my duties, my obligations and my destiny. Old enough to know that when people bowed and curtseyed to me, it was because of my God-given birthright. I was *someone*. They called me "Duchetta Anathea". The little duchess. I would have been only the third ruling duchess in all of Brugel's history. Oh, I had such lovely plans for making Brugel truly great.'

The Infanta's top lip curled in contempt as she said, 'Then *he* was born. The mewling snotty-faced brat.

---

72 *A beloved expression of Bruglers. It means someone thinks they have everything sorted out, but they've forgotten the basics. For example, if you want to cook roast beef, you must first get the cow.*

A sickly child by all accounts. Not that they'd let me see him at first. My mother had been ordered bed rest for months before he was born. I was forbidden to see her. I hadn't even known she was pregnant when the orders for her bed rest came. But I knew what was being done. They must have known a boy would be born, otherwise there would not have been such a fuss.'

The Infanta looked at the ceiling before she continued. 'I knew it was a boy the morning I was not called Duchetta. My father the Duke arrived to tell me the news. He called me *Infanta*. After that, I was called Infanta by all the staff, and bows were not made. Only nodding heads. When I was finally allowed to meet my baby brother, I was ordered to curtsey to him. A few weeks later, news arrived that my engagement was broken. Thirteen years old and my life was over. How do you like that?'

It was hard to know if the Infanta was asking a rhetorical question or a real one. Either way, Ondine didn't have an answer.

A resigned look came over Infanta Anathea's face. 'You're a good listener, and you make a good pot of tea. Your talents are wasted in the laundry. How would you like to work for me? I need a new butler.'

Warning bells went off inside Ondine's head. 'Ma'am, I'm honoured but –'

'You will be paid double the money.'

That made things interesting! 'Can I think about it?'

'What is there to think about? You are a smart girl, although from what I hear you need to pay attention in class. A good word can be said to Ms Kyryl.'

Jupiter's moons! If the Infanta could put in a 'good word' with her teacher, she could probably put in a bad word too.

'Your timetable, what is it?'

Ondine drew a mental picture of her school and laundry schedule, then she explained it to the Duchess.

'I see,' she said. 'From now on, you will fetch my breakfast before school, then work for me in the afternoon from Wednesday to Friday and then mornings at the weekends.'

'But that –'

'Still leaves you with Tuesday afternoons off. Now go and tell that wafer-thin washer-woman when you will be working for me. Then return here with morning tea, I'm feeling peckish.'

No choice at all, then. 'Yes, ma'am. Would you like fruit or cake?'

'Cake? Good luck finding that! Unless you plan on making some yourself? Now that's a handy skill to have.'

'We could . . . make a cake together? It might be fun.'

Anathea laughed and slapped the table. 'Me? Bake?' She wafted her hands in front of her, mimicking the actions of cooking. 'I don't do baking.'

'Maybe you should?'

'Don't push it.'

Head buzzing with confusion, Ondine made her way downstairs to see Draguta and tell her of her change in circumstances.

'I didn't want to take the job but she kind of made it hard for me to say "no",' Ondine said.

'Of course she did. You watch that woman, she all charm and cheer, then strikes and you never see it coming. You get whiplash keeping up.'

'I know. She gave me a compliment and it scared me.'

'Be careful, OK?'

'Thanks, Draguta.'

Chapter Fifteen

The next morning Ondine woke with a jolt. Hunger made strange noises in her belly. She barely had time to bolt down a bowl of Toots Wheat before darting off to the Infanta's rooms to start cleaning.

'I would like a cooked breakfast brought to me as well,' the Infanta said.

Ondine silently groaned at the extra workload, although she did her very best not to roll her eyes. She was used to carrying plates of food to customers in her parents' pub, but trudging up two flights of stairs with a tray of bacon and eggs and a pot of tea was difficult and potentially messy.[73]

_____

73 *Over the centuries, the Autumn Palechia had had many modern conveniences added. Ducted heating and air conditioning have made life more comfortable for the modern resident (although not for the staff, who*

With each step the tea made lolloping noises and threatened to slosh out of the pot. Her arms ached, her calves burned, her breath came out in loud puffs as she carried the heavy tray up the stairs. At last she reached the Infanta's rooms.

'Was this cooked by you?' the Infanta asked as she lifted the silver dome off the plate.

Fried-bacon smells pervaded the room. Biscuit the gummy dog stirred in his basket.

'No, ma'am, the chefs cooked it,' Ondine answered.

Without touching the food, the Infanta placed the dome back over the plate and said, 'Take it back.'

What? 'But it's perfectly good,' Ondine protested.

The Infanta's expression remained impassive, possibly because her face just didn't move all that much, but her voice brooked no argument. 'Don't back chat! I want this thrown out. I want a new breakfast cooked. I want no other hand but yours to touch my food. Is that understood?'

No! 'Yes.'

wear two pairs of fingerless gloves in the cold mornings). But none of the dukes in the history of Brugel had seen fit to install lifts. Or a dumb waiter.

193

Trudging back down the stairs, Ondine reached the kitchen and put the tray down on a side bench near the bins. Lifting the dome, she grabbed the fork the Infanta hadn't even touched and ate everything on the plate. A few minutes later she'd made a new breakfast and it was time to climb the stairs again and present the food to the Infanta, who looked none too pleased at the delay in her meal service.

With a snap of Anathea's fingers, Biscuit shot out of his basket and sat on his mistress's lap. The Infanta lifted the dome off the plate and said, 'You vouch that this was cooked by no one but you?'

'Yes, ma'am.'

'Good.' She picked up the fork and stabbed at a quivering pile of scrambled egg, then ate it. Her steely eyes blinked slowly. 'It's good,' she said at last. To Ondine's horror, she scooped more food with her fork and fed it to Biscuit. Then she put the Biscuit-slobbered fork back into the egg on her plate and ate another mouthful.

'You think I'm being difficult, don't you, child?' the Infanta asked.

I'm thinking a lot of things, Ondine thought.

'I trust you, Ondine. That is why I want all my meals prepared by you. The kitchen staff cannot be trusted. Corners are cut. Mistakes are made.'

Pangs and pings went off inside Ondine's head in frustration. The Infanta was sharing food with her dog, yet she worried about germs from the kitchen staff?

The Infanta went on: 'Everyone was made sick recently. I know it came from the kitchen. They are lazy and poorly trained. It's not their fault, of course. Proper staff were not hired. They were not screened prior to working here. Students are cheaper than people who are qualified.'

'Yes, ma'am.' Ondine tucked a stray hair behind her ear and did her best not to fidget. She had her own theories about how everyone became sick and it centred around the dog with no teeth.

'My bed will be made now and the room will be tidied,' the Infanta said.

'Of course,' Ondine replied, feeling as if she'd snapped out of a spell. She set to making the bed and tidying the room. All the while, she kept catching glimpses of Infanta Anathea and her dog eating from the same plate. Heaven help her, she just couldn't seem to look away.

'Ma'am, if I may ...' Ondine said after she'd cleared the floor, 'I must get to class.'

'Yes, of course. Go. When you finish school, you may make lunch. I would like poached fish.'

'But the Duke has banned fish,' Ondine said.

'From his plate, not mine. And it will be fresh. If you can find the gamekeeper, see if there are any trout left in the lake.'

Silently Ondine groaned at the ever-tightening squeeze on her free time. She'd been cross with Hamish for enjoying his job a little too much and now she'd gone and taken on a second job. They'd be lucky to see each other at all at this rate.

The days grew colder and the shadows grew longer. Fewer guests arrived at the palechia, making the normally bustling estate feel cavernous and eerie. The one short break Ondine had from the palechia was when she joined the school children in the main street of Bellreeve to hang up bunting for the coming Harvest Festival at Hallowe'en.

All week she juggled school and the Infanta. At the weekend she spent her afternoons in the laundry rummaging through clothes for stolen chotskys.[74] And she hadn't seen Hamish, proper Hamish, in so long, she wondered if he might be liking his job more than her.

She barely had five minutes to call her mother, who sounded terse down the line.

'But things are fine, Ma.'

'I don't care. You went behind our backs and now you're halfway across the country. You need to be home with us, you –' Oh, thank goodness, the phone started to bleep.

'I'm running out of coins, I have to go.'

'Don't you dare hang up on me! Put more coins in. Your sister is trying to organise her wedding and she doesn't know when you'll be home. Your father is furious. You come home right –'

Merciful heavens, the money ran out. Worn out from the strain, Ondine staggered back to her room, to

---

74 *Little knick-knack figurines that look like Trotsky.*

find Hamish asleep in it. Or rather, Hamish waking up with a smile on his face.

'Yer a sight fer sore eyes,' he said, giving her his charming lopsided grin that made her insides melt.

Relief made her feel as bright as sunshine. 'It's great to see you, too.' Ondine threw herself against Hamish and hugged him with all her heart.

Neither of them said anything for a while, revelling in the rare moment of privacy, content simply to gaze at each other. There are times when things need to be said, and other times, like this, when no words are needed.

In . . .

. . . a . . .

. . . book . . .

. . . it . . .

. . . might . . .

. . . look . . .

. . . a . . .

. . . bit . . .

. . . like . . .

. . . this.

They kissed, too. Lovely kisses that made her feel such utter contentment she couldn't believe she could be this happy. How silly she was so think he didn't love her. Everything would be fine. Eventually, the kissing ended and they tried talking to each other instead.

'How is school?' Hamish asked.

Ondine gave a dramatic sigh. 'Awful. Well, not awful the whole time, just most of the time.'

'What do ye mean?'

'Remember a while back, you told me we'd have a test? Well, I studied really hard for it, but I only scraped through. And now I'm doing double-duty with Anathea and the laundry, I hardly have any time to study.'

'Ye know I'll help out as much as I can.'

'Can you do my homework?' she joked.

'I'll think of something,' he said, just before kissing her again.

'Shh,' Ondine said, her ears straining for sounds in the hallway.

Hamish raised his eyebrows as if to ask, *What?*

Big exhale. 'Sorry, I thought I heard Draguta coming.' More than anything, Ondine wanted to spend time with Hamish, but their respective workloads in the palechia were making that nigh impossible.

'How about I do the next test for ye?' Hamish winked and kissed her again.

Ondine nearly lost her head, but managed to say, 'Yes, please.'

'I'm serious. I could sneak intae the teacher's office and get the answers fer ye.'

'If only.' Ondine wanted him to be quiet and enjoy the kisses. Something in the back of her mind niggled and naggled. 'But . . . you're not serious, are you?'

'I'm very serious. If ye fail at school, the Duke might send ye home.'

Home to her furious parents? No, thanks. 'But I don't like the idea of cheating.' He kissed her again but she pulled away. 'I mean it. I don't want to cheat.'

'I know ye don't want tae, lass, but ye might *need* tae.'

'But it's wrong,' she said, feeling sick at the thought. 'You really shouldn't be thinking like that.'

Hamish softly touched his nose against hers, making her tummy flip in the most delicious way. It made Ondine wonder whether he'd listened to her at all. When she kissed him again, her heartbeat thumped in her ears like hard shoes on parquet. Mercury's wings, someone was coming this way. The parting kiss Hamish delivered before scarpering off in his ferrety incarnation was almost her undoing.

Taking her seat next to Hetty the next morning, Ondine rubbed her eyes. So very tired! It had been lovely to see Hamish in private last night. A grin formed. Little zings of joy danced in her head.

'What are you smiling about?' Hetty asked.

The smile grew, but Ondine shook her head and said, 'Nothing.' She had to bite her tongue and say as little about Hamish as possible. Especially to Hetty, whose tongue ran faster than a startled gazelle. They had so little privacy here. Keeping those few stolen kisses to herself made them all the more precious.

'Good morning, class,' Ms Kyryl said as the last couple of students came into the room.

Ondine, Hetty and the rest of the class stood up, sang the national anthem way off key, recited the pledge of allegiance to the Duke and resumed their seats.

'We have a science test this morning,' Ms Kyryl said.

A groan escaped from Ondine's throat. 'Ms Kyryl, how come you're giving us another test?' she asked.

'Because there's no point teaching you things you already know. I need to know what you don't.'

That's everything, Ondine thought.

'Ten minutes' reading time and half an hour for the test,' Ms Kyryl said.

Scanning the exam pages, Ondine tried to make sense of the questions. Multiple choice gave her a one-in-four chance of getting it right, but it also gave her a three-in-four chance of getting it wrong.

Something tapped at her foot. Looking down, Ondine saw a dark ferret grinning up at her. A ferret with a wedge of paper in his mouth.

Once again she had to restrain her natural reaction. Ordinarily she would have given a bit of a squee.[75]

Sharp but not unwelcome claws latched on to her leg and climbed up. Shambles reached her lap and spat out the paper. It was damp in a few places, but what did Ondine care for a bit of ferret phlegm in this

---

75 *It's a little-known fact that the term 'squee' began in Brugel.*

situation? Especially when she looked at the note and understood its power.

Answers.

Thrilled and terrified all at once, something churned in her stomach and she thought she might be sick. They'd talked about cheating, but only in the hypothetical sense and she'd been so distracted by his kisses she hadn't been thinking straight.

At any moment Hetty might see Shambles and scream, blowing his cover. Her teacher then might spot the crumpled paper in her hand and demand to know why she was cheating – which surely would result in expulsion or at the very least a hideous form of punishment.

She cast a furtive look at Hetty. Had her desk-mate seen the ferret?

Yes. Hetty's mouth fell open and her eyes became as round as glistening marbles. Then she shut her mouth and blinked furiously. Pricks of panic spiked through Ondine. Everything rested on Hetty's reaction. Slowly – horribly slowly – Hetty's face moved through some strange emotions. As if she couldn't work out whether she should laugh or scream.

Bold as brass, Shambles crawled on to Ondine's shoulder where everyone could see him. Well, they'd all know about the ferret now. She was about to move him off when he murmured into her ear, 'Ye must lift yer grade or yer teacher will send ye home.'

Yes, but cheating? What if she lifted her grades by working even harder? It wasn't impossible. She'd just have to give up sleep for a while. Cold dread radiated from her tummy. Being sent home didn't bear thinking about. Hetty was still looking at her strangely as well.

Ondine whispered, 'He's absolutely harmless.'

Hetty swallowed a few times. 'Is that your great aunt's ferret? The one who came to afternoon tea?'

'I'll take that.' *Yoink!* Ms Kyryl's slender hands wrapped around Shambles's belly and ripped him off Ondine's shoulder.

Powerless, Ondine watched as Ms Kyryl plonked Shambles in a cardboard box and tucked the lid closed.

'This is a school, not a zoo.' From her handbag, Ms Kyryl took a small bottle of disinfectant, squirted the liquid into her palm and rubbed her hands together.

Frustration and fear of Hetty discovering more about Shambles threatened to swamp Ondine. Surely Hetty hadn't heard him speak?

'He must have escaped from his cage,' she whispered to Hetty, who looked like she was calming down a fair bit now. Thank goodness.

'Back to your tests, children,' Ms Kyryl said.

The answers lay in Ondine's hand. Casting a glance around the room, she made sure nobody was looking her way. Did she give in to temptation and cheat? Giving it another moment's thought, Ondine vowed to try her best first, and only cheat as a last resort.

Question one: What element is essential for carrying oxygen in red blood cells?

A: copper

B: gold

C: iron

D: zinc

Too easy. She circled 'C' and moved on to the next question. Confidence radiated through her – she might not need to cheat after all. The next few questions were tricky, but she knew the answers. When she turned the next page things came a little unstuck. How many bones in the human body? Name the muscle group between the shoulders. The same muscle group presently tensing up the more she tried to work out the answers. For the next two minutes she held off looking at the answers, to see if she could get any more questions right for herself first. Of the remaining twenty questions, she knew at least half the answers. But only getting half right wouldn't be enough. Hamish had just warned her she needed to lift her grades. The damp paper made hardly a sound as she opened it.[76] Andreas across the room coughed and sniffed.

---

76 *Not a bad little science experiment in itself. If you wish to tear paper silently, make sure it's wet. The same goes for opening scrunched paper – if it's wet it barely makes a sound. You may, however, find it almost impossible to read the contents.*

A few people looked his way. It gave Ondine the chance to peek at Shambles's note without anyone else noticing.

Of course! I knew that really, Ondine thought as she looked at the answers and finished the test.

By the time Ms Kyryl called, 'Pens down,' Ondine felt she'd scored at least seventy-five per cent, maybe eighty. Some of her answers were pure guesses, because Shambles's spit had smeared the note. She handed back the test papers and the air whooshed out of her lungs in relief.

For the next half hour they read about how white blood cells work in the body, how they recognised germs and defeated them. Ondine copied the diagram from the textbook into her school notebook.

Hetty leant over and whispered, 'Did you hear about the Duke?'

Fear jabbed at Ondine's nerves. How did Hetty know about that? Last she'd heard, Col had said something about him being on the mend. Could he still be sick?

'He was due to visit my parents' farm at the

weekend to Pardon the Chicken,[77] but he sent the Infanta instead. I was there, because, well, I thought maybe Vincent might come in his place. Anyway, it all went badly. I don't think the Infanta likes handling poultry. And her dog ran through the barns and ruffled their feathers. It could have been a bloodbath, except it turns out the dog has no teeth, so he just gummed them a bit and they ended up pecking him and chasing him away. You should have seen it –'

'Girls. Quiet please,' Ms Kyryl said.

Ondine should have laughed at the thought of the chickens turning the tables on the dog, but all she could think about was the Duke being sick again.

Ms Kyryl handed back the papers – all except Ondine's and Hetty's. The two of them sat at their desk, wondering why the teacher hadn't given back their tests. Meanwhile, Ms Kyryl pulled the television trolley towards the centre of the room and slotted a disk into the player.

'You two can see me in my office,' Ms Kyryl said

77 *In the weeks leading up to the Harvest Festival, the Duke of Brugel gives a pardon to a chicken – or several chickens, depending on his mood – in order to spare them from ending up on the dinner tables.*

to Hetty and Ondine. 'The rest of the class can watch last year's performance of the Harvest Pageant. Please take note and use this as a chance to memorise your lines. I want an even better performance this year.'

Guilt rooted Ondine to her chair. Hetty stood up and obeyed her teacher. The rest of the class looked at Ondine with suspicion. Somehow she found the will to get to her feet. Walking to the teacher's office, she cast a glance at Shambles's cardboard prison. He'd managed to get one claw through the thick wall. With the television on, nobody heard his gnawing escape.

Ms Kyryl took a seat behind her desk and made a gesture for the girls to sit down. Then she showed them their test papers. They'd both scored one hundred per cent. Ordinarily Ondine would feel elated, but she didn't because she hadn't earned it.

'You may explain yourselves now,' Ms Kyryl said.

Hetty croaked, 'I've been studying really hard.'

'You let Ondine copy from your paper.' Ms Kyryl's tone dripped with accusation.

'No, I didn't!' Hetty said.

'Hetty didn't let me copy,' Ondine protested, 'I've

been studying too.'

'Ondine, you are a plodder. If you'd scored eighty per cent, I'd be proud of you for buckling down. Full marks, on the other hand, makes me suspicious.'

Ondine needed to think of something, fast. 'Why is it so hard to believe I'd be good at science? I love science.'

'Come now, Ondine. You spent your summer on dream analysis and inventing horoscopes. That is about as far from science as you can get.'

'Which is exactly why I left early. I really do like science.'

An uneasy quiet rippled through the room. Hetty sniffed and wiped her nose on her sleeve. Then she looked at Ondine with tears in her eyes and asked, 'You didn't copy from me, did you?'

'No, Hetty, I promise I didn't.'

At least *that* wasn't a lie.

Ms Kyryl twisted her mouth to one side, deep in thought. 'I'm going to give you the benefit of the doubt. This time. But I'm also going to split you up. From now on, Hetty, you will sit with Andreas. Ondine will sit on her own.'

Panic spread across Hetty's face. 'But Andreas picks his nose and . . . wipes it on the desk!'

'I know,' Ms Kyryl said, handing over a small bottle of disinfectant. 'You'll need this.'

A shudder of revulsion rocked Ondine. 'Please don't punish Hetty, she didn't do anything wrong. All she's done is be nice to me. I'll sit next to Andreas.'

'Interesting,' Ms Kyryl said, twisting her mouth in thought again.

Something flickered in Ondine. Silent understanding crossed between herself and the teacher. Taking the worse punishment was tantamount to an admission of guilt. She hadn't copied from Hetty. What she'd really done was read notes from a ferret, but how did she explain that?

Hetty gave the bottle of disinfectant to Ondine.

They walked back into the classroom and Ondine took her seat by Andreas. She tried to take an interest in the rest of the play, but couldn't help watching Shambles chew his way out of the box. Instead of scurrying away to freedom, he sneaked back into Ms

Kyryl's office.

Ondine silently pleaded, *Don't get more answers for me. This whole cheating thing makes me feel sick.*

Chapter Sixteen

Funny how life turns out. One moment you're madly in love and setting out on an adventure. The next it's a beautiful Sunday afternoon and you're up to your armpits in dirty laundry.

'Not what you thought it would be?' Draguta lifted enormous bath sheets out of the machine and into the waiting basket without so much as a grunt.

Ondine shook her head. 'Am I that easy to read?'

'Yes.'

A dramatic sigh rushed out of her. 'I'm sorry, Draguta. I'm grateful for the job, but somehow I just . . .'

'You in slump.'

Ondine continued separating red socks from a

213

pile of whites. Despite all the work, it beat staying at home because this way she could still see Hamish from time to time. 'I think it's the food that's been the real surprise. Somehow I thought it might be a bit more grand.'

'Everyone thinks same. Duchess sets meal budgets. Her purse tight as fish's bum.'

Ondine laughed and said, 'But they're so rich.'

'Exactly. Want to stay that way.'

Ondine plunged her hands into a shirt pocket and pulled out a crumpled tissue. 'Draguta, how long have you been here?'

Draguta rolled her eyes, mentally counting. 'In four months, will be twelve years.'

'Wow. That's amazing! I would have been three years old when you started here.'

'Ack! Don't make me feel old.'

'Sorry.' Ondine sorted some more clothes into piles and began loading them into the washing machines. 'How come you've stayed so long?'

'Did not plan to. Like said, I lasted few months and found work suited me. And there are pay-offs.

Coming up to second long-service leave. Going to have well-deserved break.'[78]

Ondine already knew about the long-service leave because of the note she'd seen in the Duchess's ledger. She managed a polite, 'Good for you,' before changing the topic to the ball and pageant for the Harvest Festival and Hallowe'en.

'Shambles, I don't think it's such a good idea to give me the answers to the tests any more,' Ondine said that night. The ferret had snuck into her room and she'd already told him about the Infanta taking the sick Duke's place at the chicken farm.

'But it's important ye keep up yer good marks,' Shambles said. 'If ye score badly from now on, she'll know ye must hae been cheating. If yer consistently good, it's proof of yer improvement. Just make sure ye don't score one hundred per cent again.'

---

78 *In Brugel, an employee accrues eight weeks long-service leave at full pay (or sixteen weeks at half pay) after six years' continuous employment with the one employer or company. This seems overly generous on the face of it, but in reality two out of three businesses in Brugel declare bankruptcy within the first year.*

'I didn't mean to! I must have guessed right, that's all.'

Shambles gave her a friendly nudge. 'So mebbe ye *are* psychic.'

'Urgh!' Ondine rolled her eyes so high her sinuses hurt. Her ear hurt a bit too. Maybe she was coming down with a virus from sitting next to Andreas the snot-robber?

'How is Pavla? Is he feeling better?' she asked.

'Nawt really. Col thinks he's caught something. There are a few going round. Chills and all that, what with the cold weather moving in. We're checking his food and the meat is fine. Col said the salad is a bit weird, but they must be moving on to winter veg, so it's turning bitter.'

Ondine couldn't help feeling some of that bitterness herself. Here she was, working harder each day doing four jobs at once – butler, laundress, student and spy – and she didn't seem to be doing very well at any of them.

When Ondine arrived at school the next morning,

she found Ms Kyryl and Pyotr the seneschal deep in conversation over some paperwork. For a moment Ondine's stomach lurched. What could they be talking about? Pyotr remained in the classroom as the students took their places and sang the national anthem. In key.

Beautifully!

Even Ms Kyryl, whose singing voice usually sounded like a rusty saw, reached the high notes.

How bizarre, Ondine thought.

When they recited their pledge of allegiance to the Duke, they all tried to sound a little more enthusiastic about it.

Ms Kyryl said, 'Thank you, class, now if you would line up, tallest to shortest, in front of the whiteboard.'

Nobody asked any questions, but Hetty sidled up to Ondine and whispered, 'It's worming day. Everyone gets a dose.'

'Whose idea is this?' Ondine asked.

'The Duchess's.'

'No need for chatting,' Ms Kyryl said. 'The sooner we get this done, the sooner we get back to our studies.'

One by one they lined up and stood on the scales.

Pyotr wrote notes on his clipboard. Ondine couldn't help thinking her weight would make its way into the Duchess's ledger.

'You're a little heavy, better take two doses to be on the safe side,' Ms Kyryl said as Pyotr jotted down Ondine's weight. Ondine had never considered herself 'heavy' before, but, compared to the rest of the children, she did look a little taller and better filled out. More to the point, they all looked reed thin. Probably on account of their meagre diet.

The medicine tasted like chalky bananas. 'Not bad,' Ondine said to Hetty as she resumed her place in the line up.

Hetty shook her head slowly, a look of defeat on her face. 'Wait four hours, then you'll change your mind.'

'Right children, grab your scripts for the Harvest Pageant, we'll do a read-through of the whole thing from start to finish. In the next few days I want you to know your cues and get your lines word perfect.'

'I'm so excited,' Hetty bubbled as she reached for her script. 'My parents are very pleased I'm the Harvest Moon this year.'

Dread sank a hole in Ondine's stomach. Everyone was happy about the pageant except her. Because everyone else had a decent role. She'd be the one up on stage, in front of everyone, dressed as a cabbage.

That afternoon, Ondine was hard at work in the laundry. There were piles and piles of washing to get through.

'Not more vomiting?' Ondine groaned, not feeling too great at the sight of all the extra work.

'No, this precautionary,' Draguta said, sounding thoroughly annoyed. 'Every sheet, mattress protector, pillow slip, towel, hand towel, bathmat and dressing gown get washed today.'

'And every single pair of underpants by the looks of it,' Ondine said, wincing at the teetering tower of smalls.

'I hate worm day,' Draguta said. 'As if not busy enough!'

Pain buckled in Ondine's stomach, 'Excuse me. I need to go to the toilet.' She made it just in time. Damn that medicine, it ripped right through her! It took a few moments to get her breath back and she felt a little light-headed.

'You taken worse than most,' Draguta said.

'Ms Kyryl gave me a bit extra to be on the safe side.'

Draguta slapped her hand over her stomach and laughed, 'Did she? Have you been wriggling and fidgeting in seat?'

'No, I haven't!'

'Feeling more hungry than usual? Lately I have appetite of ravenous beast!'

'Of course I'm hungry, but that's because the meals here are so small!' Ondine had eaten very well in her family's hotel. Not three-course meals every night (there wasn't time), but a healthy range of fruit and vegetables and plenty of protein.

'Now you see reason for worming day. I tell you secret.' Draguta stepped closer so that none of the other laundry workers overheard them.

'Duchess in charge of catering budget. Think we eat too much. Must be riddled with worms. Every six months on dot, worm day comes and every single person in palechia must to take medicine.'

'Has anyone ever actually had worms?'

'The dogs . . .' Draguta trailed off as a visitor came into the laundry. A number of other people also turned to check out the new arrival.

Despite her roiling stomach, sunshine spread through Ondine's veins at the sight of the gorgeous man walking in. It was exactly the medicine she needed to cure her bout of malaise.

'Hello, Hamish,' she said.

A few people looked at Ondine and then back at Hamish. They said nothing, but Ondine could tell they were all dying to know who this strapping young man was. He looked effortlessly handsome, with a lock of dark hair flopping across his forehead. His clothes looked new, judging by the sharp creases down the front of his navy trousers and the starched shirt.

'Col thought ye might need an extra pair of hands tae help out, on account of it being worm day and all,' he said, smiling at Ondine.

Good Old Col. She thought how very lax her great aunt had been at the whole chaperone caper. She

221

made a mental note to thank her, next time they had a pow-wow.

'All help appreciated,' Draguta said as Hamish walked towards them. 'Here, fold sheets.'

'Aye, ma'am,' Hamish said.

Pyotr the seneschal came in with his satchel full of medicine in one hand and a clipboard and pen in the other. 'Good afternoon, everyone. If I could have your attention,' he said.

Ondine shot her hand up. 'I've been dosed already. In school this morning.'

'Ah, yes, Ondine. I have you marked down.' Then he looked up and saw Hamish. He frowned. 'Hamish, you haven't been dosed yet. I'll just add you in here.' Pyotr wrote something on his paper. 'Good, now if I can get everyone to line up, please, you can step on the scales one at a time.'

Ondine watched as everyone stopped what they were doing and obeyed the seneschal. When it was Hamish's turn to step on the scales, Pyotr wrote down his weight, then gave him a single spoonful of worming medicine. The face Hamish made caused a new roiling in Ondine's tummy and she quickly excused herself. When she came back, Pyotr was finishing up. Even the used spoons went into a bag.

'Fun time over, everyone back in work.' Draguta mopped her brow. 'On worming day, all sheets must dry in sunshine. Gardeners put up lines. Here, take baskets out and hang up.'[79]

It took all Ondine and Hamish's efforts to heft one basket out of the door. They walked through the courtyard (which hardly got any sun, as it was on the north side of the palechia) and along the gravel paths towards the south lawn. In the skies above them, shafts of sunlight streaked through the tiny gaps between the clouds. Clouds that looked dark and a bit ominous. Ondine silently hoped the rain would hold off long enough for the sheets to dry.

Turning the corner, they saw a sea of white sheets flapping in the breeze. It had a sort of modern-art-installation aesthetic and Ondine found herself smiling. In between the flapping sheets, they could

---

79 *Naturally, Draguta didn't mean hang up the baskets, she meant hang up the contents of the baskets.*

see workers' heads and arms moving, hanging up yet more sheets.

Further down the lawn, Ondine saw other workers hammering in temporary poles and stringing lines between them. Ondine and Hamish carried the basket down to the new line and launched the sheets over them. It was hard work, yet Ondine felt strangely calm and ever so domestic. The scent of freshly mown grass mingled with the lemony fragrance of washing. They both reached for the same pillowcase and Hamish's hands wrapped around Ondine's.

'Ye look so pretty with the sun in yer hair.' He curled a loose tendril around his finger and Ondine felt herself all overcome. When he brushed her cheek with his thumb, she couldn't stop the grin.

The snap and flap of sheets filled her ears. Hamish leant closer. Her eyelids fluttered shut as he pressed his lips to hers. Ondine dropped the wet towel and held his face in her hands. The gentle rasp of his cheeks on her palms made her pull back in shock.

'What's wrong, lass?'

Relief flooded through her. 'Sorry, I thought for a

moment there you were changing back.'

Hamish rubbed his cheek and smiled. 'Aye. I'll havetae shave.'

Heat raced up Ondine's neck. Shaving? That made Hamish seem so much older in her eyes. She leant forward for another kiss and felt stubble against her chin. A giggle escaped – she'd get pash-rash for sure.

Another lovely kiss made Ondine's heart kick behind her ribs and her breath started to quaver into little puffs and pants. She could never get enough of those melting kisses. They lost all track of time, standing together between the fluttering white sheets, Hamish trailing kisses all the way down her neck and collarbone. It felt so wonderful and a little bit naughty into the bargain.

'Aw nae!' Hamish pulled back and grabbed at his belly.

Ondine wailed, 'Hamish, are you all right?'

Hamish turned so pale he almost looked blue. Dismay and despair filled Ondine as she watched him collapse on the ground. Moans and groans followed. His clothes fell in a heap. After a few choice curses,

Shambles the ferret poked his head out.

'Oh, why now of all times?' Frustration took hold. Ondine screamed and kicked the washing basket as the ferret she loved ran off.

Chapter Seventeen

Apart from the sheer aggravation of having the man you love transform into a ferret at the very moment you least want it to happen, Ondine had no idea why it had happened. She no longer had Hamish's help to hang out the washing either. They'd done very little of it because they'd been so distracted. And she'd kicked the washing basket so hard the clean washing had flomped out on to the grass.

She picked up a white bed sheet and threw it as best she could over the line. Brushing off the blades of grass only made it worse: the beautiful, white, one-thousand-thread-count cotton now had natty green smudges.[80] The sheets would have to be washed

---

80 *Most of us make do with two-hundred-thread-count cotton; that is, two hundred strands of cotton per square inch of fabric, counting the up and downy threads and the side to sidey threads. Most weavers claim it's*

again. Draguta would be furious.

Walking back to the laundry, her foot hurt, her arms hurt from carrying the basket by herself, and her heart hurt because their kissing had ended way too soon.

'I'm sorry, Draguta. These sheets fell on the grass, I'll redo them. I'll stay back late if I have to.'

Draguta put her fists on her hips. 'Yes, you will. Where is helper Hamish?'

'Um . . . he had to go.' Her vision started to blur, which meant tears wouldn't be far behind. She couldn't very well expose his secret by saying he'd turned into a ferret and scarpered off.

Pyotr chose that moment to make another appearance. 'Ondine, there you are. Your great aunt is asking for you. She's had a bad reaction to the medicine.'

'She should call for a doctor, not me,' Ondine said.

---

impossible to create true one-thousand-thread-count cotton, as there is simply no way to squeeze five hundred threads vertically and horizontally into one square inch. These weavers have yet to meet the incredible craftsmen and women of Venzelemma, who achieve the impossible on a daily basis.

It was an uncharitable thing to say, but she wasn't in a charitable mood.

'Go. You are needed,' Draguta said.

'But there's so much work to do here.' Ondine wiped her sleeve over her face and sniffed.

Draguta shrugged in resignation. 'There is. Sooner you see your great aunt, sooner you come back and help.'

'As if I have worms!' From her bed, Old Col looked furious. Shambles had made his own way back and was sitting on the bedside table.

Two pink lips pressed into a thin line dominated her pale, wrinkled face. 'That woman has a nerve, lumping me in with the rest of the staff. I'm here as the Duke's guest! This is not how a hostess should treat her guests. I've a good mind to turn her into a –'

'Col! No!' Ondine jumped in before her great aunt cursed Duchess Kerala into something awful and irreversible. The image of No-Teeth-Biscuit's raw, red gums popped into her head.

'Relax, Ondine, I can't do her any harm here.

The Duke and Duchess are in the south wing. As much power as I have, I can't curse people by remote control.'

Ondine said, 'Please tell me Vincent had a dose of medicine, too? It would make me feel so much better.'

'I hope so,' Shambles said.

Ondine took in the sight of her great aunt properly. She looked so old and frail. 'Is the Duke feeling better?'

'His specialist is here from Venzelemma. We've cancelled all his appointments and have to pretend he's tied up with paperwork.'

'Is he getting worse?' This was all getting so horrible and serious and not at all like the escapade she thought she'd be having with Hamish.

'Not worse, exactly. But not any better either.' Old Col made a face and breathed in hard against the pain.

Ondine felt sorry for her great aunt. 'Pyotr said you needed me?'

'Did he? That's odd, I don't remember speaking to him.' She sucked her breath in as another pang took hold. 'Shambles, if this is anything like your pain at transformation, I am truly sorry.'

'Thanks. Yer a fine woman.' His furry face crinkled in what Ondine could only assume was somewhere between shame and sympathy. 'If ye'll excuse me.' Shambles made for the bathroom. In a few moments, to Ondine's pure relief, he reappeared as his most gorgeous human self again, clothed and complete with a shy grin.

'That's much better,' Ondine said, finding herself smiling again.

Hamish's forehead crinkled like a concertina. 'Aye. I think I know how it happened. The medicine hit me hard and sudden. It made me feel like the pain I get when I'm changing back, and so I did. Sorry aboot the lousy timing.'

Ondine shut her eyes and counted to ten.

'Oh yes? And what were you and Ondine doing at the time?' Old Col asked.

'Nothing. Can I get you something to settle your tummy?' Ondine changed the subject as fast as she could.

'Ha ha, you must have been up to no good. Maybe Hamish felt guilty and that's why he turned back?'

'Some antacid perhaps, Aunt Col?' Ondine tried again.

'That would help. And a bowl of Toots Wheat with full-fat milk,' she said, smoothing the bed covers. 'I always find that helps bind things together and move them along.'

'I'll get some from the kitchen. I wish I'd thought of it earlier, it might have helped,' Ondine said, thinking back to her own reaction to the medicine.

Old Col breathed hard against the next intestinal spasm. 'This is so annoying. I have a very important meeting this afternoon with the CovenCon organisers and I must be well. We have a lot to discuss.'

'What's CovenCon?' Ondine asked.

'It's our annual witches' convention. It's in Norange this year, of all places, so I'll have to update my passport. Birgit Howser is organising it. There's an oxymoron if ever I heard one. She couldn't organise a you-know-what in a you-know-where. Oh, come on, stop swooning at each other and get me some medicine!'

'You know, maybe we should all get out of here

232

and go home.' Ondine huffed out a pent-up sigh. 'The whole lot of them are wonky in the head. The Duchess is stashing money, the Duke thinks his sister should be sectioned. Not to mention the way Vincent turned out. What makes people behave like that?'

'Generations of inbreeding,' Hamish said.

Ondine laughed.

'He's a balloon, that Vincent,'[81] he added.

From the smile on his face, Ondine could tell he was really warming to the subject.

Old Col gave a slow shake of her head. 'Ondine, our family is far from perfect. Those who live in glass houses and all that.'

'We might have a few fights, but at least my family all love each other. I remember that night at the pub, the way the Duke looked at Vincent, as if he were nothing more than a huge disappointment. Vincent has everything he could ever want, but he's a total pain.'

'Too much money can do that to you,' Old Col said.

Hamish slapped his hands together. 'Right, weil,

---

81 *'Balloon' – somebody with an inflated ego.*

enough tongues flapping like lambs' tails. We've goat a job tae do here and I fer one plan tae get it done.'

'Oh, look at you, sounding all in charge,' Ondine said, teasing.

'I was trying tae be more polite than saying "atspish", but ye forced me hand.'[82]

'Yes, yes,' Col said, 'I know we haven't achieved much, but we'll get there.'

'I dinnae mean tae rush ye, hen, but the Duke's in trouble and we're standing round jabbering. Let's get back tae work, like.'

A wince of regret stole across Ondine. Why did Hamish have to like it here so much?

---

82 *'Atspish' – a less than stellar result.*

Chapter Eighteen

It was the end of another long day of school, butlering and homework. Ondine felt all warm and dozy as she settled into bed. Sleep embraced her like a welcoming hug. Scratching noises on the floor heralded the arrival of something small and furry.

'Pssst,' he said.

'Whah?' Ondine murmured, not keen to open her eyes because it felt so good to keep them closed. Even though it was Shambles in the room and she should make the effort. But she was so tired. Couldn't he come back later?

'PSST!' he said, louder this time.

Through the fog of half-sleep, Ondine pulled the cover over her head. But then she heard his voice say,

'I'm me again. And ye need more blankets because I'm fair freezing.'

She opened one eye and saw the man of her dreams, wrapped in two blankets he'd stolen from the end of her bed. 'Oh, Hamish, it's you.'

'Shh, don't wake Draguta,' he said.

'Fine, but you're the one making all the noise.'

'Ye have tae come with me, lass. There's something going on that ye should know aboot.'

'But I'm all warm.'

'It's the Duchess. She's not happy.'

The warmth evaporated. She wobbled out of bed and wrapped her quilt around her shoulders to stave off the chill. Her feet prickled with cold, so she reached for her shoes.

'Naw, lass, ye need tae be quiet, like.'

'Righto.' She pulled her socks on and her feet slid on the parquet floor.

'Aye, good,' Hamish said as they padded down the hallway, making barely a noise.

'Why are we going to the laundry?' Ondine asked once she realised the direction he was taking her.

'Because the chutes have ears,' Hamish said, leading her to one of the gaping black cupboard doors. 'They're like a periscope fer sound.' Hamish crouched on the floor and waved Ondine to sit beside him. She leant into his embrace and felt freshly warmed and cared for. If they weren't having to spy on people in such a drab location, it might almost be romantic.

Voices carried down the chute. 'It's the Duchess and Ms Kyryl!' Ondine said.

'Smart lass.' Hamish kissed her on the forehead.

Kerala and Ms Kyryl were chatting – complaining, really – about some kind of problem.

'I tell you, no good can come of them being here,' the Duchess said. 'Things turned strange the moment they arrived. I've never seen a storm like it. And then fish fell from the sky. I mean, don't you think that's fishy? And they have done nothing for my dear husband's health.'

Turning to Hamish, Ondine saw him make a face that said, *I know*. Understanding and worry passed between them – they were trying to help the Duke but

237

the Duchess seemed convinced they were to blame for his failing health.

'The old woman is paid far too much for doing nothing. And the girl – I tell you, cuz, there was something in her eyes when she looked at me and read my palm. As if she had nothing but bad intent towards me.'

'That's not true,' Ondine whispered to Hamish. 'She's got it in for me and I haven't done anything.'

'Ye dinnae have tae convince me,' he whispered back.

Hamish hugged her harder as the voices carried down the chute.

'I can get her expelled for you, would that make you feel better?' Ms Kyryl said. 'Set her a test she'll fail. Or catch her cheating, which I already suspect at any rate.'

'That would remove the child, but what about the old woman?' Kerala asked.

'We're done for!' Ondine exclaimed.

'Hush.' Hamish kissed her again to console her. 'At least now we know what we're up against.'

They listened harder and did not like what they heard one bit.

'The old lady has to go, Dionysia. I don't like the influence that woman has. I can't help thinking she's poisoning Pavla's mind against me.'

'Really?' Ms Kyryl asked the very question Ondine was thinking.

'He promoted her to personal secretary pretty fast. I'm suspicious. She made him stay here while I went to Venzelemma on my own. Who knows what she slipped into his food or whispered into his ear in my absence.'

Ondine's brows rose in surprise. Her great aunt had become Pavla's secretary? Way to go, Col!

'You told me he was too sick to travel.'

'That's what she said.'

'I see. Well, I can't do much about the old lady, but I can do something about the girl. Set her exams to fail, make it seem like going home is a better option, that sort of thing.'

Ondine shivered. 'We're in so much trouble. We have to tell the Duke about what she's saying.'

'Aye, but ye've seen them together. He's totally in

loave with her. If we say she's a bad egg, then we really will be poisoning his mind against her.'

'We're trying to help him. Can't she see that?' Fear and dread twisted in Ondine's gut. 'I've just noticed, the Duchess isn't slurring her words like she normally does.'

'Mebbe she's on the wagon?'[83] Hamish said, giving her a reassuring hug.

'First time for everything,' Ondine said, trying to make light of the situation.

Ms Kyryl said, 'It's getting cooler in the mornings. I can see the children's breath as they speak. Can I press you to ensure the renovations at the school are completed soon?'

'Surely it's not that cold yet? Anyway, if we want that girl gone, no point making her comfortable. Oh, would you look at the time? I must get my beauty rest.'

'Yes, of course. I'll let myself out.'

---

83 *During plagues in Brugel's middle ages, morticians would haul a wagon through town calling, 'Bring out your dead.' Passed-out drunks were sometimes mistaken for corpses and flung on the wagons. They would sober up rapidly and give up drink. Hence the phrase, 'on the wagon'.*

Huddled together after hearing such a damning conversation, something pricked the back of Ondine's mind. 'I just realised something,' she said. 'Kerala called her "cuz". I didn't know they were related.'

'It explains why the teacher is on such a good wicket. It also means ye'll have tae be on yer best behaviour in school.'

'Which means I can't cheat any more. She's already suspicious about me. She'll catch me for sure and expel me.'

'But if ye fail, she'll send ye home. I need ye here with me, Ondi, I can't do this without ye.'

His kiss made Ondine feel warm all the way through. It affected her brain like amnesia potion, making her forget everything except him.

Which is why it took them so long to get back to the room she shared with Draguta.

After another of his sweet kisses, Hamish pulled back and said, 'Is school so horrible that ye'd want tae leave me?'

'Of course not. Did I tell you we're doing a play for the Harvest Ball at Hallowe'en?' They had to keep their voices low, so as not to wake her room-mate. It had the effect of making Hamish even more delectable when everything he said sounded like sweet nothings in her ear.

'No, ye didnae. Yer in a play? Sounds like fun.'

'It only lasts for five minutes, no biggie.'

'What's your role? Queen of the Harvest?'

'Er, no. Promise you won't laugh.'

'I solemnly swear.' Hamish made the sign of an 'x' over his heart. Then he did the sweetest thing, he leant in and tenderly rubbed his nose against Ondine's.

Ondine gave a quiet sigh. 'I'm the Cabbage.'

Hamish smiled, but kept his honourable promise and didn't laugh. 'Is that so bad? Is it a speaking role?'

'I have one line.'

'That's Barry. I can't wait tae see it. I'll tell Old Col, we'll be cheering for ye.'

Ondine gave Hamish a kiss. 'Thanks.'

'What fer?'

'For not making fun of me.'

'I wouldnae do that. But lass, ye still look sad.'

Another dramatic sigh. 'I am. If I want to stay here, I have to study even harder. I'd better hit the books . . . and you'd better go.'

Even though she'd been the one to say he had to leave, it hurt to see him walk away. Her textbooks beckoned.

At school the next morning, Ondine tried not to look at the teacher. All that eavesdropping made her feel guilty. Could she look Ms Kyryl in the eye without giving away what she knew?

They sang the national anthem, sounding like a well-rehearsed choir.

For once, things were going Ondine's way. Andreas was sick and Ms Kyryl allowed her to sit with Hetty again.

'Hetty, your voice is amazing this morning,' Ondine whispered as they took their seats. 'Are you having extra lessons or something?'

Hetty blushed and her cheeks turned into little apples. 'No, I'm not, but thank you for the compliment.'

'Seriously, you should audition for Brugel's Best.'[84]

A naughty look crossed Hetty's face. 'My parents would die! They want me to become a financial advisor.'

'A what?'

'An accountant.'

'Oh!' Ondine felt slightly sorry for Hetty. She had such a chirpy, bubbly way about her. Ondine couldn't see her sitting behind a desk crunching numbers all day.

'Girls, please,' Ms Kyryl said. 'Don't make me split you up again. Open your history books to chapter eleven.'

Ms Kyryl told them off three more times for talking before they finished history. Then it was time to rehearse the Harvest Pageant. It was so nice chatting with Hetty again, Ondine forgot to hate her Cabbage role and began to enjoy herself.

After school Ondine grabbed a mortadella sandwich

---

84 *A television talent program where many contestants receive their first honest criticism. It's often so emotionally crippling it sends them back to school so they can get a proper education and do something they might actually be good at.*

from the kitchen and dashed off to wait for Hamish and Old Col by the crepe myrtle trees. She had about five minutes before Anathea would start wondering where she was. The chill wind bit at her ears and blew the last of the leaves away – the trees were bare now except for their nobbly little seed pods, and Ondine felt cold and exposed.

'Ondine, how lovely to see you here,' Old Col said as she approached. She said it loudly enough that if anyone else heard or saw them, it would look like a chance encounter. Old Col had come dressed for this early taste of winter, wearing a faux-fur hat and muff.

For a moment Ondine wondered where Hamish could be. To her deep disappointment, Shambles the ferret poked his head out from inside the muff. The wind whipped at his head, parting the fur to reveal fragile skin beneath.

'It's right freezing, so it is, and me winter coat hasnae come in yet,' he said.

A little ping of panic shot through Ondine. 'Hamish, why aren't you being you?' The last time they'd met here, he'd been his beguiling self, all lopsided grin and mischievous eyes. Now he just looked like a bundle of trouble. And not the fun sort she might enjoy either.

'Sorry, lass, havetae work,' Shambles said, with a ferrety grimace.

Another little ping went off in Ondine's chest.

Old Col coughed and looked about. 'We can't stay long, we're due at afternoon tea presently. Ondine, do you have any news?'

Ondine stopped gazing at her sweetheart-stuck-as-a-ferret and turned to Old Col. The cool wind had added some rosy colour to her cheeks, and she looked much recovered from the worming medicine. Ondine could have sworn her great aunt was enjoying herself. Getting paid to attend afternoon teas, early dinners and late soirées – who wouldn't love it? Meanwhile, she was working too hard and studying late and generally feeling as if life wasn't fair.

'The Infanta is cracked like a dropped egg. And Vincent's a total pain in the rear.'

Shambles laughed. 'No change there, then. Although, now ye mention him, he has nae given up me secret, so mebbe he's not all bad.'

'That'll be the day,' Ondine said.

Old Col's face became stern. 'Don't speak too loudly, my dear. You never know who is listening. But well done on moving through the ranks, I'm sure you'll learn a great deal from Anathea. Hamish told me your teacher is giving you a hard time. You'll have to work extra hard there.'

'Yes, Col. What little spare time I have will be spent studying.' A fresh blast of wind ripped through the trees and Shambles burrowed back inside the muff.

Right now Ondine needed Hamish to be himself. The wind whipped her dark hair around and stung her eyes. She looked away and wiped her face. It was the cold wind making her eyes water, nothing more.

'I have to go,' she said sadly. 'Anathea wants trout for supper again.'

Col tilted her head in thought. 'Interesting that she should have a taste for it. I wonder if this is her way of defying the Duke?'

'Do I get a kiss?' Shambles stuck his head out from the muff.

247

'Of course.' Ondine gave a sniff as she remembered how very much she adored kissing Hamish. Today all she could give him was a peck on the top of his furry head. She turned and ran towards the lake before the tears of frustration burst free.

Chapter Nineteen

Things did not improve for Ondine. Every morning she rose extra early to fix the Infanta's breakfast. Which, to her continued horror, Anathea shared with the dog. Then she made it to class and did her best to concentrate, then it was back to the Infanta and her bizarre demands for the rest of the afternoon. At the weekend it was laundry in the afternoons. At the end of each day, she had about an hour to cram in homework before she staggered off to bed and it all started again the next morning. There just weren't the hours in the day to study properly, so although she did her best, it wasn't good enough.

Which meant she caved in and accepted Shambles's stolen notes containing answers to her exams.

On this particular morning, classes had finished,

but Ms Kyryl asked Ondine to go into her office. Ondine wasn't thinking particularly psychic thoughts, but she knew it couldn't be a good thing to have to stay behind. When she yawned, it only made things worse.

'Ondine, please sit.'

Tightness gripped her belly. Ms Kyryl wasn't even twisting her mouth in thought – did that mean she'd already made her mind up?

Shambles scurried out from under the teacher's desk and Ms Kyryl frowned.

'I'm so sorry,' Ondine said. 'Ha–Shambles, come here, please.' She patted her knee and noticed her hand was trembling. Questions flooded her. What was he doing here? Had he broken his cover? To her relief, Shambles climbed up to her shoulder and gave her a scratchy wet kiss just below her ear.

Schh-makkk!

When would she see Hamish again, properly, with meltathon kisses and swoonworthy cuddles?

Ms Kyryl said, 'I'll get to the point. I'm not sure how you're doing it, but your marks are phenomenal. You can't be copying from Hetty because most of the time you're sitting across the class from her. I doubt Andreas is any help.'

The good grades should have been welcome news, except the teacher looked puzzled and unhappy. A nasty weight pulled at Ondine's shoulders and it wasn't because of Shambles sitting there.

'Can you tell me how you're doing it?'

It called for stalling tactics. 'Um, doing what?'

'Doing so well. When you first came here, you had trouble settling in and your work was well below the class average. When I asked you questions, your answers were generally off the mark. Now your test results are leading the pack. What's going on?'

Swallow. 'I'm studying really hard. That's why I'm so tired.'

Ms Kyryl looked unimpressed. 'Is there something you want to tell me?'

Double swallow. Shambles gave her another kiss. Ondine didn't know what to say.

Mr Kyryl gave up waiting. 'OK, let's try another way. In all my years of teaching, I have never seen a student improve so much in such a short space of time.

I am good, but not that good. Which leads me to one conclusion. You are getting help.'

A very small truck poured concrete into the pit of Ondine's stomach. She wasn't proud of having cheated, in fact, she was downright ashamed, but she'd done it because she loved Hamish so much she'd do anything to stay with him.

Ms Kyryl folded and unfolded her hands. 'Can you please tell me how you are getting help and who is giving it to you?'

Ondine looked at her blankly, because her brain had gone so very blank. If Shambles tried to help with a suggestion, Ms Kyryl would hear the ferret talking, and then Ondine would have a whole heap more explaining to do.

'Fine, I'll spell it out.' Ms Kyryl rubbed a spot on the bridge of her nose. 'I take cheating very seriously. I am on the verge of making a recommendation to the Duke that you leave the palechia school and return to your parents in Venzelemma. Do you have anything to say that might make me change my mind?'

Mercury's wings! Dry mouth, check. Tight tummy,

check. Strange hazy wobbly feeling through her limbs. Checkeroony.

'I ...' Ondine's pride shrivelled as she tried to think her way out of this mess. All she could come up with was the one excuse she really, really didn't want to use. But it was the only one that had any chance of working.

'The reason I'm doing so well ... is because I'm psychic.'

'You're *what*?' Ms Kyryl burst out laughing. 'Now I've heard everything.'

'But it's true. I spent my summer holidays getting better at it.' Or at least getting better at telling whopping great fibs.

'Oh, really?' Ms Kyryl wiped her eyes, as if the very idea could make her cry with laughter.

Zoing! An idea popped into Ondine's head. 'I can prove it. I can talk to animals. I can talk to Shambles right here. And I can help you talk to him as well. Give me your hands and I'll show you.' A surge of confidence came over her. So long as Shambles played his part, they'd bluff their way out of this mess.

'I suppose you're going to put me in a trance?' Ms Kyryl asked, one eyebrow darting up with suspicion.

'No, not needed.' Tell the truth, she had thought of doing just that. For about a tenth of a second. She'd never tried – just observed trances at Psychic Summercamp. They'd looked a bit fake, too. Something in the back of her mind told Ondine her best chance of convincing Ms Kyryl of her psychic abilities was to play things very straight.

Shambles crawled on to the table and stood up on his back legs. He looked at Ms Kyryl, then back at Ondine.

Ms Kyryl's mouth did that side-twisty thing, indicating she was deep in thought.

'Hold my hand, Ms Kyryl, then you'll be able to hear Shambles through me.'

The teacher's cool hand clasped Ondine's and the game was on. It had to be utterly convincing and completely accurate. Her future at the school and at the palechia – and therefore her time with Hamish – depended on it.

'Ms Kyryl, this is Shambles. He is my animal guide

to the spirit world.' Oh, how easily the false words came to her tongue!

Ms Kyryl twisted her mouth in a 'humour me' kind of way. Shambles stepped forward and put his paw on the back of Ms Kyryl's hand.

'It is lovely to meet you, Dionysia,' Shambles said. He spoke with barely a trace of his Scottish accent. He sounded so formal, so believable. So clever!

Ms Kyryl blinked and looked from Shambles to Ondine. Slowly, she shook her head and looked at the little ferret. A Greek curse slipped from her lips.

'*Yassou* to you as well!' Shambles said.[85]

Ms Kyryl looked daggers at Ondine. 'This is some kind of trick.'

'No, nothing of the sort. Ms Kyryl, I am sorry to upset you, but this is completely real. Even I find it hard to take sometimes. I know I professed my love for science to you. Now I'm asking you to believe in magic. But . . . do you not think it's entirely possible for science and magic to co-exist?'

---

85 Yia sou *is a friendly 'hello' in Greek. Say it to just about anyone and you'll go places, either in Athens, Greece, or in Melbourne, Australia.*

Shambles gently rubbed his paw on Ms Kyryl's turning-white knuckle. 'You can use this to tell the bairns all about irony. Aye, it's a good one.'

Panic burrowed in when Ondine heard Shambles's accent slip.

'Ms Kyryl, what would you like to know?' Ondine asked, keen to keep things moving.

The teacher drew a long, slow, breath, shaking her head. Ondine felt a bit sorry for her. This whole talking-animal caper was a lot to dump on someone.

Ms Kyryl exhaled. 'You're the psychic one, why don't you tell me?'

'OK.' It would have been easier with a bit of a hint, just so she knew where to start. As they were holding hands, Ondine figured she may as well start with them. She turned over her teacher's palms to look at the lines.

'You're left-handed, which I already know because I've seen you with a pen in your hand,' Ondine said. A little internal voice reminded her to keep this as straight-down-the-line as possible. 'In your case, the right hand is the life you were born with, and the left

256

hand is the life you have made for yourself. Now if we look at the . . . this is really interesting.'

The lines on the right hand were curved and swirly, the lines on the left were angular and straight. On both palms the lifeline cut deep and true, but on the left hand the fate line stopped short, then started again, slightly to one side of the first line.

'Ms Kyryl, you were born a creative, dramatic and emotional person, but you've carved a whole new life for yourself. It's like your parents wanted you to follow one path, but you've made a determined effort to become something else. Emotions aren't a weakness, but for you they might have been.'

'This is all very general,' the teacher said, chewing the inside of her cheek. 'I fail to see how any of this applies directly to –'

'Ambition burns at the core of your being and you pine for a lost love,' Shambles interrupted.

Zoing!

'How dare you!' Ms Kyryl withdrew her hands. 'Ondine, if this is some kind of sick joke, you can stop it now.'

Cold, clammy dread snaked through Ondine's heart. 'I apologise, Ms Kyryl. Shambles can be too blunt at times, but he calls it as he sees it. You are very, very good at your job, but the lines on your hands say you yearn for something more creative. I've noticed, lately, when we sing the national anthem, you have a beautiful voice. Did you want a musical career instead of a teaching post? Perhaps you had a patron who might have supported you if not for some twist of fate?' Ondine felt like she was grasping for ideas, but it all seemed to fit. And if she hinted at the patronage angle, her teachers' relationship with the Duchess might come to light.

'I've had enough!' Ms Kyryl glared at Ondine. 'I called you in here to give you one last chance to stay. This is not the way to do it.'

Panic exploded into full-blown fear. A strange numb feeling spread over Ondine. 'I am very sorry, Ms Kyryl. I didn't mean to be so blunt. I promise you I will never say a word of this to anyone.'

'That point is moot. As of this moment, Ondine, you are no longer a student at the palechia. I will recommend to the Duke that you return to your parents in Venzelemma.'

Something swirly happened in her head. Ondine thought she might pass out.

Ms Kyryl folded her arms across her lean chest. 'Why are you still here? Go!'

Feeling utterly wretched, Ondine dragged her feet from the converted barn and made straight for the privacy of her room.

'Great Jupiter's moons, I'm finished!'

Chapter Twenty

Panic and fear made it impossible for Ondine to think straight as she slumped on her bed. Ms Kyryl's words kept swirling in her head and all she could focus on was her imminent expulsion from the palechia.

'Aw, I'm so sorry, me love,' Hamish said.

Hot tears spilt down Ondine's cheeks. 'This is hopeless.'

She was so enveloped in her grief, she barely paid attention to the man transforming beside her. He helped himself to her beige bedspread to keep warm. His strong arms embraced her and rocked her gently.

'It's all right, lass. I'll explain it tae the Duke and ye'll be able tae stay.'

How she'd yearned to see Hamish again, but she

felt so angry and shocked, she couldn't bring herself to look at him. She'd been doing a pretty good job of bluffing Ms Kyryl until Shambles had blurted out the 'lost love' angle.

'I should never have cheated. I should have studied harder from the start and then she wouldn't have been suspicious and none of this would have happened. You shouldn't have done it, Hamish. You knew she had it in for me. You should never have made me cheat.'

'Studied harder? Nobody studies more than ye. Sometimes I think ye loave school work more than me because ye spend so much time on it. Even so, she would have sent ye home, we had tae do something.'

Coils of dread tightened the muscles in Ondine's shoulders. Going home meant facing her parents, who were still furious that she'd disobeyed them in the first place and run off with Hamish.

'Then why didn't we come up with something else?' she wailed. 'If we're so smart, how come there wasn't some other way apart from cheating? Now look what's happened – she's expelled me!'

'Nawt yet she hasnae. We'll work something out.'

'Saturn's rings, are you even listening? You were there, you saw how annoyed she was with the whole psychic thing! I should have admitted I cheated at the beginning and begged her forgiveness. Now all I've done is made her angrier.'

'It's nawt that bad. We'll work it out. Old Col will help.'

No amount of soothing words from Hamish made the slightest dent in Ondine's mood. 'I should never have looked at that answer sheet in the first place and now look where it's got me. I never wanted to cheat, it always felt wrong, but I let you talk me into it because I trusted you.' Drawing in a staggered breath, she continued her rant: 'It's this stupid palace! It's done something to your head and now you love spying and sneaking around so much you think cheating is normal.'

'So it's all me fault, is it?'

Ondine shouted, 'Yes, it is!' As soon as the words were out she both wished she'd never said them and felt glad she'd blurted them out. Shaking her head at how hopeless everything had become, her breath came in painful gasps.

A stricken look of betrayal crossed Hamish's face, followed by utter despair. Palpable silence cloaked the room. They'd never had a problem with silences before, but now it felt horrible. The longer the silence lasted, the harder it became to break it. Try as she might, Ondine was afraid to say anything more because in her present state of anger and confusion she might make things even worse.

Hamish removed his arm from her shoulder. Ondine felt the chill.

'I was only trying tae help,' he said. Then he shut his eyes and his body shrivelled away into his ferret shape.

A fierce ache ripped Ondine's heart open. 'No, Hamish, please don't go.' Not when they were still fighting, not when they hadn't sorted it out.

It was too late. He'd already reverted. 'I think I havtae.' His little ferret body waddled out of the room.

Alone, Ondine gave in to her misery and let the tears fall. She threw herself on her bed, face down in the pillow. After a few minutes of cathartic bawling, she turned the soaked pillow over to continue the marrow-deep sobs.

'What is such noise?' Draguta came in and saw Ondine on her bed. Ondine felt a bony hand rubbing her back. 'There, there, what is upset you so?'

'Nothing,' Ondine lied.

'Nothing? Then stop crying when is nothing.'

Ondine couldn't stop. She'd lost her place in the palechia school, and even worse, she'd just lost Hamish.

'So, is something?' Draguta was too smart for her own good.

It all came out in a rush. 'Hamish and I had a fight, and he walked out and now I think Ms Kyryl's going to kick me out of school because I've been cheating. I really tried hard but it wasn't enough and now it's too late because I messed it all up.'

'You have the PMT,' Draguta said. 'Need chocolate.'

With a loud sniff, Ondine wiped her eyes. Hormones would explain part of it. All the same, she'd been dealt a massive blow, which entitled her to a big cry.

Draguta opened a drawer and snapped off some squares of chocolate, then handed it to Ondine. 'Here, eat. Best medicine.'

'Thanks.' Ondine took a bite. The cocoa-and-sugar hit triggered something in her brain and she started feeling better. Draguta held her arms wide for a hug, and Ondine accepted. It was like hugging a lamp post.

The laundry mistress had been so kind, Ondine owed her some honesty. 'Draguta, I have to tell you something. You know how you're coming up to long-service leave?'

'Yes?' Draguta looked apprehensive as she sat down on her bed.

'Well, I found out – please don't ask me how – that the Duchess is being a total miser and she'll find a way to sack you before she has to pay you your leave.'

Draguta reached for her teddy bear and hugged it to her chest. 'Ptah! She did that last time. Thinks I stupid! Appreciate warning, but I prepared this time.'

'I'm so relieved.' Ondine wiped her eyes and took the last bite of chocolate. She kept her voice low. 'I thought the Infanta was bonkers, but the Duchess is something else.'

'It all be fine. I get back to work now,' Draguta said, fetching another cardigan to wear over her existing warm clothes. 'Infanta will be wanting you soon.'

'I know.' Ondine felt the chill in the air and reached for another jumper. 'I just need to get myself together before I can face her.'

Draguta left and Ondine felt misery seep into her skin. It was probably the cold as well, because the staff dormitory had no heating. She'd been sitting still for so long her muscles had started to stiffen. The little teddy on Draguta's bed offered a morsel of comfort. Ondine picked up the teddy and gave it a hug. Something jabbed her in the chest. It was like hugging Draguta again, all sharp angles and bones.

Since when did furry teddy bears have corners?

Ondine looked but she couldn't see anything amiss. She hugged the toy again and felt another jab. She gave the teddy's belly a squish for good measure and felt something hard beneath the stuffing.

Curiosity got the better of her. She turned the teddy upside down and began to look for signs of something not right. It felt a bit rude as she probed for holes. That's the problem when you're in the grip of curiosity. Even when it's rude, you still can't hold back.

Running her fingers along the seams, she found a tiny hole. She stuck her finger through and poked about – roughly where one of his kidneys would be, if stuffed toys had kidneys.

This stuffed toy had solid objects inside. Ondine tried to pull them out with her finger, but the hole was too small and the objects were too big.

If I can just . . . rip! She tore a gaping hole in the side. *Ba-dump, ba-dump,* her heart began racing at the thought of what lay inside. *Badump-badump-badump,* her heart charged faster at the thought of Draguta walking back in and finding her violating the teddy.

Mercury's wings! Trinkets, keys, earrings, brooches and even a decorative spoon tumbled out of the toy and on to the bed. Quick as a flash, she stuffed them all back into the bear and tugged on the loose threads to close up the hole.

Staring at the toy, she couldn't help a worrying thought: *Oh, Draguta, what have you done?*

Chapter Twenty-one

Shambles felt lower than a cockroach. A cockroach who'd walked into a deep pit, picked up a shovel and started digging the pit even deeper. Ms Kyryl was sending Ondine home for cheating and it was his fault. How had his well-meaning attempts to help his sweetheart backfired so badly? When they'd met in the summer she didn't have classes or exams. He hadn't realised school and studying were so important to her, but clearly they were and he'd stuffed things right up.

He needed somewhere to think, but his stomach rumbled so loudly he had to find food first. Taking care not to get under anyone's feet, he scarpered down the hall and followed the cooking smells. Judging from the pungent caramelised onion, meat and rosemary aromas, roast lamb was on the menu. His mouth watered in anticipation. He should try and take some slices to Ondine, as a peace offering. The poor hen had eaten little more than soup and bread for the past few weeks, perhaps something solid might fix her up?

On his brain went, telling him how clever he was to be able to think of Ondine when he was fair starving. Not that he'd given any thought as to how he might deliver such a meal to her in his present state. Perhaps he might find a wee bag or box he could carry the food in. What it lacked in presentation, he could more than make up for in affection and perhaps a grovelling apology, if that's what it took to get back in her good books.

As he neared the kitchen, a strident female voice echoed through the hall: 'I've never sheen such wanton washtage!'

The kitchen noises stopped. No chopping, no washing, no sounds of blenders or grinders. Mindful that people might run out of the kitchen at any moment and step on him, Shambles kept to the edges and poked his furry head around the doorway to see what was going on.

It was Duchess Kerala in full rant. She made quite a sight, her head moving madly from side to side, all without so much as a hair breaking free from her shiny helmet-do. One hand held a glass of white wine, while the other gesticulated wildly to Emphasise! Every! Word!

'Look at that pile of perfectly good food you're about to throw out! All those potato shkins can go into shoups, not the composht bins. You're throwing out the bread crusts when any chef with half a gram of shense can make croutonsh with them. And I can't believe you're throwing out half the shelery! Shelery tops taste just like parshley and you've brought that in by the truckload. And I can't believe you're throwing out the parshley shtalks instead of putting them in the casheroles! The washtage! It beggars belief!'

At this point, some people might draw breath, but the Duchess seemed beyond such mortal constraints.[86]

'What's thish? A ton of rhubarb leaves? You cannot

---

86 *It's called 'circular breathing' and is especially useful when playing the didgeridoo.*

throw thish out. I've told you before, it makesh a perfectly good substitute for spinach!'

Nobody said anything in response. Shambles looked around the room at the trembling, pale-faced kitchen staff. They looked so young, barely older than Ondine. None dared answer back.

No chance of snaffling even a morsel of roast lamb while the Duchess kept storming around the kitchen, finding more and more things to complain about, her voice growing ever more shrill with each discovery.

Tummy rumbling even more loudly, Shambles turned tail and ran back to Old Col's room. Drat, her bed was empty. The only thing to eat was a bowl of cat food one of the staff had set out in a bowl.

'Ah, weil, when in Brugel.' Shambles took a deep breath and a small bite.

After a few mouthfuls, he started to feel better. But then he thought past his hunger and a fresh pang of regret hit him. He needed to make it up to Ondine, but huffing fish-breath all over her wouldn't help if he wanted to kiss and make up.

It was imperative he find some mouthwash to

get rid of the lingering fishiness. He trotted into the bathroom and jumped on to the sink. Not in one leap – even a ferret has his limits – but two leaps. Floor to toilet seat – ooops, nearly fell in, must remember the lid's not always down! – then to the edge of the sink. He found a tube of toothpaste and managed to chew the flip-top lid off.[87] Stepping on the tube, he forced out a neat white pipe of minty paste. A few licks later, his mouth filled with foamy freshness and he felt really pleased with the results.

At that moment, Draguta Matice walked into the bathroom with arms full of fresh towels and screamed, 'Aaaaaah! Rabies!'

'Hnnnnggggff!' He tried to respond but he had a mouth full of foam. In desperation he spat out as much as he could into the sink, but the white bubbles coming

---

87 *Aren't flip-top lids on toothpaste wonderful? It's so easy to snap the lid back in place. In the days when you had to screw the lid on, many time-poor people would forget to replace the lid. Because clearly, it was soooo much effort to screw one tiny little lid back on the tube. It's enough to drive you completely insane.*

It's no coincidence that the introduction of flip-top lids on toothpaste tubes in the early 1990s dovetails neatly with Brugel's plummeting divorce rates.

from his mouth only made Draguta scream louder.

Draguta dropped her bundle on the bathroom floor and ran out of Old Col's room, shouting all the way, 'Pyotr! Pyotr! Rabies!'

No, no! Shambles forgot about the height and leapt to the ground. Crack! He landed hard on the floor, smacking his chin. Pain lanced through him. His head went all fuzzy and wobbly. If he'd had a chance to think, he would have descended in two stages, back to the loo seat, then the floor. Desperation had made him forget how small he was and how far he'd fall. Trying to shake out the pain only made it worse.

Ye daftie wee bampot, ye've broken ye jaw!

Still not thinking – he seemed to be doing a lot of that – Shambles ran after Draguta to make her stop. She didn't know he was really Hamish, but if he could explain himself, she might realise her mistake and stop screaming. He called out, 'Wait!' but his jaw hurt so much it came out like 'waaaad' and even he barely understood it.

People came rushing towards Draguta's screams,

adding to the commotion. Maids, visitors, Pyotr the seneschal and, worst luck of all, Lord Vincent.

'I'll handle this,' Lord Vincent said, raising his booted foot.

Arrggghhh! The blood froze in Shambles's veins as the size eleven sole filled his vision. Pain or no pain, he bolted sideways to avoid certain death and scarpered back into the safety of Old Col's room.

Not safe for long! Everyone from the hall poured into the room and began talking at once.

'Where did it go?'

'Over there, look!'

'It's under the bed.'

'Is that it over there?'

'Throw a blanket on it.'

'Someone get the dog-catcher!'

'Someone get a gun!'

Trembling with fear, Shambles cowered under the bed. He wiped his mouth with his furry front paw to clear away the foam. Not gentle enough! Fresh pain speared his jaw. A little bit of sick burnt his throat as he feared for his life. Any second now one of them would look under the bed and it would be goodnight Shambles.

Wiping his mouth again – gently! – he managed to get rid of the remaining gobs of toothpaste. It still looked bad because his front legs were streaked with saliva. If anyone saw him, they could mistake his wet limbs for profuse sweatiness. The only option left to him was transforming into his human shape. If he concentrated hard enough and fixed Ondine's smiling dark eyes in his mind. Sure, he'd have a mountain of explaining to do when he crawled out from under the bed without a scrap of clothing on. But at least he'd be their size, and he'd be able to take on Lord Vincent on a level playing field.

'What's going on?' a woman said.

He knew that voice. It wasn't Ondine, but Old Col. Maybe her presence could bring him round? He anticipated the maelstrom of lurching and twisting as he willed himself to become human. But nothing happened.

'Your ferret has the rabies,' Draguta said. 'We must capture, before he bites anyone.'

'He hasn't got rabies,' Old Col said. 'Whatever gave you that idea?'

From his hiding place under the bed, Shambles saw Lord Vincent's heavy boots stamp about the floor.

'How do you know it's not full of disease?' Vincent said.

'It had foaming mouth!' Draguta added.

'Nobody has rabies,' Old Col said. 'That ferret is my pet. He is vaccinated and in perfect health. I have the vet bills to prove it. Now if you don't mind, you're in my room and I'd like some privacy.'

Lord Vincent snorted contempt. 'You're a guest in this palace and you'll do what you're told.'

'Hold your tongue!' Old Col snapped right back.

'Abwath –' A strange noise came from Lord Vincent's mouth.

Shambles peeked out from his hiding place to see the Duke's eldest son holding his tongue between his thumb and two fingers. In fact, he didn't seem able to let it go.

'Wha-hab-oo-dundame?' Lord Vincent cried.

'I told you to "hold your tongue". You're lucky it

wasn't "shut your face", then you'd be in real strife,'
Old Col said. 'It will wear off when you reach the
other side of the palechia.'

It took all Shambles's willpower not to burst out
laughing. It was probably a good thing, because
laughing would hurt like crazy.

Vincent looked furious and stomped out of
the room.

'Show's over, may I have some privacy please?' Old
Col said.

When everyone else had left the room, Shambles
craned his head out from under the bed. It hurt to
speak, but he needed to thank her. 'Tha' was goo'
magic, Col.'

Old Col grinned. 'Yes. I rather think it was. Now,
why are you even more difficult to understand today?'

Chapter Twenty-two

Melancholy cloaked Ondine as she tidied the Infanta's rooms. For some reason, Anathea wasn't being a total cow and had refrained from telling her off every minute.

'Where is my happy Ondine?' the Infanta asked after half an hour of heavy silence.

Ondine wiped her face, trying really hard not to bawl in front of her employer. But her chin wobbled and her vision started blurring. 'I had a fight with my boyfriend and now I don't think he ever wants to talk to me again.'

'You have time for a boyfriend?'

'Apparently not.' Would this horrible pain behind her ribs ever go away?

'You love him?'

'With all my heart.'

'And he walked away?' The Infanta's face seemed to soften.

'Yes.'

'He let you down. Now you know how I felt,' she said. 'It won't be the first time. Mark my words, you will be let down time and time again.' Imperceptibly, the Infanta's chin trembled, but she turned away.

It felt so strange to be sharing this moment of honesty with Anathea. Something shifted between them, Ondine could feel it. For the first time, she saw things from the Infanta's point of view. Fate had taken her fiancé, the man she might have grown to love and spend the rest of her life with. Yet the moment she'd lost her title, he'd given her the flick.

Steeling herself for some kind of rebuttal that would put her back in her place, Ondine asked the question that had nagged her for some time. 'I know your first engagement fell through, but what about later on?'

An icy glare greeted Ondine. '*He* was no better. I do not even say his name. I was young. My head was lost. We had three beautiful daughters together, but it wasn't enough.' The Infanta shook her head and ground out the next sentence: 'He wanted a boy.'

'History repeated itself,' Ondine said.

'That would have been preferable.' Anathea drew breath and Ondine could only wait, and wait a bit more, to hear the rest of it.

'There was a boy born, but it was not by me. A week later I was served with divorce papers. And that is all that will ever be said of it. If you bring this up again, you will be dismissed immediately. Is that clear?'

Stricken with equal amounts of fear and sorrow, Ondine only nodded and hastily got back to work.

Pyotr arrived at the Infanta's door. 'Ondine, the Duke will see you now,' he said.

The bottom dropped out of Ondine's world. Not that she was feeling particularly psychic, but she knew being summoned to the Duke's rooms couldn't be good news. But then a little spark of hope surged – if the Duke had asked to see her, he must be feeling well enough to see people. That had to be good, surely?

Feeling wretched for herself, Ondine followed Pyotr

to the Duke's office. The Duke looked a bit strange, as if he hadn't completely recovered from whatever ailed him. Perspiration sprang from Ondine's face, neck, armpits and elbows. Not from nerves but because of the temperature – it was roasting hot in here, with four heaters on full blast. As Ondine removed her scarf and fingerless gloves, she noticed Old Col looking calm but flushed in the face. Hamish was there too, in Shambles form, on her shoulder. Guilt spread through her at the sight of Shambles, because he looked so utterly pitiful. Oh, how she wished she could apologise to him and take back everything she had said. But this was not the place for domestic reconciliations. That's if reconciliation was on offer. Judging by the way he kept his ferrety gaze away from her, there might not be. Which set off another fresh burst of guilt and sorrow.

Ms Kyryl the teacher was also there, her face firm and set, like a ... well, like a disapproving teacher, really.

Resentment towards Shambles sliced through her. If she hadn't cheated – if he hadn't encouraged her to cheat – she wouldn't have given Ms Kyryl enough ammunition to bring this situation to the Duke.

'Ondine, thank you for joining us,' the Duke said.

Pyotr fetched a chair for Ondine and put it beside Ms Kyryl. Ms Kyryl nodded as Ondine sat down and cast another of those disconcerted looks at Shambles, her soft Adam's apple bobbing up and down.

The Duke spoke in a thin, wavering voice, which indicated he had a fair bit of recovering to do. 'Ms Kyryl, Colette and I have been discussing your scholastic performance and I have several concerns. All things considered . . . you might be better off returning home to live with your parents and attending your local school.'

'But I . . . I'm working so hard, please don't make me go.' It felt so stuffy in here Ondine thought she might gag. She loosened the top button of her shirt but it made no difference. Without being asked, Pyotr walked around the room and switched off the heaters.

The room fell silent for a moment, except for the suddenly noticeable ticking of the wall clock. *Tick, tick, tick, tick.*

Every tick of the clock counted down the moments until her expulsion.

Not only was Shambles not even looking at her, he said absolutely nothing to help her.

The Duke got to the point: 'Ondine, you have been here several weeks, but it's not such a long time that your education would suffer if you returned to your previous school.'

Tick, tick, tick, tick. Her mind raced. Naturally, they couldn't talk about spying in front of Ms Kyryl, so she tried very hard to come up with some other way of explaining how she could still be useful here.

The Duke continued, 'Pyotr tells me you have been working in the laundry. I have heard no complaints and in fact Miss Matice sings your praises. You have been a credit to your great aunt in that regard. However, a laundry position can easily be filled, so it would put the palechia at no disadvantage if you were to leave.'

Ondine automatically nodded agreement, then blinked as she realised something important. 'Um . . . Your Grace . . . I recently began butlering for the Infanta.'

'Oh, really?' With an effort, the Duke sat a little straighter in his chair.

Ding! went Ondine's brain. The door of opportunity creaked open a fraction. Maybe that mad Infanta had saved her skin?

'Yes, Your Grace. The Infanta requires me to prepare all her meals myself. She says I'm the only one she trusts.'

'Does she now? How very interesting.' The Duke stroked the edges of his split moustache before turning his steely gaze to the teacher. 'Ms Kyryl, thank you for your time.'

'Yes, Your Grace.' Ms Kyryl bowed her head and walked out.

A cool gust of air from the corridor wafted in, helping to clear Ondine's head for just a moment.

After the door clicked shut, the Duke looked at Old Col, then at Ondine.

'Do go on,' he said.

'Um.' Ondine knew she had to say something good. Her future at the palechia depended on it. But what had she seen or heard from the Infanta that might prove useful to the Duke?

A dreadful thought took hold. Perhaps Shambles refused to say anything because he thought she should be going home?

The Infanta's words rang in her ears: *You will be let down.* Ondine couldn't stand it. She didn't want to credit Anathea with foresight, but Shambles's silence seemed to confirm it.

Maybe everyone would be better off if she went home? If only she had some kind of sign she hadn't completely stuffed things up with Hamish and he would eventually return to her in Venzelemma.

Duke Pavla locked eyes with Ondine and leant forward, which served to accentuate his widow's peak. 'You must tell me everything. Even the things you think might not be important. Little things that go unnoticed can sometimes turn out to be very important.'

'Um,' Ondine said again, as her mind reeled back to her first meeting with the Infanta. 'I think Aunt Col told you about the dog soup.'

'Yes, and thank you for the warning.'

'My pleasure. Well, we got talking. Or rather, she

kind of lectured me. She said she didn't like so many new people being here in the palechia. I mean, all the new employees who don't seem to have much training. Maybe they aren't very good at handling food and that's why we're getting sick?'

'Interesting theory. Anything else?'

'She asked me to tell her everything. You know, if I saw or heard anything strange. So I said I would. And now I'm working for her and cooking all her meals.'

'I see. Anything else?'

The full intensity of the Duke's attention gave Ondine an idea. 'Your Grace, just before I tell you about Anathea, I have to ask about my friend Draguta Matice. She is due for long-service leave and I think the Duchess wants to sack her before the leave is due so she can save money.'

She might be able to secure Draguta's continued employment. And she would be able to tell Draguta she'd spoken up for her. Maybe then her friend might explain what all those expensive trinkets were doing stuffed inside her teddy bear.[88]

---

88 What Ondine is relying on here is the 'double coincidence': the

She thought she'd been really clever, because she hadn't said anything about the ledger or the secret bank account. Unfortunately, she'd hadn't been clever at all, because Pavla's face creased, like he'd just smelt something horrible.

'Do not bring my wife into this, it will get you nowhere.' He turned to Col, 'I heard about what happened with Vincent earlier today. Just between us, I was quite grateful for your intervention, but my dear wife was inconsolable. I'd be most grateful if you would do your best not to upset her any further.'

'The Duchess objects to me using magic?' Col said.

'That is putting it mildly. She was tremendously upset and would rather the three of you were gone. I made it clear you were here for a very important purpose, but I fear if she is upset again, I may have to ask you to leave.'

idea that the information she gives the Duke has the same value as the information he needs to hear. She's also relying on the information she will subsequently be able to give Draguta being of the same value as any information Draguta may give to Ondine (about why she's padding her teddy with precious objects rather than fluffy stuff). So really, she's relying on the 'quadruple coincidence', and the chances of that happening are virtually zero.

'Yes, Your Grace,' Old Col said.

Ondine's mind creaked and snapped and whirred and clicked at this new piece of information. They would have to be extra-extra careful about saying anything to the Duke about his wife, because he'd most likely take her side. If they wanted to keep their jobs, they might have to keep stump.[89]

A look of frustration crossed Duke Pavla's face. 'Do you have any useful information about my sister that might be linked to my declining health?'

Ondine thought she might be sick with fear. 'I'm sorry, Your Grace. I haven't noticed anything else. Yet.'

'Then you'd better notice. Stay close to Anathea and tell me everything you see or hear. Is that understood?' His words filled Ondine with fear and

---

89 *'Keeping stump' is an old Brugel idiom about staying quiet and being clever, and your deepest desires will come to you. It refers to the classic Brugel fable of 'The Fox in Disguise', who strapped branches on his limbs and sat on a tree stump with his mouth wide open for so long, the forest creatures couldn't help but get closer and closer to get a better look at the strange tree. Eventually the dim forest sweeties walked straight into the fox's mouth and he got everything he wanted.*

It may also be a mishearing of the phrase 'keeping stumm', but nobody in Brugel would know what you were talking about.

hope. Fear that she'd better come up with something, and hope that she might be able to stay on a bit longer and repair things with Hamish. 'And you, Shambles and Miss Romano, had better come up with something soon, other than guests stealing silverware, or I'll reconsider your employment.'

Gulp!

As they left the Duke's office with his threat ringing in their ears, Ondine felt completely overwhelmed by the task at hand.

'We are really up against it, Col,' she said.

'You don't say,' Col replied.

'What happened with Vincent, by the way?'

'I shut him up.'

'Nice one.' Ondine wanted to give her great aunt a high five. Her feeling of quiet triumph soon evaporated as she waited for Shambles to say something to her. Anything would do. Despair wound itself through her system, growing more palpable with each passing minute of silence.

By the time they reached Old Col's room, Ondine's nerves were strung out. Col placed Shambles on the end of her bed. Then she turned to Ondine. 'So, what happened between you two? Did you have a fight?'

'No,' Ondine lied.

'Nnn,' Shambles mumbled. The first noise to come from his lips and it wasn't even a proper word. To Ondine, he was completely out of sorts. When he started gesticulating with his paw in front of his face, she wondered if he was making a 'go-away' gesture.

Old Col put her hands on her hips. 'You're uncharacteristically quiet, Shambles. What gives?'

'Ah oke eye aw.' He didn't really speak, it was more a case of the words sliding out sideways.

'Are you sick?' Ondine reached down to touch his furry face and he recoiled. *Oh no! Now he doesn't even want me touching him*, she thought. 'I'm so sorry about everything I said. I take it all back. Please talk to me again.'

'You did have a fight,' Col said. 'I knew it.'

Feeling utterly wretched, Ondine's vision went blurry with fresh tears. 'Yes, we did.'

'Ondine, you'd best be running along. The Infanta will be waiting,' Col said gently.

'In a minute.' She dragged her sleeve over her eyes

to dry them. If Shambles would just say something reassuring she would feel so much better.

With a groan of pain, Shambles began transforming into a human. Blessed relief filled Ondine's heart and she quickly grabbed a blanket to keep him warm. Then she ripped the cover off the bed to make another layer of warmth for him. In this part of the palechia, Hamish would freeze.

Hamish looked like he might be sick as he finished transforming. 'Aw, thanks hen,' he said, pulling the blanket around him. Despite the cold, beads of sweat dotted his brow. 'I ken talk again, thank goodness fer that.' He tenderly rubbed his jaw, 'Aww, that's handy to know, eh, Col? I broke me jaw leaping awf the basin but it's all fixed now.'

'You broke your jaw?' It didn't seem possible, but Ondine felt even worse than before. She and Hamish were supposed to have a *connection*. All this time, she thought he'd been ignoring her. Instead, he'd been in so much pain he couldn't even *talk*. And she hadn't even *realised*!

'I'm so sorry, Hamish,' she said again. He still

hadn't said any of the soothing words she needed right now, like *It's fine, I love you,* or *I'm sorry too, I hope you can forgive me.* Maybe he didn't forgive her. Maybe he preferred being a ferret because it was becoming too painful to be a man? Then shouldn't he avoid the pain by staying human all the time instead? There was so much demanded of them. And Ondine didn't have the benefit of changing into an animal, yet she was still expected to work the espionage angle just as much as Hamish. It was exhausting.

'The Infanta is not known for her patience, child,' Old Col said. 'You two can make up some other time. Hamish, you need to keep an eye on Lord Vincent. He and Kerala are up to something, I can feel it in my waters.'

Ondine didn't want to leave, she'd much rather stay and talk things through with Hamish. But instead of asking her to stay, Hamish gave her a sad look and said, 'Ye'd best be going then.'

Which Ondine took to mean he didn't want her with him. She turned to leave before she started a fresh bout of bawling.

Chapter Twenty-three

'I would like some biscuits made,' the Infanta said, as Ondine prepared her pot of tea and slices of lemon. The way the woman spoke made Ondine want to roll her eyes. Everything the Infanta said implied someone else had done it, or should do it. And whenever she spoke about something bad happening she had that knack of making it seem like someone else's fault.

'Yes, ma'am. I'll go down to the kitchen and do it.' The thought of spending a bit of time in the kitchen, away from the Infanta, held great appeal.

'You know something? They could be made here.' Anathea raised her hand and pointed vaguely to the left. 'I've been told there's a kitchen next door.'

'Next door? You're kidding?' Ondine still found

it hard to guess the Infanta's mood, because her face remained so immobile. But from the woman's tone, she sounded serious.

'See for yourself. I think there is a connecting door somewhere – oh, look, if that table is moved, there's a latch to be found. It's either a kitchen or a storage room. It's never been used.'

How bizarre! Ondine grunted as she shifted the table and found the latch. It was easier to see the doorframe now, because she knew what to look for. But if you didn't, you might think it was a shoddy join in the wallpaper.

She turned the handle in the top of the dado and pulled the door towards her. It opened with a groan, as if waking from a hundred-year sleep. Beams of light streaked in through the dusty windows. Ondine found a light switch near the door. Sleepy fluorescent tubes buzzed and flickered into life. The air smelled musty and dry, as if the room had lain undisturbed for decades.

'Mercury's wings! What a great kitchen!' Ondine walked around, her footsteps stirring up dust motes on the terracotta tiles as she assessed the room. The old electric oven belonged in a museum. It looked like it had never been touched. When Ondine opened the refrigerator, she held her nose in anticipation of biohazard, but it was empty. The freezer door put up a fight. When it finally came free, Ondine discovered the inside was completely iced up. She leant down and switched it off at the power point.

'Has anyone ever used it?' she called out to the Infanta.

'Probably not. Certainly not me.'

Ondine would be able to prepare the Infanta's meals here instead of down in the kitchens. She set to wiping dust off the counters.

The Infanta said, 'About those biscuits?'

Saturn's rings, does she never let up? 'Yes, ma'am?'

'I was thinking. Perhaps the biscuits should be made by me?'

Double-take time. 'Um, have you ever made them before?'

'There's a first time for everything.'

Oh dear! 'OK, then. First thing, take all your rings

off and wash your hands. I'll find us some aprons.'
Sure enough, the kitchen had several pantries. Inside
one, Ondine found everything she needed except
ingredients. Probably just as well, because any food
remains would have been supporting new ecosystems
by now.

'I'll head downstairs and get the food.'

In the kitchens she very nearly collided with the
Duchess.

'Ondine? What in heavensh name are you
doing here?'

That's right, the Duchess wanted her gone. In her
peripheral vision, Ondine saw pale, trembling people
who looked as if they'd just been thoroughly told off.
Ooops, very bad time to arrive.

'My Lady Duchess.' She made a quick bow of
respect. 'I came to collect ingredients so I can cook for
the Infanta.'

'Really? She's not happy with the copioush free
meals I shupply her?'

Oh dear, the slurring was back and it wasn't even
that late in the day. Ondine didn't know where to look,

so she kept her eyes lowered. 'Your Grace, I can come back later if you like.'

'You've got one minute.'

Ondine wasted the first ten seconds of that minute in mute shock, before she sprang into action and grabbed a tray. Despite the Duchess's tight rein on food supplies, she at least found enough ingredients to make biscuits and pancakes. A small bag of flour, some butter, sugar, salt – they were easy to find but she needed more. Where was the chocolate and crystallised ginger? The pantry was so neat and ordered, with everything labelled – it was an obsessive-compulsive's dream. She found the ginger but no sign of chocolate. The Duchess hadn't kicked her out yet, so she reached for the refrigerator and grabbed a bottle of milk and a couple of eggs.

'I'm glad I didn't give you two minutesh, you would have cleaned me out,' the Duchess said.

'Thank you, Your Grace,' Ondine said, before making a hasty bow and an even hastier exit.

'Was there trouble?' Anathea asked when she returned.

'Just your sister-in-law keeping an eye on the food supplies.'

'That woman.' Anathea rolled her eyes and shook her head, making Ondine giggle in shared sympathy.

For the next half hour, she and the Infanta got their hands dirty making pancake batter and biscuits.

'This is good fun,' The Infanta said.

They had flour all over the counter top and themselves, but they didn't care. Ondine couldn't get over the change in the Infanta. 'I'll start cooking the pancakes,' she said. 'Now, the rule is, the first one is always a bit of a mess.'

'Hah! Just like marriages!' Anathea said.

Ondine laughed, marvelling at this new Infanta and how friendly she could be when the mood suited her. Which sent a little ping of worry through her, because Duke Pavla had instructed her to report everything back to him. What could she say? Your sister's not such a bad old sort after all?

They rolled the biscuit dough into balls and flattened them on the trays with their fingers. They pressed the ginger pieces in, making patterns and smiley faces.

'Would you like to lick the bowl?' Ondine wondered if she'd gone too far in this new, informal atmosphere developing between them. How confusing that she should be having such a sweet time with the Infanta while her relationship with Hamish felt like it was falling apart.

'No, but a cup of tea wouldn't go astray.'

'I'll get right on it, once I've put the tray in the oven,' Ondine said.

'No need.' The Infanta placed her hand lightly on top of Ondine's. 'The pot of tea shall be made by me.'

Ondine wasn't sure if she could cope with any more surprises.

The Infanta washed her hands, removed her apron and walked back to her rooms. Ondine remained in the kitchen, humming a quiet tune as she scraped the messy pancake off the pan and started a new one. Giving in to temptation, she had a bite. Ugly but delicious!

The sound of footsteps in the other room were

followed by Duchess Kerala's strident voice: 'Why are you not bowing to your bettersh?'

The demand for obedience had Ondine recalling her hideous encounter with Lord Vincent. Although she couldn't see the Infanta, Ondine assumed Anathea made some kind of bow, because she heard the Duchess say, 'Thash better.'

'Your Grace, by what honour do I have the privilege of our meeting today?' the Infanta said.

'The Duke has inshtructed me to invite you to the Harvesht Ball,' the Duchess said in a tone that could only be described as pained.

'My brother is the very milk of human kindness,' Anathea said.

Ondine remained in the kitchen. Hiding away seemed the safest bet as she listened to the women trying to be civil to each other.

'I trusht you will behave yourself this year,' the Duchess said.

'I shall be the very model of gracious behaviour.'

'Good. That is all.'

When the Infanta came back to the kitchen, she

had a scowl on her face. An actual scowl! Her neatly plucked eyebrows were clamped down and there were ridges in her forehead. 'Oh, that woman! Comes in here soaked to the gills and tells me to behave myself! She should be pushed down the stairs. She's so drunk everyone would think it an accident.'

'Mmm,' Ondine said as non-committally as possible. All the while uncharitable thoughts criss-crossed her head. She found herself completely agreeing with Anathea. On the other hand, the Infanta wanting to cause harm to the Duchess meant she finally had something useful to tell the Duke. Even if it was only an empty threat. But what should she do? Save her skin or save this new-found friendship?

When the biscuits and pancakes were ready, they sat down together and ate them, with the pot of tea the Infanta made. The tea wasn't awful, as such, but Ondine knew she could make better. Not that she said so, because Anathea looked really pleased with herself.

'Come here, Biscuit,' the Infanta called to the dog. He bounded on to her lap. She dipped her biscuit into her tea and fed it to the dog.

A biscuit for Biscuit.

Ondine couldn't help recoiling when Anathea dunked the rest of the Biscuit-sucked biscuit into her tea a second time.

When Ondine woke up the next morning in her cold room, Draguta was already up and dressed, and about to leave. Ondine had to act quickly.

'Wait. I need to tell you something,' she said.

'Oh yes?' Draguta's shoulders slumped. 'Don't make me late. Duchess is more horrible than usual.'

'Try not to be upset,' Ondine said.

'Impossible. I am upset.'

Oh dear. Ondine gulped. Taking a deep breath, she said, 'I know about your teddy.'

The woman's eyes turned to ice. 'Why you say "teddy"?'

There seemed little point in pretending ignorance. 'I didn't mean to pry. I found out by accident. I was feeling really fragile after I'd had that fight with Hamish and I gave your teddy a cuddle because he looked soft and warm. But he was all lumpy.'

'You snoop!' Draguta leapt back to her bed and grabbed the stuffed toy, giving it a squeeze to make sure its contents were in place.

'No, it wasn't like that!' This was all going so badly! Ondine wrapped a thin dressing gown around herself to keep out the early morning chill. 'I found out by accident . . . but . . . I couldn't help wondering . . .'

'Why I am thief?' Draguta placed the teddy under her pillow.

'I won't tell anyone.'

'Hah! Have not lasted years in palace by trusting sweet-face girls.'

If Draguta had smacked her she couldn't have hurt her more. 'But we're friends,' Ondine said, caught in confusion.

'I have no friends,' Draguta said.

Before she could think, Ondine blurted, 'But that's terrible!'

'Ack! Don't look full of sorrow.' Draguta shook her head, put her hands on her hips and paced the room a bit. She threw her hands in the air and said, 'Ack! I grow soft. Kerala sacked me before. One month before last long service. She found me . . .' she looked up, as if asking the heavens for guidance. Or forgiveness. 'Was private. Duchess found me. She said instant dismissal. I left, no savings. Came back two weeks later and begged for old job. Ha! Thought Duchess kind to let me back. At first. Then people talk. I put it all away in here,' Draguta tapped the side of her head. 'It was set-up, Duchess sacked me to save money. I know she will do again, I waiting for axe to fall. Teddy is compensation.'

'Oh, Draguta, I'm so sorry.' Ondine moved in for a hug, fully expecting a rebuff. Instead, Draguta threw herself into Ondine's arms. All sharp angles and pointy bits.

Draguta wiped her face. 'Looks bad, but I never steal. I draw line at that. Never take money what isn't mine. But if Duchess and silly friends leave things in pockets when throw out washing, I keep. Not big things. Little bits and bobs they not notice. Is not stealing. Is collecting.'

They stood on shaky ethical ground. On the one hand the Duchess had schemed to sack someone to save money – stealing Draguta's entitlements with a workplace loophole. Draguta was stealing by way of opportunity, but they were items that had gone unnoticed by their owners. Is it theft if it falls in your lap and the previous owner doesn't even realise?

'I promise I won't tell a soul,' Ondine said, thinking about all the people she couldn't tell. It made her heart ache that little bit more to think she couldn't even tell Hamish, because he didn't seem to want to talk to her.

Chapter Twenty-four

Ondine sat down on a rickety chair in the ballroom wearing her Cabbage costume for the Harvest Pageant. It was an ugly meringue of a dress, which sapped her confidence. However, it succeeded brilliantly at being a fabric cabbage – all layers of green lace and padded foam built around a succession of hoops. Even the ruffles around her neck looked just like a cabbage's outer leaves.

Ms Kyryl was on stage, directing the rehearsal. In one hand she held a banana. The moment she finished eating it, she called for a lunch break.

Ondine nibbled on a cheese sandwich made from crusts of rye loaf. She looked over to see Ms Kyryl peel her jam sandwich apart and add anchovies and potato crisps to it.

Ondine lost her appetite.

Over by the doorway, a small ferrety shape darted behind the curtains. The shape moved to a quiet corner behind the stage. Any moment now, he'd dive into the costume trunk and transform into his lovely self.

'Oh, there ye are, lass,' Shambles said from behind a prop tree.

Why didn't he grab some clothes and become human? Ondine gave thanks for small mercies that at least he was talking to her again.

Keeping her voice low so as not to attract attention, Ondine murmured, 'Hamish, I'm sorry for everything I said before. I really am.' Perhaps using his proper name would encourage him to be his proper self?

He shifted back and forth on his paws and looked at the ground. 'Aye, ye cut me good. I was only trying tae help ye, lass.'

'I know, but . . . I was really upset.' Ondine fidgeted with her cabbage costume. 'I thought maybe you might say sorry for making me so upset.'

With possibly the worst timing in the world, Lord Vincent stepped into view. Looking his usual smug self, he said, 'That costume suits you.'

'Watch it, caramel yoghurt,'[90] Shambles said.

'How very gallant of the ferret to defend your honour,' Vincent said with a sneer.

Sickness spread through Ondine at the sight of him. As far as she was concerned, the less she had to do with him the better. 'What do you want?' she asked.

'It's, "What do you want, My Lord", to you.'

Ondine closed her eyes hard, but they rolled behind her lids anyway. 'Fine. What do you want, *my lord*?' She said it in such a way that Vincent would know she hadn't capitalised the letters.

'I want you gone. From the moment you arrived we've had nothing but bad magic. The storm, the fish rain, outbreaks of food poisoning, and now the seneschal seems to know what I'm about to say before I say it. He's always been good at anticipating people's needs, but he's never been able to read minds before.'

'How can any of that be my fault?' Ondine said.

'Because you're a bad egg and you're spreading

---

90 *Someone with excellent lineage who turns out bad. The combination of caramel, being golden and scrumpy, and yoghurt, being so lovely and delicious, should be fabulous, but instead it's horrible.*

bad magic wherever you go.' Vincent said, glaring at her.

'Watch it,' Shambles said, rearing up on his hind legs and exposing his nippy wee teeth.

Across the room, Ondine saw Hetty whisper something to Ms Kyryl. Fear spread through her at the thought that they might have overheard Shambles. Instead, Hetty and Ms Kyryl both stood up and got all fidgety. A blush stole across Hetty's face. Nope, it wasn't Shambles making them pay attention, it was Vincent. Hetty was ga-ga for the Duke's son. If only she knew what he was really like!

Vincent stood his ground. 'Because of you, an entire coven of witches is demanding an audience with my father to discuss all this messy magic. Why don't you save everyone the hassle and just leave?'

Oh, he made her cross! 'Because he wants us here, OK? You probably haven't noticed, because you only think of yourself, but your dad's sick and we're trying to find out why.'

'He was fine before you lot arrived, so if you want him to get better, you should get lost.' He looked her up and down and sneered at her costume. 'If you're not gone by the first of November, I'll have you arrested for trespassing.'

With that, he sneered again and marched off. Not a moment too soon as far as Ondine was concerned. Out of the corner of her eye, she saw Hetty giving a dramatic sigh, as if the world's most famous movie star had just walked by.

'We have a saying in Scotland about people like him,' Shambles said.

'I hope it's rude.'

'Waste of time if it's not.'

Ondine laughed and tried to look on the bright side. 'Maybe he's right? Maybe we should go home.'

'And leave all this? I don't know aboot ye Ondi, but I'm *loaving* it. First real job I've had in years. I've never felt so useful or important. Each week I'm on a different watch, it's so exciting.'

'But . . . my parents would give you a job just like that.' She clicked her fingers. She also thought, *And you're important to me*, but couldn't say it over the lump in her throat.

'But that wouldnae be a proper job, not really. More like a family obligation. And I thought ye liked me being responsible?'

Mist covered Ondine's eyes.

'Aw, naw, hen, dinnae cry. I'm truly sorry fer upsetting ye. And I know the teacher is giving ye a hard time, but I'm not sorry fer getting ye the answers. It was the only way tae save ye from being sent home.'

'But . . . we should have thought of something else.'

'I know. But there wasnae time. I felt lower than a worm when I saw how much I'd let ye down.'

'Thank you.' Ondine wiped away a tear of gratitude.

'Now the Duke knows yer working fer the Infanta, Ms Kyryl can't bother ye no more. I'm proud of ye, hen. There's bound to be plenty ye can tell the Duke about his mad sister, no?'

'No. That's the problem.' Ondine felt her spirits sagging. 'There's nothing to tell.'

'Sure, there must be. That Infanta, she's always up tae something.'

'I wish I shared your confidence.'

Some reassuring kisses would have come in handy at this point, but her true love remained a Shambles-ferret.

'As much as we cannae stand Vincent, he had a point. There has been some strange magic round these parts,' Shambles said.

'Strange doesn't begin to cover it. This place is off-the-scale weird. And have you heard the children sing? They used to sound like mangled cows, but now they're amazing.'

'Aye, true. And have ye seen what Ms Kyryl's having fer lunch?'

'It's disgusting.'

Across the room, Ms Kyryl finished eating her sandwich and began wrapping slices of salami around wedges of apple. Nearby, the rest of the school children scoffed their lunches. They sure were eating plenty. Maybe the cold weather made them hungry? If they hadn't all had their dose of worming medicine, the Duchess would be convinced they were infested with parasites. Hetty held her bowl of food up to her mouth and shovelled it in like she was starving.

Everyone ate so noisily Ondine and Shambles could continue their conversation without being overheard.

'I bet you've been giving the Duke plenty of information about Vincent,' Ondine said to him.

Shambles shifted on his paws, as if the floor were made of lava. He looked up and swallowed, his accent full of remorse. 'Apart from the obvious, that he's a total pillock, I goat nothing.'

'What do you mean, "nothing"?'

Shambles climbed on to her lap, but kept his voice low. 'I know, I'm shocked as weil. It was a total bust. I snuck around fer ages, listening as hard as I could. I tried going through diaries, but there was nothing. I thought I might get something when the Duchess arrived in his rooms. She talked with him for a while, but I swear they said nothing incriminating. The most she's ever said is, "One day all this will be yours, ye need tae be ready", but that's it. I thought she'd say more, but she didnae.'

'They know we're on to them. Tell me, Shambles,

when you were listening, did you see them, or were you hiding?'

'I was hiding, of course.'

'Right. So maybe they were saying one thing, but it meant something else. Or maybe they were passing notes and you didn't see it?'

'Yer a smart girl. Ye can see why I need ye here to help make sense of all this. Nice costume by the way.'

Ondine ignored the compliment, because she felt so ungainly. 'He must be planning something.' She wondered if she were being suspicious merely because she couldn't stand Vincent, or if something really was going on. 'If you've got nothing, what are we going to tell the Duke? You're going to have to find out *something*.'

The Duke had threatened their eviction if they didn't get more information. A gleam of hope flickered in Ondine's mind – she would go back to her old school, where the lessons made sense and they wouldn't make her dress as a lumpy vegetable. Except then Hamish wouldn't be happy working for her parents in the pub. Why could nothing be simple?

'Eh . . . we might have tae tell him about the Duchess's secret stash,' Shambles said.

'I'd hold off on that. He doesn't like to hear bad things about her. Did you see his face when I talked about Draguta? If it came down to it, he'd take his wife's side over ours. And there's no point telling him Kerala drinks too much because everyone knows it, he just can't see it,' Ondine said.

'Aye, it's a real shame when people can't see what's right in front of them,' Shambles said.

'Children, places, please,' Ms Kyryl called out.

Ondine swayed to her feet and flumped out her costume to get it back into proper cabbage shape.

'Unless,' Shambles piped up, 'yer sure ye havenae goat anything on the Infanta? Sure and she'd be worth something?'

Heavy guilt weighed her down. 'The Infanta declared she'd love to push the Duchess down the stairs. But I'm sure she was only wishing out loud.'

'Aye, there's bad blood between those two.'

'You've got that right. But . . . I want to keep that between us for now,' Ondine said.

'Aw nae! Don't tell me yer starting tae *like* her now?'

How could she explain her feelings when she didn't even understand them herself? 'Kind of. I mean . . . she's not all that bad once you get to know her.'

'Not that bad? She could be the one behind the Duke's troubles, and yer sticking up fer her! Ondi, love, ye have tae tell the Duke. If ye don't give him something, he could send ye home.'

'Shambles, maybe that would be for the best,' she said heavily. Sure her parents would ground her for the next month. Maybe the next year, but she knew where she stood with her family.

'Aw nae, dinnae think like that. I need ye here with me, Ondi.'

'But everything's going wrong.'

'Ye can't go!' Shambles's voice cracked. 'Aw nae, ye look so sad, yer breaking my heart.'

Ondine thought, *And you're breaking mine.*

Chapter Twenty-five

The next day, Ondine and Infanta Anathea made fresh pasta together and cooked it with parsley, basil and butter. Ondine felt they'd forged some kind of bond, which only made her feel more wretched at the thought of ratting on her.

When they had finished eating, Pyotr came to the Infanta's rooms. Ondine's heart lurched behind her ribs.

'The Duke will see you now,' he said to Ondine.

'Oh yes, and what's all that about?' the Infanta asked.

'I don't know,' Ondine said, although she had a fair idea. Guilt churned in her tummy.

When Ondine arrived at the Duke's office, Hamish was already there. Back in handsome human form in smart clean clothes. He looked so lovely, standing tall as she walked in, with a lock of hair flopping over his forehead. Her hands itched to brush it away. Circumstances prevented it.

'Ondi, I'm a waiter again, I'll be working at the Hallowe'en Ball. I'll be able to watch ye in the play,' he said.

Oh dear. 'That's . . . nice,' she replied.

'I don't have much time,' the Duke said, his forehead creased in pain. Something scrunched behind Ondine's ribs at the sight of him – he should be getting better but instead he looked worse. This time, his office was freezing cold and she had to lock her jaw down to stop her teeth chattering.

'I need to be in four places at once,' the Duke said. 'Ondine, Hamish tells me you have some news?'

A cannonball to the gut couldn't have hurt more. Ondine looked at Hamish and couldn't believe he'd dropped her right in it.

A look of shame crossed Hamish's face and he said in a low voice, 'I wouldnae be doing me job if I didnae tell him what ye told me.'

Her mouth dry, Ondine swallowed.

'I'm waiting,' the Duke said, rising from his chair

and packing papers into an attaché case. A couple of times he winced and touched his side. One of the kitchen staff came in and delivered the Duke's elevenses – a tray of savoury pastries stuffed with spinach and feta. One of them was already cut in half. Old Col must have tasted it first.

The room felt so cold it was difficult to talk, but Ondine gave a small cough and spoke: 'The Infanta admitted to me she would like to push your wife down the stairs.' She wished the ground would open up and swallow her.

The Duke shook his head and frowned. He didn't look cold. If anything, his cheeks were pink, as if he were hot. Annoyed, even. Did that mean he wasn't happy with the information? In which case she should have lied and said she had no information. Sweat broke out on Pavla's forehead and he breathed hard. Then he seemed to collect himself and gave Ondine a solemn look. 'I am sorry you had to hear that. But I am grateful you told me. It's important to tell me these things. You may have saved my wife's life. Thank you, Ondine.'

If it wasn't so cold, her jaw would have fallen open in shock.

The next day Ondine went to the kitchen to collect ingredients for lunch. Just as she was about to leave with her basket of vegetables, herbs, milk and eggs, Duchess Kerala arrived. At close range, Ondine could see the dark line around her face where the mask of make-up ended and her neck began.

'Where do you think you're going with that?' The Duchess pointed at Ondine's food with a plump finger. Her free hand held a glass of red wine, even though it was barely half-past breakfast.

'It's for the Infanta, Your Grace,' Ondine said, bobbing a quick curtsey.

'Oh yesh, the woman who wants to push me down the shtairs! Well, she'll not have that.' The Duchess pulled out the eggs. 'Or that.' She took away the parsley. 'Or that.' Removing the bottle of milk.

No chance of an omelette now.

'You may go.' The Duchess dismissed Ondine with a wave of her hand, and although her head moved, her brown helmet remained stiff as a lump of wood. 'And tell that woman she's lucky to have anything. All the support we give that freeloader and this is how she repaysh us.'

Good thing the Duchess had not seen the rashers of bacon underneath the onions, otherwise she would have taken them too. Ondine got out of there as quickly as she could. When she reached the Infanta's rooms, things rapidly deteriorated.

The Infanta took one look in the basket and said, 'Are you here to cook for me or poison me?'

From one mad woman to the next. 'This is all I could get.' The best way to deal with the Infanta's bad mood would be to get on with the cooking. It would at least keep her hands and mind busy.

'There are fifty dozen eggs produced in the chicken house each day. You are friends with the girl there. You're telling me none could be had?'

Ondine began slicing onions. 'Your Lordship, I did get some, but Her Grace the Duchess took them from me. I was in no position to argue.' They weren't even the nice red onions, which don't make you cry as much. These were the extra-thrifty white onions that burned your irises with the first cut.

'You seem to be on such good terms,' the Infanta raised her voice and added a layer of sarcasm. 'Because I was accused of wanting to push her down the stairs!'

The ground was never going to open up and swallow Ondine, so she should stop wishing for it. Her eyes burned and it wasn't the onions' fault. A horrible silence filled the kitchen. Ondine couldn't find the strength to look at Anathea.

'I am really, really sorry.' She put the pan on the heat and slapped in a dob of butter. Anything to keep busy. 'I really am. Really.'

'I thought you could be trusted!'

The onions sizzled in the pan. Ondine wiped her eyes with her fingers, which only made her eyes sting more. 'The Duke made me tell. He was going to send me home if I didn't say something.' She made a start on the celery, stripping the string away as best she could.

'I will have my tea made now,' the Infanta said, her voice cold and threatening.

322

Ondine turned off the hob to stop the onions burning and reached for the kettle.

'I am so disappointed in you,' the Infanta said.

Something cracked in Ondine. 'I said I was sorry!' She dropped to her knees and clasped her hands together in supplication as tears poured down her face. 'Please find it in your heart to forgive me, Your Lordship. The Duke is paranoid, the Duchess is a drunk. They think you've got it in for them. I know that's not true, but they're *crazy*! I had to tell them something, because if they send me home, I'll never see Hamish again.'

The Infanta took a step back to stop Ondine crying on her shoes. 'Pull yourself together. I can't stand snivelling.'

Ondine grabbed the edge of her apron and dried her face.

'Hamish is so important that for him you'd betray my trust?'

'I didn't think of it like that,' Ondine said. 'He works here in the palace, for the Duke. So if Pavla sends me home, I'll hardly ever see him.' Would the

Infanta notice Ondine was too much of a coward to answer her question?

'Why would you be sent home?'

Deep breath. 'Because I was cheating on my school tests and Ms Kyryl told the Duke to expel me.'

The Infanta shook her head. 'You're a smart girl. Why would cheating be needed?'

'Because my marks were so low Ms Kyryl was going to send me back to my parents. And she's close to the Duchess and I think the Duchess hates me too. So Hamish got the answers for me but I did too well and she got suspicious.'

A slow blink, as if the Infanta had to count to ten. 'This Hamish thought he was helping, and instead you were let down. I told you. It is always the way with men. Hamish is just a man, and, as with all men, you will be let down by him.'

Mind whirling, Ondine had no comeback. Because as much as she didn't want to believe her, the Infanta was right.

'He has already let you down. Trust me, he will again. I have been let down by all the men in my life.

My daughters, too, were let down by the men in their lives. You will be let down by the men in yours.'

No. Not Hamish. *He's not like that,* Ondine said to herself, but all the while a horrible thought nagged at her. Hamish had blabbed to the Duke about the Infanta and that should have stayed private. If he'd kept his mouth shut, she wouldn't be in this position. Oh, why did things have to get so messed up?

Anathea looked down at Ondine. 'When will my cup of tea be made?'

Chapter Twenty-six

The morning of Hallowe'en felt so cold Ondine could see her breath as she got out of bed. Tonight she would be a cabbage on the stage. The thought should have filled her with dread and embarrassment, but she had far bigger things to worry about. Vincent had threatened to evict them tomorrow, which meant she and Hamish and Col had to find out who was making the Duke so sick, and how. They needed solid evidence. Today.

If they failed, Pavla might become so sick he could die. Then Vincent would step in and take over. They couldn't let that happen.

Pyotr knocked on her door. 'Your great aunt needs you.'

'What is it this time?'

'She is dying.'

Bang! Ondine sat bolt upright. 'What?' Immediately her mind returned to their journey on the train, when Old Col had spotted the the shape of a coffin in the tea leaves. Had her great aunt seen her own death coming?

'Apparently,' Pyotr said. 'The doctor is with her now.'

That's strange, Ondine thought. Pyotr seemed to answer the question she didn't even ask out loud. That might explain how he was always in the right place at the right time. Lord Vincent's accusations played in her head – maybe she *was* responsible for spreading bad magic? But for that to be true, she had to be a bit magic herself, and she didn't have a magic bone in her body. If she did, for starters she'd magic herself a nice warm coat.

Heart hammering with fear, Ondine followed Pyotr to Old Col's room and found her in bed. Her skin had a grey pallor. Beads of sweat gathered on her brow.

The doctor looked up, holding Old Col's wrist, and acknowledged Ondine and Pyotr as they walked in.

'It seems to be kidney stones. They are very painful. It may also be some food poisoning at the same time,' she said. 'I will have to run some tests.'

'Must be something I ate in Norange,' Col whispered.

Ondine's eyebrows shot up. 'You've been to Slaegal?'

'Yes. Nipped over for twenty-four hours but had to come straight back. I'm trying to help them organise the next CovenCon. They should bring it back here. There is some strange magic about.' Col seemed exhausted by saying these few words. 'A bunch of monkeys couldn't be less competent.' *Blurgle* went her stomach.

The doctor interrupted them. 'You need to stay hydrated and flush it out of your system. I'm recommending you drink a litre of cranberry juice per day. You'll also need to take charcoal pellets to help get the toxins out of your system.'

Old Col's stomach made the strangest noises.

Ondine shared her worries with the doctor. 'The Duke didn't look very well last time I saw him either.

Like he was in pain. Do you think he might have kidney stones too?'

Shock played over the doctor's face. 'Has he been eating foods rich in oxalic acid?'

'Ah . . . like what?' Ondine asked.

'Spinach, too much salt, too much meat.'

Pyotr nodded. 'I will take you to him directly,' he said.

'Good.' The doctor picked up her bag.

'Wait.' Old Col coughed and tried to sit up. 'Stay, I need a witness.' The effort of sitting wiped her out. She closed her eyes as more sweat gathered on her brow.

Pyotr retrieved some papers from the nearby table. 'Your great aunt has made her will, she needs two non-beneficiaries to witness her signature.' Pyotr then picked up a pen and placed it in Old Col's clammy palm. He grabbed a book off the side table to support the paper. Old Col opened her heavy eyelids and made a spidery signature on both papers.

Panic ate through Ondine. 'But . . . Aunt Col, you're not dying. You just . . . probably feel like you are.'

329

Pyotr handed the papers to Ondine. She couldn't help smiling when she saw Hamish would inherit everything.

'Um, I'm not eighteen. Am I even allowed to sign?'

'Good point.' Pyotr gave the papers to the doctor instead.

A doctor in the midst of drawing up a needle full of clear liquid.

'What's that?' Ondine asked.

'Are you allergic to anything?' the doctor asked Col.

'Nothing gets to me, usually,' Col said, beads of sweat growing over her top lip.

'Good,' the doctor said. 'This is a strong analgesic, which will treat the pain and give you some rest for a while. Now, I really must be attending to the Duke.'

'Is Aunt Col going to be OK?' Ondine asked, all the while wondering why Col and the Duke were sick but Hamish wasn't. At least, not last time she checked. Then it hit her – Hamish didn't eat green leafy things so he'd probably missed out on whatever was making Col and the Duke sick. Then she remembered something else – when Hamish transformed, he left his illnesses and injuries behind. Thank heavens he could change into a ferret, it had probably saved his life!

The doctor turned. 'I expect your great aunt will make a good recovery. But it depends on what she's ingested. Now, this is very important. If you hear of anything strange going on in the kitchens, you tell me, all right?'

'Oh yeah, sure.' Great. Someone else who wants information. Just Ondine's luck. She really sucked at being a spy, because she knew nothing.

The moment the doctor and Pyotr left, Col murmured something. Ondine stepped closer.

'Sorry, Ondi,' Col said, 'this has all become very serious.'

'You're telling me!'

'Must be Duchess doing . . . this.'

'I don't want you to panic, but if we don't get something on the Duchess or the Infanta tonight – and the way I see it, it has to be one of them – then Vincent's going to evict us tomorrow.'

The doctor's needle was doing its work, because

her great aunt slumped back against her cushions and could barely put two words together.

'OK, don't talk, just two blinks for yes, one for no, OK?'

Two blinks.

'Right. So we know the Duchess is siphoning money into a secret account.'

Two blinks.

'And we know the Duke probably doesn't suspect a thing.'

Two blinks.

'And people are sick, including the Duke. So it's the Duchess slipping poison into the food?'

Two blinks.

'But what good would it do her to kill her husband? I thought they were in love? If she doesn't love him, why not get a divorce?' The twig snapped. 'Ah, but if she got divorced, she'd be out of the palace and she'd have no money. But . . . Aunt Col, I'm really no good at this. If the Duke dies, it all goes to Vincent. But he's too young to – Mercury's wings, the Duchess would rule on his behalf, wouldn't she?'

Two blinks.

'So.' Ondine sighed and felt a headache coming on. 'How do we tell the Duke?'

Three blinks.

'What does three blinks mean?'

'Means . . . I don't know.'

When Ondine returned to her room, she found a furious Draguta cursing her name and the Duchess's under her breath.

'You!' Draguta made a spitting sound, her face full of fury. 'Thought were friends, but friend stabbed me in back!'

'I haven't done anything!' Ondine splayed her palms out in surrender.

Draguta snatched her teddy and stuffed him inside a jumper, then squashed the jumper into her small suitcase. 'Duchess seek me out. Makes example of me in front of whole staff! Call me snoop! Says I go through her things! I never touch her things. Everything fine until you come . . .' The rest of her words made no sense, as Draguta reverted to her mother tongue.

'But I didn't say anything! I even stuck my neck out with Duke Pavla so I could *protect* you!'

'Protect? Ptah!'

'I'm sorry.' It came out as a squeak. Guilt turned Ondine's stomach into cement and her voice sounded thin and wobbly. 'Why did she call you a snoop?'

'Something about wine glass and book few weeks ago. Said she waited to now so that all linen clean for Harvest Ball! Ptah! Not matter, Kerala never make sense at best of times. She want me gone, I gone.'

It *was* Ondine's fault. And a bit of Hamish's as well. She played dumb but knew exactly what Draguta was talking about. The glass of wine they'd left when they first found the ledger, to confuse the Duchess into thinking she'd left it there herself. Clearly, it hadn't worked. Heart thumping, eyes misting, hands shaking, Ondine slumped on to her bed. Nasty, clanging clunks echoed around the room as Draguta snapped the locks on her case.

Silently, Ondine cursed her decision to follow Hamish to the palechia. Everything had gone so badly wrong, right from the start. Nothing in her life had ever been so messed up. She couldn't help thinking the entire palechia had to be cursed.

And then a horrible little voice in her head said it wasn't the palechia's fault, it was hers.

'Please, Draguta, don't be angry with me. I tried to help. Really, I did,' she pleaded.

'Should have kept mouth shut.'

Apologies were getting her nowhere. 'The way I see it, the Duchess would have sacked you anyway. I know you're angry with her, but don't take it out on me!'

'Of course, is all about you!' Draguta hefted her suitcase and made for the doorway. 'One day I come to your restaurant. I be big shot. I order best of everything. Then I puke all over floor!' With that, she stormed down the hall towards the servants' entrance.

Ondine dissolved into a flood of tears.

Chapter Twenty-seven

O ndine slipped away from the dress rehearsal for the pageant. Col had rallied in the past hour so she brought her a bowl of comfort food – mashed potato and gravy.

'I was poisoned,' Col said to Ondine. 'I'm entitled to feel sorry for myself.'

'Have you thought of a way to warn the Duke?' Ondine asked.

'No.' Old Col shook her head. 'And the more I think about it, the more I'm convinced he can see no wrong in the Duchess. We're going to need irrefutable proof before he'll believe us.'

Ondine felt frustrated. 'But there's no time for that! We just have to explain and hope he'll listen.' She reached for the box of charcoal pellets and shook ten of them into her palm. They left smudgy grey marks on her skin.

'Yes, yes.' Old Col grabbed a glass of water, popped one pellet in her mouth and drained half the glass in one gulp. 'Now it's your turn.'

'I don't see why I have to —'

'The doctor said this is the best treatment for this sort of thing. In your case, prevention is better than cure.'

'Is Hamish all right?'

'Fit as a mountain goat. Lucky devil.'

'Where is he?'

'Working in the kitchens, as a waiter. He's doing his best to find out the source of the food poisoning since it's not just me who's ill.'

Ondine gagged as she tried to get the tiny pellet down her throat. It seemed to grow in size the closer it got to the back of her tongue. Would it go down or come flying back out?

'You're a good girl, taking care of me,' Col said. 'I'm sorry I haven't been around as much as I should have. And I haven't been nearly as good a chaperone as I promised your mother I'd be.'

'That's OK, Aunt Col, you've had a lot to worry about.' Ondine was quite glad her great aunt had been so busy. Otherwise she would have had even less time with Hamish.

Col gave a knowing chuckle. 'Are you nervous about the pageant tonight?'

Ondine grimaced. 'No, just very embarrassed.'

'Well, don't be. The Cabbage is a very important part. I'm sure you'll get a big cheer.'

That night Ondine took her place in the darkened wings, beside her fellow cast members. She sent a silent prayer of thanks that the play would be over in a few minutes.

A quick peek through the gap in the curtain had shown a packed ballroom. People were wearing the most amazing costumes. Grand ball gowns. High wigs with feathers. Baroque pantaloons. And that was just the men! Amongst the wide skirts were women dressed as monsters, sailors and soldiers. Vincent was in attendance, wearing an army uniform. There were also at least two dozen witches. Not classic witches with long black skirts and pointy hats. These were true Brugel witches, who wore earth-coloured tunics with thick trousers and heavy travelling cloaks. On their backs they carried multi-pocketed backpacks. The rest of the costume consisted of warm hats with ear-flaps and on their feet, strong boots. Clothing designed for travel on foot or horseback, not broomsticks.

Sure it was Hallowe'en, but how unoriginal that so many women dressed as witches, Ondine thought. Perhaps there was a special deal at the costume shop?

Even Aunt Col had come as a witch. Judging by the way she virtually inhaled every passing canapé, she'd made a full and, quite frankly, remarkable recovery from her illness and was back to tasting every morsel of food before the Duke had any of it.

How Ondine wished this night would be over soon. Butterflies flipped in her belly at the thought of going on stage in front of so many people. She took a few deep breaths and steadied her nerves. That's when she heard two female voices, growing nearer. One of them sounded like Old Col, the other voice she didn't know. They were muttering something, trying to keep it private, but Ondine couldn't help straining her ears.

I shouldn't. But I am here to spy, she thought, as she took a step back and listened as hard as she could.

'. . . need to move CovenCon to Brugel, this is where the weird magic is,' Col said.

'Agreed,' the other woman said. '. . . feels like epicentre . . . so strange.'

'Doesn't begin to cover it.'

'. . . growing stronger.'

'You feel it too?' Col said.

'Oh yes. It's this ballroom. Has anything strange happened here?'

Ondine couldn't help rolling her eyes. This ballroom was where Old Col had first turned Hamish into a ferret. It didn't surprise her that it could be a centre of strange magic.

'So strong,' Old Col said.

Just as Ondine thought *gee her voice sounds close*, her great aunt stepped around the corner. Followed by the other woman. And Ondine found herself staring into the glistening round eyes of Brugel's First Minister!

Gulp!

No words came out. The two women – both dressed as witches – stared at her, boring holes right through her. Well, she *had* just been sprung listening to them. And she must look an absolute sight in her Cabbage costume. Any nerves she'd had about going on stage were now completely overtaken by fear of what her great aunt might do to her.

'It's her!' The First Minister said, her mouth dropping open in a most unparliamentary way.

Ondine looked behind her, but saw only the boy cast members. She turned around again. The First Minister kept staring right through her.

'Me?' Ondine felt sick right down to her frilly green socks.

'Yes, you! You're doing all this,' the First Minister said.

'I rather think she is,' Old Col said, making Ondine feel even more confused. Her great aunt knew she didn't have any magic. Maybe she was just going along with it, like the time she'd made Ondine read the Duchess's palms?

Another gulp. 'I haven't done anything.'

'It *is* you.' The First Minister was beginning to creep Ondine right out. 'There is something about you. You have the strangest magic, it's seeping out of your pores. You don't even realise, do you? You're like a sieve.'

'But I'm . . .' Ondine didn't know what she was, only that she didn't understand a word of what the First Minister was saying. Maybe she'd been at the plütz?

'You're due on stage, there's a girl,' Col said. 'Better get to it.'

Head swirling in confusion, Ondine felt only too glad to take her leave. She found her position on stage behind the lowered curtain and tried to think straight. There was no argument that the palechia was full of strange things, but they weren't her fault. She hadn't made Pyotr psychic, or taught the children and Ms Kyryl to sing. Or caused the fish to fall out of the sky. Had she?

Her great aunt must have been trying to impress the First Minister, that's all. Yes, that sounded completely reasonable and believable.

342

A hush fell as the curtain parted and Ms Kyryl walked to the centre of the stage, to make the opening announcement. 'Your Graces the Duke and Duchess of Brugel, Madam First Minister . . .'

Glancing about the crowded room, Ondine saw the First Minister take her seat.

'. . . distinguished guests, ladies and gentlemen. Welcome to the Harvest and Hallowe'en Ball at the palechia. As is traditional, the night begins with the children's pageant. Without further ado, I present to you the Palechia School children.'

Ondine quickly crouched into position and waited for her cue. All thoughts fled, including what she was supposed to be doing up there. A huge roar of applause filled the room as the curtain parted to reveal their colourful, cardboard set. Suddenly she didn't feel so bad. She could get through this!

Farmer One and Farmer Two strolled on to the stage with their tools. The crowd broke into applause.

'Our months of toil will soon be rewarded,' Farmer One said as she hefted her cardboard hoe over her shoulder.

'That is true,' Farmer Two said, enunciating clearly. 'In fact, you could say our labours will soon *bear fruit.'*

The audience roared with laughter and cheered.

Mercury's wings, what an easy crowd! Ondine thought.

'Here is the apple, so sweet and ripe,' Farmer One said.

The boy playing Apple spun around and twisted himself from the branch of a cardboard tree, as if the farmers had just picked him. The audience broke into fresh applause.

Farmer Two moved over to the vegetable patch. 'And here is the Turnip, here is the Cabbage!'

Andreas stood up and said, 'I am Turnip,' then gave a bow.

That was Ondine's cue to stand up and deliver her line, 'I am Cabbage.' As she leant forward to take her bow, her skirts flew up in the air behind her. The audience roared with laughter as Andreas the Turnip peeked behind Ondine and pretended to be shocked. Just as they'd rehearsed it.

As she did a little twirl, she cast a look at Sun and

344

made a sweeping gesture with her hand. Cue Sun stepping sideways offstage.

'Oh no, we still have much work to do, but the sun is leaving us,' Farmer Two said.

'It will soon grow dark,' Farmer One said.

'The light is here,' a voice said from offstage. Hetty, dressed in her silvery lunar costume, shimmied into position. 'I am Harvest Moon. I will help you.'

The crowd went crazy. Ondine couldn't get over what an enthusiastic audience they had. Making her way backstage as the play moved into the final scenes, Ondine found Hamish waiting for her.

'Lass, ye were great up there,' he said, smiling at her.

Ondine shrugged away the compliment, too distracted by Hamish looking so gloriously dashing in his waiter's outfit.

Hamish stole a quick kiss that made her feel beautiful despite her frumpy costume. 'Here, I grabbed some food from the kitchen.'

Ondine took a pastry. 'Oooh, these look nice, what's in them?'

Hamish shrugged. 'Silver beet and feta. Well, it

might be spinach, it might be rhubarb leaves.'

Ondine nearly choked. 'Rhubarb leaves? You're kidding?'

Confusion swamped Hamish's face. 'No, I'm not. I heard the Duchess tell them tae do it, tae save money, like.'

'No way!'

'Sure. She told them to stop wasting food and use potato skins in the soup, rhubarb and celery leaves in the pastries. They've been following her orders ever since.'

Ondine's body grew cold all over and she put the pastry back on Hamish's plate. 'Rhubarb leaves are toxic!'

'They are? But . . . the food's full of them! It's the Duke's favourite snack!'

Ondine stared at the plate of pastries, each one a neat rectangle of tasty death. Instantly her memory reeled back to the time Old Col had upturned the teacup on the train and declared, *That's not a carriage, dear, it's a coffin. What a shame, that means somebody's going to die.*

'Great Pluto's ghost!' Ondine gasped. 'Col didn't get sick in Slaegal, she was poisoned right here. Throw these in the bin. We have to stop people eating them.'

Ondine charged into the ballroom and ran directly towards the Duke. He was dressed as a Baroque dandy with a gold cane. She nearly lost her footing as her voluminous skirts buffeted the shocked guests.

The Duke looked pale as he leaned on his cane. In his other hand, he had a pastry.

'No!' Ondine screamed as she ran. 'Don't eat the green ones!' All the while she kept silently begging, 'He can't die. The tea leaves can't come true!'

The Duke's mouth fell open, his eyes became round and frightened at the sight of the human cabbage hurtling his way.

'They're killing you!' Ondine yelled as she launched herself towards the Duke. Everyone in the room gasped as she became airborne. She whacked the pastry out of the Duke's hand and managed to knock over a waiter with a tray of food at the same time. Oooof! She landed with a thud in a shower of hors d'oeuvres.

'What is the meaning of this?' The Duke looked ready to explode.

Before she could censor herself, Ondine cried, 'Please, Your Grace, you musn't eat the food. It's got toxic rhubarb leaves in it. It's the Duchess's fault, she told the chefs to do it.'

'How dare you!' the Duke thundered.

Oh no! Ondine had completely forgotten about the Duke not wanting to hear anything bad about his wife. But this time it couldn't be helped. If the Duke wanted to survive, he had to listen. Which meant Ondine had to draw every last skerrick of courage and tell him what she knew.

'Please, Your Grace, rhubarb leaves are poisonous. That's why you've been so sick. That's why Old Col got sick too. The Duchess told the kitchen staff to use them in the food and she knew the pastries were your favourite!'

'But –' the Duke started.

'I did noshing of the short!' Duchess Kerala strode towards them, glass of red wine in hand. She'd come dressed as a soldier, like her son, and the scowl on her face really made her look the part.

By this time, Hamish and Old Col had caught up with Ondine.

'Yes, you did!' Ondine's voice trembled as she faced down the Duchess. The entire room went quiet and she felt sick with fear. 'Hamish overheard you, didn't you, Hamish?'

Everyone looked at Hamish.

Out of the corner of her eye, Ondine saw the Infanta, dressed as a 1920s movie starlet. The Infanta looked at Ondine and slowly shook her head. As if to say, *Now you will see. Hamish will let you down.*[91]

The room was full of people, but it was so quiet Ondine could hear Hamish shifting his weight in his new shoes. All the while she kept hoping, *No, he won't let me down. I know it.*

Time stretched to the point of snapping.

Silently, Ondine prayed, *Oh Hamish, please say something.*

'Aye, that's right,' Hamish said.

---

91 *Except she probably would have said, 'You will be let down by Hamish,' because of her penchant for the passive voice.*

Relief washed over Ondine at those three words. She couldn't help smiling as he continued; every word from his lips strengthened her claim.

'I saw ye tear strips off the kitchen staff for wasting food,' he said to the Duchess.

'You're lying,' she answered, taking another sip of wine.

Palpable tension rippled through the room.

'Mebbe if ye didnae drink so much, ye might remember,' Hamish said.

The crowd gasped at the massive breach of protocol.

Jupiter's moons, but things were getting ugly! Yet at that moment Ondine had never felt more proud of Hamish.

The Duchess looked angry enough to shoot darts out of her eyes. 'You have no right.'

A lesser person would have withered under the Duchess's glare. Everyone stared at Hamish, most of them probably wondering who he was and how he had the nerve to say such things to the Duchess.

'He has every right.' The Infanta stepped forward, and if Ondine didn't know better, she could have sworn Anathea was smiling. 'If your drunken behaviour has put the Duke's health at risk, then this man is doing the right thing.'

'You would shay that,' the Duchess said.

Ondine cast a quick look around the room. She caught Old Col's glance and noticed her great aunt staring daggers at the Duchess. 'You will speak the truth!' Old Col commanded.

The Duchess made a strange sound in the back of her throat and clamped her teeth together, refusing to speak. In the crowd behind Old Col, Ondine saw a lot of the witchy women huddling together, discussing things in murmured tones. She suddenly wondered if they were not pretending to be witches, but were real witches in real life.

'I don't feel so well,' the Duke said, turning pale.

Everyone gasped.

Ondine thought they were all being pathetic and cowardly. 'Well, don't just stand around. Someone get a doctor!'

The Duke slumped into Ondine's arms. He was so heavy, she couldn't hold him up. They fell to the floor in a flumph of green cabbage skirts.

Luckily for the Duke, there were three doctors in attendance at the Harvest Ball, one dressed as a ballerina, one as a lizard monster and the third as another witch. They laid him on a chaise longue in one of the libraries.

'It's kidney stones,' the doctor dressed as a witch said. She was the one who'd treated Old Col and the Duke earlier. She made the Duke swallow a tablet the size of his thumb. 'If what you say is true, and he's been eating rhubarb leaves, then he's lucky to be alive.'

Ondine breathed a sigh of relief.

'Oh, my dear darling,' the Duchess said, smothering her husband's forehead with kisses.

The Duchess's words didn't ring true to Ondine. She looked at Hamish and he looked at her. While everyone else fussed over the Duke, Ondine and Hamish snuck out of the room.

'Where do you think you're going?'

Ondine knew that voice. Oh, why did Vincent

have to turn up now? He stood right in front of them, blocking their path.

Squee! 'It's you!' cried another voice that Ondine knew.

Brilliant! It was Hetty, and she'd just walked around the corner in her shimmery moon costume.

'Sorry, Hetty, you have tae take one for Brugel,' Hamish said. Quick as a flash, he grabbed her and threw her in Vincent's path. There were grunts of frustration (from Vincent) and shrieks of glee (from Hetty) as she smothered her idol in kisses.

'Nice one!' Ondine said as she and Hamish charged the rest of the way to the Duchess's rooms.

Her cabbage costume was so wide she knocked things over. They had to stop for a moment as Hamish helped pull the material over her head. She felt stupid standing there in a green polo neck and tights, but it was agility she required, not the latest fashion. Together they negotiated all the polished breakables. In the bedroom freshly arranged ginger lilies filled the air with such a cloying smell Ondine sneezed.

The ledger was still there in its hiding place. The hand-written balance sheet too.

'We need them both, otherwise the Duke won't believe us,' Ondine said.

'I know.' Hamish unscrewed a bottle of white wine. 'We have tae sell this right. We have tae stand absolutely firm.'

'What are you doing?' Ondine asked.

'Drinking some courage.' Hamish necked the bottle and took a good swig. A strange expression came over his face.

'Bad vintage?' Ondine thought the wine had turned.

Hamish stared at the bottle. 'It's . . . it's nawt wine at all. It's apple juice!'

Chapter Twenty-eight

'Apple juice? That makes no sense.' Ondine reached for the bottle and took a deep sniff. The sweet tang of apples filled her nostrils. She took a swig anyway and tasted the truth.

Hamish had already moved on to a bottle of red wine. The label may have boasted a harvest from the previous decade, but, judging by his face, it might have been bottled last week.

'Grape juice,' he said, offering it to Ondine.

She sniffed and tasted this one too. Although there was no alcohol content, her head started spinning. 'But . . . if the Duchess is always a bit soaked, why are these bottles full of juice instead of wine?'

Hamish shook his head, then picked up another bottle and twisted the cap. 'Hear that?'

'No.'

'Exactly. No crinkly sound, no seal breaking. These bottles have all been emptied and refilled.'

'By who?' In her head, Ondine heard her mother say, *By whom, darling.*

'By the Duchess. She's not a sad old drunk at all. She's as sober as the day is lawng. She just wants everyone tae think she's wasted so that nobody suspects anything.'

Ondine felt her eyes grow wider at the thought. 'No wonder she could put so much away, it was all an act.'

'Exactly.' Hamish grabbed two bottles and put them under his arm, then he picked up the ledger. 'Ever notice how uncomfortable everyone is when she's wobbling around, getting all shouty? Ye look the other way. Ye don't want her tae target you, because she's a raving drunk. Except in this case, we're all looking away so that we won't notice what she's up tae.'

'That's so clever!' Ondine blurted.

'Ondi, me love, she was trying tae kill her husband!' Hamish said, leading them back to the hallway.

'She did it right in front of us. You were there in

the kitchen and you watched her yelling at the staff, but you didn't realise.'

Hamish's voice dripped with sarcasm: 'Thanks fer yer vote of confidence.'

They jogged back to the room where the doctors had taken the Duke.

'Oh, Hamish, I've just realised,' Ondine gasped. 'You said the Duchess told Vincent, "One day all this will be yours." She really wasn't just saying that as a figure of speech.'

'Aye: I only hope we're not too late fer the Duke.'

Laid out on the chaise longue, the Duke looked stricken. Perspiration ran in rivulets down his face. His hair stuck to his scalp in wet dregs.

The Duchess sat weeping by his side while the three doctors discussed the situation amongst themselves in the corner. In a nearby chair sat the First Minister, and next to her, the Infanta.

'I think we'll need more than doctors,' Ondine said.

The Duchess turned around and looked daggers at them. 'Get these intruders out of here,' she commanded.

'It's over, Kerala,' Hamish said, holding up the two bottles of not-wine. 'We know yer dirty wee secret.'

'I have no secrets!' the Duchess said.

'I think you do.' Ondine's mouth turned completely dry. 'My Lord Duke, I am so very sorry you have to hear this, but your beloved wife has not only been poisoning you, she's been stealing from you, too.'

The Duke whimpered but said nothing.

The Duchess screamed at them, 'Are you trying to kill him?'

'No, but you are,' Ondine said, her heart hammering behind her ribs. 'We know the wine is just for show. It's only fruit juice. We have the ledger, and we have your secret bank account details.'

'How dare you!' the Duchess said between clenched teeth.

The Duke whimpered some more, from the pain in his kidneys and probably the pain in his heart.

Old Col stared at the Duchess as she muttered a dark spell under her breath, ending with the hideous threat, 'speak truth not lies or the next Duke dies.'

Ondine noted that she cursed the next duke, not

the current one. The Duchess didn't care if the current duke died, but she cared very much about Vincent. No Vincent, no chance to rule on his behalf.

The Duchess grunted and tried to clamp her mouth shut, but Old Col's stare worked like a drill, digging through layers of obfuscation. The Duchess's words came out as a strangled snarl: 'I did it for Brugel.' Exhausted, she collapsed on the floor in defeat and said nothing more.

From his sickbed, Duke Pavla whimpered again.

The First Minister spoke up: 'I shall convene an urgent sitting of the Dentate first thing on Monday.'[92]

'Does this mean Lord Vincent will still be the new Duke?' Ondine said as she and Hamish returned to the ballroom. They'd grabbed some warm trousers and a coat so Ondine no longer looked like a green bean. In the ballroom, the party atmosphere had evaporated – as it should, considering the circumstances. People had stopped eating the food because of Ondine's warning.

---

92 *The Dentate is Brugel's equivalent of Parliament. 'Dentate' means 'the place with teeth'.*

However, the police wouldn't let anyone leave, so the band kept playing, even though nobody was dancing.

'I hope not.' Hamish shuddered at the thought.

'So who will be the next Duke?'

'I think the First Minister is checking the constitution right now.'

Speaking of which, the woman herself walked into the ballroom. 'Ah, there you are,' she said, making a beeline for the Infanta.

Ondine and Hamish were close enough to overhear without having to strain their ears.

'Your Grace, I have checked the constitution for the line of succession. It states that while the Duke is incapacitated for reasons of physical or mental ill health, the closest relative over the age of twenty-one shall rule in his stead, until such time as the Duke makes a full recovery or dies.'

The Infanta's jaw dropped in shock.

'Do not be alarmed, the doctors expect Lord Pavla to make a full recovery in time,' the First Minister said.

Ondine leant closer to Hamish, an act that made

her brain a bit fuzzy. 'Does that mean Anathea will become Duchess of Brugel?' she whispered.

'It seems so.'

Everyone in the ballroom stood and watched as the First Minister, dressed as a witch, made the Infanta, dressed as a silent film star, place her palm on a bound copy of the constitution and recite the *pledge of Brugel*.

The Infanta recited the oath word perfect, with a steady voice.

The First Minister shook the new Duchess's hand, then made a deep curtsey. 'Thank you, Your Grace.'

A team of waiters appeared with flutes of champagne and began handing them out. Hamish grabbed two flutes and offered one to Ondine.

The First Minister held her glass aloft. 'I propose a toast. To Her Lordship Duchess Anathea the First of Brugel.'

'Anathea the First,' everyone said. Ondine and Hamish raised their glasses and took a sip.

The bubbles tickled Ondine's nose. Would anybody notice if she plonked in a sugar cube to improve the taste?

'Your Grace,' Ondine said, performing a quick curtsey as Anathea turned to her.

The room fell silent again.

Anathea gave a nod and the briefest of smiles in return. 'My brother's health is paramount. He is being well cared for, thanks in part to you. If anything is needed by you, you have only to ask.'

Ondine's heart leapt into her throat with gratitude. She seized her chance to repay a debt. 'Actually, there is one thing. Could Draguta Matice have her job back, please? The previous duchess sacked her and . . .'

Murmurs rippled through the crowd as people said, 'rude girl', 'ungrateful' and 'pushing her luck'.

Another small smile and Anathea nodded. 'It will be done.' She stepped forward, the ruling Duchess of Brugel, and shook Ondine's hand to seal the deal. Then, in a low voice, she said to them, 'You must be Hamish. When things calm down a bit, you must tell me exactly what kind of employment you performed for the Duke. Your skills will be in great demand in the coming months.'

'Aye,' Hamish said.

Ondine reached for his hand, silently hoping he wasn't about to accept another position to keep them in this strange place during the winter.

The whole time, the First Minister hadn't taken her eyes off Ondine, making her feel under suspicion for something. 'You are a very clever girl. I am going to invite you to lunch at the Dentate very soon.'

'I would be honoured,' Ondine said hardly daring to believe it. The First Minister unnerved her, but maybe over lunch she might loosen up? Time would tell.

Displaying his knack for being in the right place at the right time once more, Pyotr approached and made a low bow. 'My Lord Duchess, to you and your household, I offer my services.'

'Oh yes,' Anathea said, sounding guarded. 'And what services would they be?'

'In whichever way you see fit, Your Grace. I served at Duke Pavla's pleasure. I now offer my services and loyalty to you.'

Ondine couldn't help thinking how quickly Pavla had made his move. 'I need some air,' she whispered to Hamish.

'Aye, I could use a clear head meself,' he said, leading her to the rear gardens. They put their barely touched champagne glasses on a side table.

'Where are you going?' A police officer approached. 'We will need your statements.'

'We're just going out to the bonfires,' Ondine said.

'As long as you don't leave the grounds.' This was said in a tone that made Ondine feel like they were in trouble.

'Aye, we'll not go anywhere,' Hamish said, putting a warm hand on Ondine's back as they walked outside.

The cool air helped clear Ondine's head. She pulled her coat collar up to protect her neck. Hamish draped a protective arm over her shoulder as they approached the bonfire. The full moon had been two nights ago. They would have had a fat orb in the sky tonight if not for the cloud cover.

There were several fires instead of one large one, spread over a vast area. People milled about each blaze, basking in the warmth of the orange and red glow. Those wearing especially flammable costumes stood back a little more.

As is the custom, people were writing their regrets on slips of paper and casting them into the flames, as a way of saying goodbye to the past and cleansing the future.

Ondine shook her head and said, 'I think I've had about enough excitement for one night.'

'Aye, lass, me too.' Hamish gave her a devastating smile that turned her legs to noodles.

'I haven't written a note.' Ondine reached into her pockets for a scrap of paper and came up empty.

Hamish looked about and saw some more witches. Steam rose from their warm drinks. 'Could I trouble ye fer a pen and paper?'

He must have given them one of his trademark smiles, because the three witches giggled and gave him a pen and a whole pad of paper.

'Thanks,' he said, then turned to Ondine.

They found a quiet part of the garden, near one of the smaller fires, and sat down on the damp ground. Ondine pulled her coat around her tightly. The paper felt too small to fit all her regrets and bad habits.

She wrote, 'I don't like telling lies.' Below that she wrote, 'I don't like spying on people,' and, 'I don't like getting other people into trouble.' No sooner had she written that than she had another regret: 'I wish I'd stayed at home.'

When she read her note back, she squished her mouth up in thought. She and Hamish had just saved the Duke's life and prevented Kerala from poisoning her way into power. If they'd stayed at home, the Duke might be dead by now.

She crossed the last line out.

'Ye writing an essay, lass?' Hamish said, resting his chin on her shoulder to see what she'd written.

The cold wind kissed Ondine's cheeks and she angled her body so that Hamish became a windbreak.

'What did you write, Hamish?'

'Not much.' He showed her the paper. On it he'd written, 'I wish I'd spent more time with Ondine.'

'Oh!' She choked back a sob, then grabbed her paper, turned it over and quickly wrote, 'I wish I'd spent more time with Hamish.'

Hamish pulled Ondine into an embrace and kissed

her. It warmed her body from the inside, while the cold air settled around them and prickled her skin.

Ondine pulled away and breathed through her nose. 'I think I can smell snow,' she said.

Hamish's eyebrows shot up in surprise. 'Ye can smell the weather? Ye sure yer not psychic?'

'I'm sure.' Ondine grinned and said, 'Close your eyes, breathe through your nose. Smell that clean, cold, ozone-y kind of smell.'

'But it's only the last of October.'

'You don't believe me?'

Hamish grinned, then shut his eyes and followed Ondine's example. His nostrils flared. He ducked his head and sneezed.

Ondine laughed and hugged Hamish again. 'Come on, let's warm up.'

Hand in hand, they walked towards the edges of a fire. The cold air clung to their backs, the bonfire thawed out their faces. Ondine scrunched up her paper and threw it on to the burning heap. It dissolved in the flames, sending a plume of tiny sparks into the night sky.

Hamish fashioned his paper into a dart and threw it lower down. It turned black, held its shape for half a second then dissolved into flaming vapour.

It felt so lovely standing near the bonfire, Ondine didn't want to leave. They stood together for a good ten minutes, balanced between the cold air and the blasting furnace. A step closer and they'd burn, a step back and they'd catch a chill. Hamish put his arms across her shoulders. She snuggled into him, feeling protected.

'Well, I'll be a –' Hamish nudged Ondine to look at the sky. 'Look, Ondi, it really is snowing.'

Ondine blinked. Flurries of snow flitted through the sky, evaporating as they touched the bonfire. She looked back towards the palechia, to see soft flakes landing on windowsills and the tops of perfectly manicured hedges, dusting every surface like icing sugar.

Ondine smiled and said, 'Told you I could smell snow.'

Hamish pulled Ondine into an embrace and kissed the tip of her cold nose. 'I'm deeply sorry fer the trouble I put ye through. I should hae thought of a better way tae help ye than cheating at yer school tests.'

Tears blurred her vision. 'Oh, Hamish, I'm sorry for the way I reacted. I know you were only trying to find a way to help me stay here with you.'

He hugged her a little bit tighter. 'Ye broke me heart every time I thought ye might be leaving.'

'I didn't like fighting with you. I'm not cut out for it,' Ondine said. 'Everyone here is so messed up it's contagious.'

'Aye. Mebbe we should go back tae yer parents' pub.'

Lightness filled her. He wanted to go home? She wiped her eyes. 'You'd do that for me?'

'In a heartbeat.' He gave her one of those grins she'd come to love. The ones that made her feel all warm and melty inside. And a bit giddy in the head.

She kissed him with all her heart. The kind of kiss that told him how much she wanted to put all this craziness behind them. He returned her ardour tenfold, making her wonder how she'd ever doubted his love in the first place.

When they pulled apart, he brushed away a fresh

tear from her cheek. 'Then why are ye still crying?'

'Because I feel so guilty for doubting you. The Infanta ... I mean, I guess she's the Duchess now. Anyway, she filled my head with doubts and I was silly and tired and stressed enough to believe her. She said you'd let me down. Her words were like poison and –'

He silenced her with a kiss that sent firecrackers off in her head. When he eventually broke away, he looked short of breath.

Snowflakes fell on their hair and shoulders, but Ondine felt warm right through. 'I wish we could stay like this,' she said.

'Aye, me too.'

The sounds of the orchestra inside the banquet hall drifted outside. Hamish took Ondine's hand, bowed over it and said, 'May I have this dance?'

Ondine giggled and put her hand on his shoulder, ready for a Brugelish three-step. They took a few steps this way and that, before the snow and cold wind made her hands freeze. She pressed her arms around him, under his coat.

'What kind of dance is this?' he asked.

'It's called a snow-shuffle.'

Hamish chuckled. 'Aye, I like this dance.'

They shuffled and snuggled, in that thin zone between the bonfire and the cold air, as snow swirled around them, heralding the onset of winter.

'I love ye, Ondine.'

She held herself against his warm chest and said, 'And I love you right back.'

Acknowledgements

Thank you to my readers. I hope the past few hours between the pages have been great fun.

Monumental thanks to my husband, for challenging me to come up with bigger and better ideas.

To my clever agent Suzy Jenvey and the talented team at Egmont, especially Leah Thaxton, Philippa Donovan and Rachel Boden. Thank you for sharing my imaginary friends with the world. Thank you for pushing me to work harder. But mostly, thank you for making this writer's dreams come true.

ONDINE

One boy, one girl, one spell to be broken...

ISBN: 978 1 4052 5458 8

Ondine is starting
to hear voices . . .
Or is that her pet ferret talking?
It is indeed – Shambles, a cheeky
ferret with a wicked sense
of humour and a broad
Scottish accent!

If all that wasn't strange enough,
Ondine soon discovers that
Shambles is a man under a
witch's spell. What on earth
would he look like as a man?
Her heart starts to flutter
– love is blind after all . . .

EBONY MCKENNA

BREE DESPAIN

The Dark Divine

Daniel looked up at me. His dark eyes searched my face. There was something different about those too-familiar eyes. Maybe it was the way the orange light from the streetlamp illuminated his pupils.

Maybe it was the way he stared without blinking. His eyes made him look . . . hungry.

ISBN: 978 1 4052 5458 8

A PRODIGAL SON. A DANGEROUS ROMANCE.
TRUE LOVE'S FIRST KILL.

EGMONT PRESS: ETHICAL PUBLISHING

Egmont Press is about turning writers into successful authors and children into passionate readers – producing books that enrich and entertain. As a responsible children's publisher, we go even further, considering the world in which our consumers are growing up.

Safety First
Naturally, all of our books meet legal safety requirements. But we go further than this; every book with play value is tested to the highest standards – if it fails, it's back to the drawing-board.

Made Fairly
We are working to ensure that the workers involved in our supply chain – the people that make our books – are treated with fairness and respect.

Responsible Forestry
We are committed to ensuring all our papers come from environmentally and socially responsible forest sources.

For more information, please visit our website at www.egmont.co.uk/ethical